THE Forest of Mayhem

ELLEN KING RICE

Also by Ellen King Rice

*The EvoAngel (2016) A Wishing
Shelf Book Award Winner*

*Undergrowth (2018) An IPPY Silver
Medal winner for best regional fiction*

*Lichenwald (2019) An IPPY Gold Medal
winner for best regional fiction*

Larry's Post-Rapture Pet-Sitting Service (2020)

The Slime Mold Murder (2021)

Praise for *The EvoAngel*

*"Compelling characters and plot with a little fungi
thrown in! A FINALIST and highly recommended."*

THE WISHING SHELF BOOKAWARDS

Praise for *Undergrowth*

*"Nothing says Pacific Northwest better than mushrooms,
lush forests and gray, rainy days… Rice's multi-
generational story combines a murder, mushroom
research and disturbing backwoods encounters."*

*"As compelling and hard to set aside
as a box of chocolates."*

Praise for *Larry's Post-Rapture Pet-Sitting Service*

*"The characters are delightful and well
developed as the plot clips along."*

*"I got hooked on the first page, and couldn't
put the book down till I finished."*

Dedicated to the Indie Writers of Olympia
Thank you for your words and actions of support.

Many thanks to Don Henise and Andrey Zharkikh for letting their photos be used as a reference for Duncan Sheffel's illustrations.

This story contains a fictional workshop on fears inspired by material from Patricia Marcantonio's program to the Pacific Northwest Writers Association in 2021. Information on Patricia and her books can be found at: www. patriciamarcantonio.com.

The biological details of the species found in the woods are as accurate as I can make them.

Learn more at: www.ellenkingrice.com

Cover and book formatting by Damonza.com

Illustrations by Duncan Sheffels.

Paperback ISBN: 978-1-7338276-7-6

ePub ISBN: 978-1-7338276-8-3

Tamiasciurus
douglasii

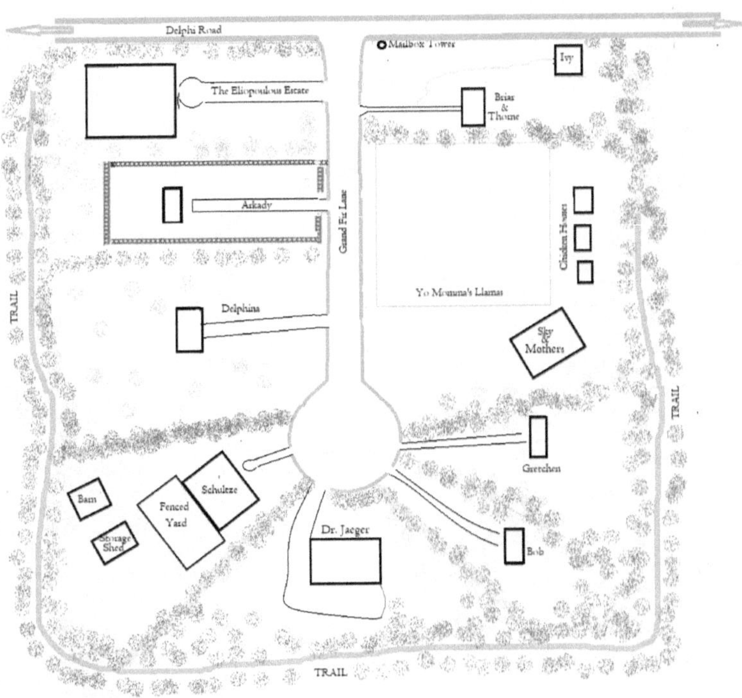

Delphi Road
Mailbox Tower
Ivy
The Eliopoulous Estate
Brias
&
Thorne
Arkady
Grand Fir Lane
Chicken Houses
Delphina
Yo Momma's Llamas
TRAIL
Sky
&
Mothers
TRAIL
Gretchen
Barn
Schultze
Fenced
Yard
Storage
Shed
Dr. Jaeger
Bob
TRAIL

CHAPTER ONE

Nature has always had more force than education.

VOLTAIRE

Thursday, April 30 - 9 a.m.

"MY PROTAGONIST WILL be wearing a kilt and carrying a claymore. And he would have a military jacket with, ah, epaulets. Oh. And a war bonnet, with eagle feathers."

"Cliché, cliché, and cliché with a double-side of truly horrible cultural appropriation." I sounded shrewish. I didn't care. "You must be joking."

Gretchen used the tip of her hiking stick to send a rock skittering off the trail into the undergrowth. Gretchen is a large woman of sixty-five years. She has a bum left knee, but she primarily uses the staff as a tool to dominate her space. As if she wasn't already intimidating with a mannish cut to her silver hair, and her stumping about with thick legs wrapped in gaiters, ending in heavy-soled boots.

She sent another wayward rock bouncing out of the way. "This hero needs to be complex!"

"Make him schizophrenic," I muttered. "That'd be different."

Gretchen came to a stop as her blue eyes turned to very blue ice chips. Rain streaked down, soaking us both. "Kami, that's petty and unkind. You are jealous. And you need to stop it."

I frowned. Then sighed. She was, as always, completely correct.

Everything was wet. A breeze was lifting the hem of my Gore-Tex jacket, sending a cool current up my backside. I fumbled for a tissue, knowing it would be wet too.

Gretchen kept her eyes on me. She could be relentless.

There was nothing to do but laugh. "You stinker!" I cried. "You were pulling my leg! A kilt, a claymore, epaulets and eagle feathers?"

"The funny thing is, it'd probably sell well."

And it would. Gretchen's racy romances were paying her mortgage. And then some. With four ex-husbands, two current lovers, and a life of saying "yes" more than "no," she had the experience and imagination to write lurid sex scenes. With each installment, she steamed up the pages and sent her book sales climbing.

In contrast, my recent space adventure had landed with a thud when a major author published a similar tale a week after mine launched. Despite being first out, my book stumbled, in part due to my modest marketing budget that was not well-targeted.

Hindsight is known for '20-20 vision', but such clarity can be depressing. I'd coasted on getting advance copies out to reviewers and hadn't used even my modest connections, being too embarrassed to flog my book to family and peers.

I had skipped press releases too. And book giveaways. I hadn't even really considered the release date, thinking all days were the same.

Alas, nobody buys a book on Superbowl Sunday. Not when

the game was at even odds and between two of the nation's most popular teams.

In short, I had not only screwed up the book launch with cheapness and distraction, I'd also stumbled, bumbled and pretended the basics didn't apply to me.

The book launch had not paired well with the sadness and exhaustion that accompanied the sorting through of my parents' estate. At age thirty-five, I felt eighty.

Meanwhile, the major author had major money for buying ads on social media. He also had help to wrangle invites for talk show interviews. And… well… he was a "he." In engineering-and-math-based science fiction, it matters. It shouldn't, but it does.

My book earned tepid reviews suggesting derivative writing, all accompanied by pitiable sales.

I had known misery after booting a philandering husband to the curb and dropping out of grad school, but this winter had been worse.

Depressed? Who wouldn't be?

Gretchen took on my rescue. As March winds gave way to April rains, she insisted we tramp the woodland trail behind the backyards of the homes on our rural road. This was our third walk.

"Chin up," Gretchen ordered. "Look around. What do you see?"

"Wet woods. Wet jackets. Wet everything."

"Be more specific."

"Argh." A lecture was coming. However, Gretchen tended to be both salty and insightful. And anything was better than thinking about the current status of my life.

I looked up. "The maples have leafed out, the skies are gray, and the lichens on the branches are plumped up."

"Excellent. I'm glad you remembered to notice the lichens. Keep going."

"The stripes on the Douglas fir are accentuated with black fuzzy stuff."

"A mold. Not harmful, but distinctive. Continue."

My eyes narrowed. "And there's a brown lizard on that tree trunk." I squinted. "Brown, pebbly top. Orange underneath."

Gretchen swiveled to look. "Ah. A rough-skinned newt. On a tree trunk! That's highly unusual. They normally are walking on the forest floor. It's not a lizard. Poisonous. Don't eat it."

"Not a problem. I've had breakfast."

Gretchen grinned. "Cheeky is good. Today we are *flâneuse*, the feminine of *flâneur*, which is, of course, the literary stroller, the amateur detective, retaining our individuality while taking in details of the urban landscape."

"Darling, I hate to disappoint you, but we're in the woods." I wiped my nose again with the wet tissue. "We're soaking wet women ignoring our task lists."

"*Au contraire*," my companion answered. "We are adventurers, and the forest is a thriving city, inhabited by the industrious, the beautiful, and the conniving. We have the charming, and we have the complex. All ours to observe and contemplate."

Gretchen waved her walking stick toward the tree trunk. "Our newt is deep in an arms race. It has the same toxin as a puffer fish, but the local garter snakes have developed a tolerance, and they will eat newts."

Her eyes sparkled as she added, "It becomes complicated. The snake has to evaluate just how much poison is in that particular newt, because some newts have developed a high level of toxin. And the newt isn't immune to its own poisons. It takes in a serving of poison to itself every time it deploys a dose. There are layers of things happening all at once."

"There can't be snakes out. It's too cold." I shifted my feet, looking down at the fir needle duff. Garter snakes are harmless to people, but I didn't want to be stepping on one.

"It's a bit early for snakes to be out," Gretchen admitted. "But the arms race is real. The newts get more and more poisonous as the snakes adapt to tolerating more of the toxin."

"And I care because?"

"Because some of the newts are so far down the development path that they contain enough poison to kill a person. Easily." She nodded at the newt, now creeping in slow motion further up the tree trunk. "And you can use that in a story."

She winked. "Or in real life."

It was easy to laugh. "You are referring to my sister-in-law, right? I may yet throttle her, but no 'eye of newt and toe of frog.' Not yet, at any rate." I grinned at Gretchen. "Although Ashlee can be a toad at times. Are we finding any real toads today?"

"I'm not sure they're in our area. I should look that up." Gretchen moved off the trail to study the newt. "Let's try for a close-up photo."

Her voice was casual as she pushed through the knee-high salal. "Ashlee is wanting you to move faster?"

"Of course."

Ashlee had opinions on the sorting through of my parents' estate, although the word "estate" was a rather decorative word to describe the large, but poorly-maintained, pseudo-farmhouse and several outbuildings, all crammed with the collections of two people who'd had a fortune for indulging in their passions.

Eventually, however, my mother's kidney failure coincided with my father's lung cancer.

Mom and Dad died within weeks of one another, having spent their fortune.

In my grief, I had blundered on, refusing to postpone my book launch, certain the world would see the merits in my story.

The world hadn't.

Now Ashlee, my sister-in-law, hoped for spectacular value in the dusty shelves of Japanese ceramics, vintage clocks, collectible dolls, duck decoys and Depression glass that filled the farmhouse and storage sheds.

Ashlee and my fraternal twin, Kent, had two little girls. Kent ran an ice cream store in downtown Olympia, but business was spotty. Money went out faster than in.

"Ashlee insists my parents were shrewd." I sighed. "Dad could be. My God, you should have heard him negotiate the fee on the furnace repair. That was the night before he died. He got fifty dollars knocked off."

"You had a furnace repair after hours?" Gretchen whistled.

"The repairman was great." I dabbed at my nose. "Of course, I was bawling my eyeballs out while Dad was hacking up the last of his lungs, so it may have been the pity discount." I shrugged. "Dad chatted him up and insisted on talking deals. Wednesday Hump Day special. He sold cars before buying a winning lottery ticket, you know."

Gretchen laughed. "He sounds shrewd. You think he knew collecting?"

"Sometimes. There's lots of tourist junk. Dad told us he was leaving real treasures, but he was such a positive, chatty guy. It's not easy to assess."

I kicked another fir cone into the undergrowth. "This morning I learned a jackalope might fetch two hundred dollars, eBay being my new friend."

"A jackalope?"

"Appalling taxidermy wherein a deer's antlers are attached to a bunny's head. Bird wings on a muskrat brings in a lot more. We may have one of those, too. There's a whole shelf of stuffed animal weirdness."

"Oh, joy."

"No kidding." I shuddered. "I try not to think about it."

"This may be a female." Gretchen was close to the newt now, taking photos. "The males tend to have smoother skin in the spring breeding season." She straightened up. "These newts breed in the late summer at high elevations and in the spring down where we are. When she meets up with a male, he may spend as much as two days stroking her to get her ready for mating."

"How do you know all of this stuff?"

"Second husband." Her eyes glittered with a harshness that surprised me.

"He was a biologist?"

"Nope," Gretchen said. "Military. He was a real donkey's butt to the kids. The best way to survive a weekend was to get them out of the house first thing Saturday morning. I'd load the kids up, and we'd head to a nature walk. Shelton, Aberdeen, Centralia, Tacoma, Auburn. Anywhere. We'd go on the tour, eat lunch, then get home as Captain Donkey Butt was headed out to golf. Mandatory sex Saturday night. Church on Sunday morning. If there wasn't a football game on Sunday afternoon, I made sure to get the kids out of the house again."

"Geez. I'm so sorry."

Gretchen shrugged. "I survived bad times. Nature-bathing helps. You're going to survive your bad times too."

"I hope so." I kicked another fir cone, using a left-footed cross like a soccer player. "I'd better do the sword collection soon. They may be valuable." I looked up at my dear, wise friend and confessed. "I'll do better with all the swords out of the house."

Gretchen's blue eyes took on a different sort of flintiness. "We'll load them up today. I'll follow you to the house."

"No." I exhaled. "I'm not going to slice myself open with a katana, whether it is a pseudo-Japanese knock off or an expensive, authentic relic. Kent can pick them up. He likes that sort of thing. He and Ashlee can research and sell them."

"You sure?"

"Yes. I'll call him today."

"What's your brain saying?"

"That I'm overwhelmed and unhappy with the work ahead. My thoughts are weirding me out, but I'm still functional."

"Good." Gretchen took one last photo and walked to stand inches from me. Peering into my eyes, she said, "I lost Captain Donkey Butt to suicide. Even my kids don't know that. They think he died in a training accident, but he killed himself with his service revolver."

"My God. I am so sorry."

"Me, too. I was close to divorce, but it was horrible to lose him." She shook her head. "After that, I moved the kids to Oregon, and I started as a pot seller."

"Weed or ceramics?"

"Both." She sniffed. "I was not using all my brain cells for a long while."

Gretchen reached out and put a hand on my very wet sleeve. "Kami, you don't want to mess around with depression. It is a very heavy load. If you're having end-it-all thoughts, let's get help."

"My misery is mostly situational. I'm just exhausted." The wet tissue was beyond useless, but I used the wad to wipe my nose anyway. "I wanted an estate buyer to haul everything away, but Ashlee's right. There's a real possibility we'll do better if we go piece-by-piece. We should at least make a good review of what we have."

I sighed. "Ugh. I hate that she's right, and I hate that I hate that she's right."

Gretchen snorted. "Right as in a treasure or two is in with all the tchotchkes?"

"Yep. There's gold in them thar knick-knacks." My sigh rivaled the wind ruffling the trees. "And lucky me, I get to be the miner."

We left the newt and returned to the trail through the woods, Gretchen stumping along in front, scattering rocks with her walking stick.

"Star-crossed lovers," she said.

"Excuse me?"

"That's what you need in your life. And I happen to know a pair."

The April rain intensified. The wind picked up. I said, "Are you sure I don't just need a nice cup of tea and a trashy novel?"

"Nope. Real life Romeo and Juliet. Only their names are Sky and Juno. They live on our road. Seventeen years old, and her parents are dead set against the romance."

"This helps me how?"

"The kids could research your stuff. They could photograph things and write up the product blurbs and do the postings. They'd jump at the chance to work at your place. I know they would."

"In a very large house with lots of nooks and crannies. In nine months, they could name me as godmother to their 'whoops' baby!" I shook my head. "Let's not make my life more complicated."

Gretchen's right arm came up, making a dramatic sweep to encompass the woods. "Vibrant life is all around. Embrace living. Empower love." She smiled. "You'd be okay. I'm projecting on the romance. Sky's had a crush on Juno for a couple of years. So far there's been oodles of tension and no action. You could help them along."

"Oh, goody." My jeans were damp to the knees as rain came blowing down the trail. The gray clouds were roiling with a sudden new intensity. I was keen to get home, grateful as I was for the outing.

My gratitude to Gretchen had me be politely curious. "What's with the parents? Republicans versus Democrats?"

"That'd be too easy." Gretchen's voice dropped into a chuckle. "We do have that one Republican pair on the corner. The Eliopoulous family. But these are the neighbors across the road – on my side. Sky's mothers run the llama and egg farm."

"Okay. Green metal roof, and the big pens full of, well, llamas."

"Too right. Yo Mommas' Llamas."

Our neighborhood consisted of homes on five to twenty acre lots spread out down a long gravel road. I hadn't met all of my neighbors, although I knew names from gate signs.

My life had been too full with parental care and writing to be sociable. Days could go by without me spotting a rural neighbor, which worked well for my cranky, sad self.

"Juno lives next door to the llama farm," Gretchen said.

"The place with the *Visualize Whirled Peas* sign?"

Gretchen nodded. "Militant vegans. On a mission."

"Free range eggs are not acceptable?"

"Nope. The Yo Mommas' Llamas farm has the most pampered flock of chickens on the planet, but consuming unborn chickens is deeply offensive to Thorne and Briar. They're on a mission to end animal industries, and the Llama Mommas aren't having it. There's heavy feuding fueled by an assortment of herbal teas."

I couldn't help it. I laughed. "Very Olympia."

"Indeed."

With a ripple of thunder, fresh rain cascaded down. As billowing sheets of water obscured the woods, I felt water wicking up my jeans to soak my underwear.

How typical. I thought I couldn't be more miserable, but, once again, I had underestimated Mother Nature and My Life.

"Isn't spring wonderful?" Gretchen bellowed. "The stage is being set for so much new growth."

Taricha
granulosa

Chapter Two

Thursday, April 30 - 10:30 a.m.

MY WILD WATCHDOG, a small Douglas squirrel, set up a chattering complaint as I dripped up the side steps to the kitchen door of my parents' funky olive-green farmhouse. The little squirrel had taken up residence in the trees next to the house during the winter, and now she chattered at perceived intruders, including me, who had lived here over a year.

My parents had purchased the rambling home when I was in college. I'd loved it straight away for the wide-planked wood floors, generously-sized rooms and abundant windows. The exterior was an odd color scheme with the olive-green house being topped by a gray roof and accented with berry-red gutters, and bright yellow doors, all of which were grimy now.

I unlocked the algae-streaked door, accompanied by the high shrills of the squirrel.

"You're better than a dog," I called.

The squirrel went into overdrive as I squelched inside. I stripped down on the inside door mat. There was no one home to see me in my goose-bumped nakedness, which suited the hell out of me. My wet clothes could wait on the welcome mat until I felt like doing laundry.

There were a few joys I'd discovered in having a large, rural home to myself. Wandering about unclothed was one. The house had been built in the 1980s to look like it was from the 1880s, which meant it came with a mighty furnace and abundant insulation.

It was a toasty home.

I carried my phone and sauntered, naked, down the main hallway, then up a staircase to an old-fashioned bathroom with a deep tub. Turning on the taps and rejoicing at the quick steaming water, I added bubbling bath soap. A few minutes later and it was heaven to wiggle toes in the hot water as the suds reached my chin.

A walk with Gretchen was a good excursion, even with the downpour of cold, late April rain.

There hadn't been many happy moments in the past year. So many things had been a struggle.

The months ahead didn't look to hold much joy either. My happiness began to dissipate as I contemplated the tasks to come.

I blinked, sniffed and frowned. It was time to entice my twin into taking on some of the estate shedding.

It had been easy to speak with confidence to Gretchen about getting the things moving, but now I found myself squirming with discomfort. My brother's life was very full. Thursday mornings, however, he had an assistant to open the ice cream shop.

Taking a breath, I reached for my phone and typed a text, "Ready to make some $$? Stop by?"

An affirmative thumbs up chimed in quickly. "10 min," my brother messaged.

"Damn." I'd hoped to stay in the tub until the water cooled. Still, task shedding and improving my mental health were the goals. The game was on. I emerged from the water, rosy and clean.

After a few hasty pats with one of my mother's deluxe towels, I made another naked dash through the house, this time to a bedroom overlooking the back meadow.

I'd claimed the room as mine when I had moved in to care for my parents. They had been frail and needy from the start, which meant I had simply dumped my worldly goods in the gracious room.

Today I yanked a clean T-shirt out of the laundry basket and rummaged for a semi-clean pair of jeans from a pile on the floor.

Speed was important. I wanted to greet my brother with a sword. Our father had been a sucker for weaponry, and Kent was too.

Unfortunately, the sword collection had been popping up in my mind every night as I struggled to sleep. I was too often haunted by a mental picture of what a fine blade could do against a wrist. It was time to take positive actions before a negative action became alluring.

I clattered back down the staircase and headed to our father's office, a room I'd avoided for weeks. Two of three overhead light bulbs were out, and I hadn't summoned the strength to fetch a ladder to remedy the issue. The office was a dim place, crowded with belongings.

The door opened smoothly enough, coming to rest with a bump against a heavy wooden chest. I clicked on the remaining light and tried not to see the thick film of gray dust that covered every surface. My heart stuttered a bit as I took in Dad's big office chair.

I made my eyes move to the wall to the left. There, on a high shelf, sat a prized Japanese katana, resting on an elegant wooden stand with the sword's scabbard cradled underneath the blade.

It would be foolish to stand on Dad's wheeled chair to reach the high shelf. I dragged the wooden chest closer to make an enormous step. With a stretch I could lift the entire array, which ended up being heavier than I expected.

My legs shook, but I was able to lower the whole apparatus to the desk. I scrambled down, took a new grip on the sword, sheath and display stand and hustled out to the kitchen.

Kent's Civic was already turning down the long drive to the farmhouse. I galloped back to my father's office and flung open the closet. Pushing aside coats that smelled altogether too much of my father, I found four stacked wooden cases. I grabbed two and sprinted back down the hall to the kitchen to lay the cases on the counter.

Three swords would have to do. I knew there were more stashed elsewhere in Dad's office, but we could start with these.

I rinsed my now grubby hands and took a few calming breaths, trying to look nonchalant as my brother came in the kitchen door.

Kent stepped onto my pile of wet clothes, swear words coming easily as he rocked for balance, all of which amused me.

"Sorry about that," I said. "I had a walk in the rain. Thanks for coming."

"Sure." Kent pulled me into a fast hug. His eyes were already on the katana as he released me. "Oh, man. That beauty!" He moved closer, bending down to take in the details of the exquisite sword smithing. "It's dirty, but you can see the hamon line."

One of the lovely things about having a twin is seeing yourself. Kent has my russet curls, round face and square jaw.

Alas, our father's fascination with all things Asian had begun early. My given name is Kamiko, and my brother is Kento. With our stout Western bodies and pale, round faces, we look at home hoisting steins of lager in an Octoberfest beer garden. I'm busty enough to fill out a dirndl nicely.

Kamiko and Kento don't play well with the surname Schmidt.

For years I had a reflexive wince when a new teacher called out "Kamiko Schmidt?" always with an air of uncertainty.

Our parents had been unapologetic. We'd been miserable until a middle school P.E. coach Americanized our names.

It wasn't that we hated our names. We had, like most schoolchildren, hated being different.

Today my twin straightened up, smiling. "I remember when Dad bought this. He was so excited. You're right. This is worth some money." The smile shadowed as Kent added, "If we can find the paperwork."

"Yep." I hunched up my shoulders. "It might be under 'sword' or 'katana.' Dad's filing was terrible."

"I know. The papers might be under 'Japan.' Or 'Collectible.'" Kent shook his head. "I think we bought a katana on the 2014 trip. Maybe a 2014 file?"

"Great." I folded my arms and sniffed. "That's about when Mom bought a new dryer, so maybe I can figure out if that screeching sound can be fixed under a purchased warranty if I can find the 2014 folder. Dryer receipt with a sword receipt. That sounds about right."

Kent looked a bit ill, like he'd swallowed a frog.

"What? You think I'm wrong?" I asked.

"No. You're absolutely right. Dad's filing system isn't a system." Kent looked at me, steady, twin-to-twin. "I need you to know that Ashlee is wound up. She thinks you're goldbricking out here."

"What?" I waved a hand towards our father's den. "She's seen that mess!"

"I know. I know."

I couldn't help myself. Ranting was better than breaking into tears. With a most excellent sneering tone, I said, "I was all for calling in an auction house. She's the one who says we're going to come out ahead if we go through all this stuff ourselves. And you're not helping. Any."

"I know." Kent looked beyond miserable. "We're cramped. The girls have lots of needs. She's overwhelmed, and I don't know if I'm coming or going."

He sighed. "Money is so damn tight. I really think the shop will pick up this summer. People are going to be traveling, and there'll be events downtown."

I relented. "But you have to get through most of May, right?"

"Yeah. Things should pick up as soon as we have some sun, but it'll be June before we're really busy." His fingers drummed on the kitchen counter. "Could we get this house on the market next month?"

My rage dissipated. Kent was trying to find a way forward, and I could hear his exhaustion.

"It'd be crazy making," I said, flapping a hand at the sword. "Maybe we can do the nice stuff faster. Can we sell this katana without the paperwork?" I managed a weak grin. "I'm an eternal optimist. Hell, I even thought I could write books for a living."

"You can." He looked down at the sword. "We will get so much more with proper documentation. This was made with immense skill. With the paperwork, we might get thousands. Without, maybe a couple hundred."

"It matters," I said.

"Yes. For Japanese katanas, documentation matters a lot." Kent straightened his shoulders. "We can do this. We have to. It would be a tragedy for the history of this piece to be lost. We've got the history. We just have to sort out where the hell Dad filed it."

"And the others?" I jerked my thumb at the two long boxes I'd fetched. "There's more in the den closet."

"Let's hope all the documentation is in one file marked 'Katanas,' or it's a long path to payday," Kent said.

"Sweet Jay-sus." I had harbored hopes that Kent would remember more about the swords and be keen to take them home to do a fast, lucrative marketing plan. I'd be safer from my dark ruminations, and we'd make money.

Now I was realizing that was ridiculous. Kent and Ashlee had a cute, but overstuffed, bungalow and two very little girls. There was no room for processing estate items. Ashlee would be apoplectic at the idea of weapons coming in the door. For all their collectability and grace, the katanas were serious blades.

The swords had to stay with me.

My stomach swooped and roiled. I took a steadying breath and made a silent vow to find a sleep aid so my nights would not include mental images of blades on wrists.

"You okay?" My twin's face showed his lips coming together just as mine did when I was worried.

"I'm overwhelmed. Each item has to be researched. I have to measure the thing, take pictures, write a description, and then the real fun begins. I upload the whole bundle and pray for results."

A groan escaped me as I added, "And then it either is total crickets with no interest, or the emails start arriving with questions I struggle to answer."

I scowled, "Would you say Dad's jackalope is in good, fair, or moderate condition?

"There's a difference?"

"Good is better than fair. I think that both 'good' and 'fair' are under the moderate umbrella. If I'm wrong, then the buyer might ask for a refund."

"Jay-susss!" Kent's eyes roved around the kitchen. I could see him look up at the row of cookie jars lining the perimeter of the upper cabinets.

"Right," I nodded at his surveillance. "Each one of them should get that treatment. An hour, or more, per cookie jar. Some of those are rare collectibles."

Kent shook his head. "I can't help you with the cookie jars.

If I took one of those home, the girls would be into it right away. It'd be chipped by dinner time."

"I know. They're little girls." I moved to the sink to fill the tea kettle and took in my brother's tightly hunched shoulders. "What's really going on?"

"Whadya mean?" Kent's question was too innocent. I shot him a hard look, bringing my eyebrows down to augment the glare.

Kent shifted on the kitchen stool. He finally said, "Ashlee bought a product line."

"No!" I set the teakettle down on the burner with a thump. "One of her mother's Ponzi schemes?"

"Multiple Level Marketing opportunities are not all Ponzi schemes."

"Most of them are." I turned the burner to high with a frown. "I can't believe Ashlee did that."

"She can't either." Kent slid off the stool and took down two mugs. "She told me Glynnis called with a 'fabulous entry deal,' and it caught her at a weak moment."

"That I can believe. Glynnis is a terror."

Kent licked his lips. I knew that 'tell' because I had the same one. There was more to confess here, and he didn't want to share it.

I plunked tea bags into the mugs and said, "Spill the beans. Which line did she get and how much?"

"Essential oils."

"Great. Any product Ashlee doesn't sell can be gifted. Everyone can smell like vanilla or cinnamon all year after Christmas. For the next ten years."

"Not funny."

I poured hot water into the mugs and gave my twin no quarter. "How much?" I repeated as I set the kettle back onto the burner.

"Five thousand."

It was a good thing I'd put down the kettle because I would

have dropped it. My mouth worked like a goldfish, opening and closing with no sound. Finally, I croaked, "Five thousand *dollars?*"

"On the store credit card."

"No!"

"She feels bad," Kent defended his wife. "She's going to do her best to move the product."

"To make her money back, she'll have to enroll other salespeople."

Kent shook his head, "Nope. We agreed she is not going to do that. She's going to sell the product she has and be done."

"Five thousand dollars of essential oils must be boxes and boxes of stuff."

My brother's sigh was expansive. He followed it with a second sigh. "I can't park the car in the garage."

"I don't get it. Ashlee's smart."

"It has nothing to do with smarts," Kent snorted. "It's her desire to make her mother proud, and to rescue me from a business I can't run well. Glynnis said she knew someone downsizing an essential oils collection, and this was a chance to get in on the ground floor. I was in Seattle for a couple of days for a training course. Glynnis drove over to stay the night with Ashlee and the girls. By the time I was back, Ashlee had signed. The stuff was delivered the next day."

He squeezed out the tea bag and tossed it into the trash. "I would say 'ground floor' was really 'ground-down Ashlee.' It's hard to stand up to a sales pitch from Glynnis."

"Can Ashlee unload this great opportunity to someone else?"

"She's trying. It's hard to do much at the computer with the girls."

"But she thinks I should be churning out the sales here." My bitter tone made my brother's shoulders rise and tighten.

"She says a novelist cranks out thousands of words, so why

aren't you?" Kent put his hands around the tea mug. "Kami, I know you hate this stuff, but doesn't she have a point?"

"All writing is not the same." I responded with a sneer. "It's like ice cream. You can power through a pint of Chocolate Crunch, but you can't handle a scoop of Double Licorice. Lots of people can tell a story and are not able to write a sales blurb or a synopsis. I *can* write blurbs - I just hate them."

I sat down on the kitchen stool next to my brother and made my voice take a neutral tone. "I told you. There's also a ton of work assembling the material. It's exhausting."

Pointing at the katana on its stand, I confessed. "I'm having nightmares about cutting wrists. I'm okay, but I need to stop that road from building further."

"Shit!" Kent's eyes went wide.

"I'm not going to. There was just the thought you could take the swords home and do some of the research and write up yourself. You'd see what I'm talking about, and I'd get these things out of the house."

"I can't have blades at our place. The girls…"

"Got it. What was I thinking?" I shifted my weight and grimaced. "Gretchen knows two high school kids. She says they could be hired to help process stuff."

"Can you get them, like fast?" Kent's shoulders were still hunched up.

Eyeing his tension, I asked, "Besides Ashlee dropping five grand on stupid stuff, what's up?" I held up my hand, extending a pinkie. It was our secret handshake. Pinkie-to-pinkie meant "I'm here for you, but no bullshitting me."

Kent wrapped his beefy pinkie around mine. "The reason Ashlee caved and went for the product line purchase is because we're thirty days behind on the store rent. She actually got twenty thousand dollars of product, so she was thinking – for a moment

– that it was a screaming deal. Glynnis, of course, was pounding that line, for sure."

"Christ on a crutch."

Kent snorted. "It gets better." He released my pinkie, which was fine. I knew he would continue to be frank.

"How does it get better?"

"Glynnis is coming back here." Kent paused. "She's staying with us while her condo is painted and recarpeted. She wants to sell her place."

"Well, Bro, the girls *are* her grandbabies."

"Doesn't mean I'm happy about it." Kent scowled. "She'll be in my face and on my case about improvements I can make. She also acquired a dog. A little yappy thing."

"You poor man. Is there someplace else she can stay now that she has a dog?"

"Dearest sister. Twin of my heart," Kent began.

"No!" I shook my head. "Absolutely not. She is not staying here."

CHAPTER THREE

Neither a borrower or lender be.

POLONIUS IN HAMLET. ACT 1 SCENE 3

Thursday, April 30 - 11 a.m.

I WAS UNRELENTING. Based on my previous handful of interactions with Glynnis, I knew her presence would, in no way, help me process my parents' belongings. Quite the opposite. Glynnis could be very persuasive. If she were staying with me, I might end up thinking one of her programs was actually a smart investment.

To his credit, Kent didn't try too hard to convince me to house his mother-in-law. He finished his tea and left, giving me a hug and a wry smile after rinsing his mug and shrugging on his jacket.

"We'll get through this," he said.

I gave him a fierce nod, but found myself blinking back tears as he backed an old Honda Civic down the drive. Five years ago, we'd each had a top-of-the-line Lexus.

Now there was too much to do and not enough cash on hand. There were financial outfits who were keen to lend quick cash while the estate went through probate, but my research made me wary of them.

The downstairs toilet gurgled ominously when I flushed. I stalked out to the garage to look for the plunger, feeling that a backed-up toilet represented my life when an idea blossomed.

What about a home equity loan? Would the respected credit union where my parents, Kent, and I had banked for years extend a home equity loan to the estate? We could get the house in shape with hired help and get it on the market.

I abandoned the plunger hunt and ran back into the house.

Forty-five minutes of intense computing later, I had an on-line application submitted for thirty thousand dollars.

As I stood up and stretched, I felt we had a chance of gaining approval for the loan. Housing costs in Thurston County, like so much of the rest of the nation, had soared in recent years. My parents had no mortgage. It was a low-risk loan for the credit union.

We could do so much with the added cash flow. The roof could be replaced and the driveway re-graveled. Both should be done before the house went on the market.

And the loan could give Kent and Ashlee a bit of breathing space.

We'd have to be careful. With our history of spending, Kent and I could mow through thirty thousand in an eyeblink. We had been accumulating better money management habits too slowly.

A weak sunbeam slicing through a dirty window let me know the morning showers had passed. I felt empowered enough to fetch the mail.

I have a love-hate relationship with mail. I adore cards and packages. I hate bills and flyers. The past week had been so miserable that I hadn't collected the mail even once. It was depressing to acknowledge my college friendships had wilted during a long year of parental care. There was no one out there who would be sending me a card. Surrounded by knick-knacks, I'd also severely curtailed my on-line shopping. There would be no interesting packages arriving.

Shouldering a canvas shopping bag, I set out for the neighborhood mail tower.

My parents' farmhouse sat at the end of a rural spur road. The meth epidemic of the early 2000s resulted in constant theft from rural mailboxes, so the eight households and one real farm on our spur went together to buy an industrial mail tower, anchored in concrete and lit by a rare county streetlight.

The hike to the mailbox was actually one of the few occasions when I might have a neighbor-sighting.

Our neighbor to the right was a surgeon, Dr. Jaeger, we rarely saw. His house was also in the farmhouse style, but his was meticulously maintained behind a border of giant rhododendrons. Tall Douglas fir and one droopy-topped hemlock rimmed his flat and very green backyard.

Next to Dr. Jaeger lived Bob, a retired mycologist and part-time folksinger who was one of Gretchen's favorite lovers. Today Bob emerged from his drive, walking slowly. He was, as usual, skinny, shaggy and smiling. He often wore a lurid tie-dyed shirt, stained mountaineering pants and hiking boots. Today the shirt was long-sleeved, and he'd added a fleece vest.

"Mail?" he called.

"Yep! I am prepared for the onslaught." I wiggled my elbow, making the canvas bag flap. "I haven't picked up in a week, but I'm feeling brave at the moment."

I waited for Bob. He was walking slowly with his shoulders forward. My heart clinched as his old man's tilt reminded me of my father's decline. I didn't know Bob well, but his confident stride had been noteworthy all last year whenever I'd had a Bob sighting.

Bob joined me and I deliberately set a very slow pace as we walked past the entry to Gretchen's drive. Both Bob and Gretchen had long, cedar and Douglas fir-lined driveways with small homes at the back of the five-acre lots.

The Yo Mommas' Llamas farm was next to Gretchen's place on the north side. Its entrance configuration was open, with no trees. The llama farm had a small shed by the drive with a table display offering cartons of free-range eggs. They also had a padlocked pay box welded to a massive metal fence post. Five-foot-high stout fencing paralleled the road and divided the farm into several pastures, each dotted with llamas. There were chicken runs at the back of the property, next to a large, single-story home.

"They've been having more issues," Bob said, waving at the two women who were loading a metal feeder with hay.

"With each other or with the neighbors?"

Bob snorted. "Monika and Xiulen are solid. The asshole vegans and the feral cat lady are being snots about the egg sales."

"Gretchen mentioned something about that. Delphina has feral cats now?" This was my neighbor to the left. I rarely saw her, but I knew her to be a large woman with a soft cloud of brown hair and four or five cats. She ran a book-indexing business from her home. I'd only spoken to her a handful of times, but had always found her to be smart and pleasant, if perhaps a bit shy.

"Delphina?" Bob shook his head. "No. She's cool. Keeps to herself. Even better, she keeps her cats in her garden. She's great."

He pointed at the *Visualize Whirled Peas* sign on our right, standing in front of a row of head-high huckleberry bushes. The rainbow-hued letters stood out against the flat black sign board. "These guys and their tenant. You got the name change memo?"

"Ah." My mind stuttered for a moment before I recalled a penciled note on unattractive handmade paper. I said, "Belinda and Steve are now going by Briar and Thorne."

Bob's snort was half a grunt. "Yeah." His voice deepened as he quoted, "To better reflect our mission to move the world to a sustainable, vegan path." He followed the broadcaster's tone with a sigh. "It pisses me off that I about ninety percent agree with them. I just don't like their approach. Seems like you could be doing some other things than harassing your neighbors over their little egg stand."

He frowned. "And they're even free-range eggs! Those are some happy hens!"

"So, Belinda, I mean Briar, is into feral cats?" We were past the vegans' drive and now near the mail tower, also backed by high huckleberry bushes.

"No. Sorry. Got side-tracked there. See the little house?" Bob pointed at a clever wood trailer structured like a caravan from a fairy tale. It was possible to get a clear look through a gap in the bushes. "That's their renter's place. She now goes by 'Ivy,' which is a hell of a name."

Something Gretchen had said on an earlier walk popped up in my brain. "Ivy is an invasive species?" I ventured.

"Yep. Horrible stuff. Right up there with Scotch broom. Bad news for the Pacific Northwest. We need more ivy like we need more commuters."

Bob sniffed, "That feral cat rescue stuff is madness. Bad for birds."

We each opened a box on the mail tower. My family's box was crammed with letters and advertising. As I scooped and unloaded into my canvas bag, Bob said, "I read your book. It's pretty good."

I tried not to wince. I pasted a smile on and said, "Didn't Gretchen tell you that writers like superlatives? Just throw in a 'marvelous' or at least an 'unexpected.' We're fragile things."

Bob snorted as he pulled out a paltry two envelopes. "You're not fragile. But I see your point. I tend to understate stuff. Let me start over. I thought you wrote a clever book."

"Ah. 'Clever' I'll take. Thanks."

Bob turned and raised his eyebrows. "I did leave a five-star review once for one of Gretchen's books, *Susan's Flight of Wild, Wild Love.* I said the sex scenes were incredibly realistic."

I stopped at the road edge, the now-heavy canvas bag bumping hard as I halted. "The black feather scene? That was you?"

Bob winked. "Tail feather straight from the Yo Mommas' Llamas Australorp rooster."

"I'm not sure I'm ready to go that far for a book review." It was hard to keep from giggling.

"It's just one way," Bob shrugged. "I'll find something to go with 'clever' and get a real review up for you. You did a good job."

"Thank you," I said. "I need to do a lot more asking. Gretchen's on my case to do more. I'm supposed to ask for reviews, buy some ads, and start my next book. I just don't have the energy."

"Too much mail," Bob said. "I know you've had a lot to do."

"It's been nuts." I looked down at the bag that now was bumping my side as we walked. "I'm going to hope this is all recycle bin stuff."

As we made a return past the *Visualize Whirled Peas* sign, I asked, "Do you know the teens? Gretchen said there's a girl and boy?"

"Actually, there's three teens on this street. They're all high school seniors, which is why you don't see them a lot. Kids are crazy busy these days."

"Too bad. I was hoping to hire some sorting help."

"Your timing might be pretty good for that. Senior year finally lets up in May. The kids have their projects done, their college acceptances in. Sometimes they do have time on their hands."

Bob nodded at the sign. "Briar and Thorne's daughter is named Juno. Tall, pretty gal. Nice. Then Monika and Xiulen's son is Sky. I like him a lot too."

"Okay. Where's the third kid?"

Bob jerked a thumb over his shoulder. "Cadence Eliopoulous. Dark hair. Small. At the mansion."

It wasn't really a mansion. The peaches-and-cream, mock-Victorian house across from the mail tower was the biggest, grandest thing in the neighborhood, and our only right-leaning neighbor. I'd seen luxury cars in the drive and Republican signage in the yards, always professionally printed and upright. The signs disappeared promptly after each election and the extensive grass lawn would again be groomed to perfection.

"You're not a fan," I said.

"Peach is not a Northwest house color," he grumbled.

A small brown bird with a stubby, erect tail alighted on a distant tree stump and began a sweet, trilling, then staccato song.

Bob pointed, "Pacific Wren in shades of brown. A true lyricist, close to nature, strutting his stuff for the ladies. There's a Northwesterner."

"Small, short feathers," I observed.

"Ah, but he knows what to do with them." With that Bob sketched a salute and left me for his long driveway.

Raindrops began again as I hurried up my own drive. I realized the one neighbor we hadn't discussed was the one I found most interesting. We had not talked about Arkady.

Chapter Four

*Everyone is prejudiced in favor of his
own powers of discernment.*

PLINY THE YOUNGER

Thursday, April 30 - 11:30 a.m.

ARKADY'S PLACE WAS a one-story, leaf-green home nestled between Delphina's place and the peach mansion of the Eliopoulous family. He'd moved in about the time I had returned to write and care for my parents. His lot had formidable six-foot cedar plank fencing and pragmatic but minimal landscaping.

My mother had gathered coffee-klatch intel that Arkady worked from home, doing some sort of design work, and he was divorced. "Sounds like it was messy," she'd said. "You should chat him up."

I hadn't been too keen on the idea of bonding over imploded relationships. My own wounds were far too fresh. But I had noted, from a distance, that Arkady had a full head of black hair and broad black eyebrows. He was a muscular man with arms that swung easily as he walked.

My interest was shaped, no doubt, by how little socialization I'd had in the last year. Our next-door neighbor, Dr. Jaeger, was aloof and rarely home. Besides, his tastes seemed to run to the temporary. At least I'd seen a succession of females who would arrive on a Friday to depart on a Saturday, never to be seen again.

Our other bachelor, Bob, was easy to adore, but he was past seventy, and Gretchen had snapped him up – or at least kept him busy when she needed a sensory refresher for writing her latest lurid chapter.

Arkady was the only single male in my age group that I knew. Snorting at the despair in this as the mail bag slapped against my side, I used my arm to hold the top of the bag closed as the rain shower intensified. The rhododendrons edging the road held fat buds that would soon burst into large blossoms of pink and red. Two Pacific dogwoods towered over the rhodies and were already covered with ivory flowers.

May was going to be beautiful, even if estate-sorting glutted my days. This last day of April held hope in its light, even as rain showers descended, then abruptly halted.

I was almost to the house when I saw a woman exiting our barn. Stunned, I stepped under the overhang of the garage and stared.

Two long, brown braids of hair emerged from her brightly striped cap. The braids descended to her waist. She wore a long, red-and-violet tiered skirt and a black sweatshirt. Her feet were in gray wool socks and leather Birkenstock sandals, an odd and very Olympia combination. She carried a bulging daypack.

She smiled and waved, then flipped a long braid over her shoulder before advancing.

"Hi! You must be Kami," she called.

"Indeed." I gave her a hard stare. "And you are?"

"Ivy!" She advanced, hand out. "I live down by the mail tower in that Little House. I'm a friend of Briar and Thorne."

I shook her hand, but didn't add a smile.

"I knocked on your door, but I guess you didn't hear me," Ivy said. Her voice tone was apologetic. "I was out for a walk, and I just couldn't resist taking a peek in your barn. Forgive me for being curious."

My inner bullshit monitor was screaming at me. My best move now was to gather information, so I went with, "If you're looking to stable a horse, we're not set up for boarding."

"Oh, no. I can see that."

"Okay." The barn had three stalls and a tack room, none of which held horses or saddlery. I hadn't been out to see the condition of things for months, but I recalled there were bins of holiday lights, and a couple bales of moldy straw we'd used for Halloween decorating. There was also half a vintage tractor, a small boat on a boat trailer with flat tires, and a riding lawn mower that actually ran. It was unlikely she'd seen anything of value to take, but I didn't like the look of her full daypack.

Did we have any small items of value in the barn? My mother had a few small gardening tools. There was also a tool caddy with an assortment of screwdrivers.

I recalled a task on my to-do list was to wrestle the blade off the riding mower and take it to town for sharpening. The grass could use a trim as soon as a dry day permitted. I should have had Kent give the nut a yank. Too late now.

Ivy was talking as my mind was wandering. My brain regrouped, and my mouth managed, "Again, please?"

"Your barn is perfect for a barn cat! I'm a volunteer with *Freedom for Ferals*, a cat rescue group. We have several animals that would really thrive at a location like this. These are healthy, spayed cats who need an outdoor lifestyle. They've been vaccinated, and they make excellent mousers."

I thought of Bob's remark at the mail tower. "Don't outdoor cats eat birds?" I asked.

"It's really not a problem," Ivy said. "Birds fly."

"Babies don't." The words were out of my mouth in a flash. One of the advantages of being an almost Ph.D. in the sciences was a well-developed ability to zero in on logic holes while ignoring social niceties. My time at grad school had definitely shaped me.

Ivy's brown eyes went hard as her mouth firmed into a straight line. Ms. Charming transformed into Ms. Pissed when challenged. Interesting.

She said, "I can send you information from our group. We've documented bird life around several of our re-homing projects."

I sincerely doubted the independence and accuracy of such an agenda-sponsored project, but I went with, "My parents have passed away, and I am working hard to resolve the estate. There's lots to do so the house can go on the market. I'm really not in a space to take on pets."

"They wouldn't be pets," Ivy began.

"Not interested. This is not the time." I shifted the heavy mail bag and added, "Today there's a ton of mail to process. Nice to meet you."

Ivy nodded a goodbye. I had the satisfaction of watching the rain intensify as she walked down the drive, daypack bouncing as she went. I can be marvelously petty at times.

My small victory in refusing a barn cat had me feeling satisfied until I was inside. I went to my "office," which was the end of our large dining room table. The next task was to dump out the contents of the mail bag and begin pitching ads into the plastic recycle bin resting at my feet before ripping open the non-ad envelopes.

I was making fast progress until the words, *Dear Ms. Eliopoulous* caught my eye. I paused and reviewed the envelope. It was addressed to my neighbors.

Mail mis-sorts happen all the time. The solution is usually to slide the wrongly-delivered piece into the slot in the mail tower for outgoing mail, but this time I had opened the envelope.

I scanned the letter to see just how bad a faux pas I'd inadvertently made.

It was awkward. One line in the letter said, "We expect immediate payment as this account is ninety days past due." The text pled for a Republican PAC to pay its venue rental bill. Apparently, Eloise Eliopoulous was treasurer for the group.

Eloise was a lot of things. I sorted through the rest of the mail pile and discovered she was also receiving officer's mail for the County Republicans, the South Sound Conservatives, the Western Washington Arts Improvement Union, and two more community organizations.

Half my mail bag was mail for her.

I really should return this mail to the tower immediately. I hadn't checked the mail for a week, so some of this mail may have been misdelivered for days.

Rain was now pounding the roof and lawn. It was no time for a pleasant return walk to the mailbox.

Sighing, I stuffed the dunning letter back into its envelope and wrote, "Opened by mistake. Sorry," on the outside before sacking up all of the Eliopoulous's mail. Muttering this deserved a prize, or at least a chocolate bar, I collected my rain jacket and dashed out to the garage. The mail tower was only a few hundred yards away, but this time I would drive.

Of course, the windshield and windows of my cranky old Mazda were fogged. I scrubbed a small hole in the moisture and backed the car down the drive.

It was not my day for efficiency. When I reached the end of our road there was a maroon sedan parked in front of the mail tower. As the rain poured down, I couldn't see who was in the car, but a man's shouting pierced the clatter of the rain. Someone in the maroon car was shouting into a cell phone. Between my misted windows and his, I could barely make out the man's profile.

My choices stank. I could sit in my car, waiting for an opportunity to pull up to the mail tower and keep dry, or I could get out of my car to walk to the tower. If I got out to get the mail returned, I'd be receiving my second soaking of the day.

It dawned on me that I could turn onto the main road and find a place to turn around. That would at least let me pull up to the mail tower within arm's length of the driver's side.

Since the yelling was ongoing, it was time to move on.

I pulled out around the maroon sedan and crept my vehicle down the main road to a safe turnaround point. I returned to the mail tower just as the maroon sedan turned down our lane.

Feeling victorious that a soaking had been avoided, I slid the wrongly delivered mail into the outgoing mail slot. Our mail lady would re-sort it to the right box.

It dawned on me that I could have delivered the mail stack to the Eliopoulous home. They had a covered front porch. Or I could knock and hand over the mail in person.

But I wasn't willing to drive up a driveway to deliver a few pieces of mail. I'd ducked out on interacting with others during the weeks of my parents passing because of my emotional exhaustion, but I now seemed to be taking People Avoidance to new levels.

It was something to think about.

My cell phone chimed just as I finished. It was Gretchen. I rolled up the car window and took her call.

"Forecast is dry for tomorrow morning," she said. "You up for another walk?"

"Sure." Gretchen was an easy companion. I asked, "Oh, Goddess of All Things Nature, do feral cats eat baby birds?"

"Hell, yes. Is Crazy Ivy trying to tell you otherwise?"

"Yep. She thinks I have the perfect barn for some mousers."

"Better talk to Bob before you do that. He'll be furious if we have a feral cat colony on the street."

"Not happening at my place," I promised. "Hey, while I've got you. Who drives a maroon sedan?"

"On our street?"

"Yeah. A guy was parked in front of the mail tower for a bit. He was yelling."

"Bob has a truck. Dr. Jaeger has a blue BMW. Could it have been Arkady?"

"Maybe?" I wasn't sure.

"We can rubberneck from the trail," Gretchen said. "We could look to see what car is in his driveway."

"Hmm. I could write in the early morning and fit in spying about ten."

"You're on," she said.

CHAPTER FIVE

*The Mayday distress call is based on the French
word, m'aider, which means "help me."*

A MAYDAY CALL IS USUALLY REPEATED
THREE TIMES FOR CLARITY.

Friday, May 1 – 7 a.m.

THE FIRST OF May dawned cold and clear, which is great weather for writing.

I started the morning with a bowl of oatmeal and two cups of coffee. I kept myself from checking email, knowing it was too soon to hear from the credit union. Worse, email was a writing drain. If I spent half an hour deleting all the 'supplements for you' and 'donate now' emails, my creative muse would be on holiday for the morning.

Rolling my shoulders, I sat at my laptop and opened my guide to plotting a novel. Walling off my inner voice of anxiety, I went to the Basic Starting Point. Who is the Main Character, and what does the MC want?

I scrolled through the standard list. A Main Character might want to 'find love.' That was a classic. Worked for one Kami Schmidt.

Next on the list of suggested motivations was 'Save the World.' I mulled that option for a moment and discarded it. I didn't feel strong enough to dust. Saving the world seemed a bit much of an undertaking.

This took me to 'Earn Respect.' My eyes flooded with tears as a wave of grief welled up. I felt for my poor, sad novel launch. Being brutally honest, I had wanted my parents to be proud of me after my failed marriage and bombed-out Ph.D. effort.

If I'd had my ex-husband's respect, then he wouldn't be my ex.

Sniffing, I wiped my eyes with my sleeve. My nose kept running. I went to the bathroom for a tissue and tried to mop up my face. There was no trash can, so I tossed the tissues into the toilet and flushed.

The toilet gurgled and the water level rose to the rim of the bowl before slowly receding.

The choking toilet was altogether too much. Bawling, I leaned against the pseudo-Victorian wallpaper of the little bathroom and howled as tears rained down. I leaned over the sink to splash my face, only to cry some more.

There was so much missing from my life. My parents. The comradery of Graduate school. Nights of dreamless sleep. Finances that had been stable with knowledge of family resources at hand should there be a surprise expense.

All gone now.

I even missed the skunk who was my ex, who had run up twenty thousand in debt on our credit card while amusing himself with porn and gambling.

Now needing to pee saved me. I definitely did not want to tempt fate by using this downstairs toilet. I ran upstairs, used the toilet in the main bathroom, and took a moment to look out an upstairs window.

The ivory flowers of the Pacific dogwoods in the woods behind the house shone like candles against the dark green of the forest. The cold, wet days of April were done.

As I shuffled back down the wide, wooden staircase, it occurred to me that 'earn respect' might be what was motivating Eloise Eliopoulous. Why the hell else would a woman put herself into that many organizations?

It was almost time to meet Gretchen. I started to close my laptop file and my eye landed on the next Main Character Goal on the suggestion list. 'Rescue or protect.' That had Gretchen all over it. Her main characters were forever out there, doing good, at the rate of eight books a year.

"Compare and despair," I told my inner critic. "That's her. Not you."

Gretchen's main characters were always flawed, a Standard Operating Procedure for storytelling. I thought about Ivy, who was out there rescuing cats, but sure as hell did not like being challenged.

What did Ivy carry in that bulging daypack?

I needed to check the barn carefully. There was a pegboard with hand tools and a potting bench. Wasn't there a cute garden gnome on the bench? Was it a collectible? There was nothing cat-friendly that I could recall.

Shutting the laptop, it was time to give myself some Life Points for thinking about my next novel, even if I hadn't yet written a word.

Gretchen was on time. She patiently waited as I found my jacket and donned my trail shoes. As we walked to the woodland trail, I told her about the maroon car at the mail tower.

"It was pouring. I drove down to the tree farm on Delphi to turn around. Whoever it was had a long phone call," I sniffed, "He had to have seen me waiting. It was a bit rude, really."

"Might have been Arkady," Gretchen said. "His social skills aren't great. Hey, look at this!"

She pointed to a pink-bodied snail with a dark mahogany shell making his way across the trail. "Pacific Side Band Snail. Out for romance!"

"Is this a guy or a gal?" I took out my phone to take a picture and realized that an aerial shot would produce a photo that would resemble a mahogany golf ball.

"Go ahead. Get down there," Gretchen said. "Get a side view."

I would have never knelt down on the trail in the wet days of April, but this sunny start to May seemed to be another world. The slow pace of the snail made it easy to take a dozen clear pictures.

"Snails can be both male and female," Gretchen said. "They are hermaphrodites who have amazing lovemaking. This little one doesn't see well, or hear, so there's a hunt on to find the slime trail of a potential partner. Once there is a meetup, there will be hours and hours of cuddling and exploring."

"Hot stuff?"

"Actually, it's a bit of a brawl. They stab each other with love darts."

"Do what?"

Gretchen grinned down at me. "There are calcium carbonate bony structures in the snail. It uses these slivers, or "love darts" to impale the partner. The dart injects hormones that encourage the partner to accept sperm. Both snails have a penis, and they can both give and receive sperm."

"Ok." I stood up. "Are they both moms after that?"

"Nope. Each one is trying to be the father, not the mother, because, duh, being a mother is hard work. There's goop on the love dart to protect the injected sperm from rejection, so the guy with the biggest, baddest, fastest love dart is more likely to get the other snail to be a mother."

"Damn."

"There's more," Gretchen said. "Even though they cuddle for hours, they aren't very accurate with the love darts. Sometimes a snail will launch a dart, and it will pierce the head of their partner. An ugly outcome for the lovers."

"You are making me feel a bit better about being single," I said.

"Single, but not alone. You do have friends and family."

"Right." I took a breath. "I started doing a little reading about main characters and goals this morning. It's a pre-warm up to a warm up to having a thought about writing another book."

Gretchen embraced me. "Yes! This makes my day!" She let me go, beaming as she tucked her hands into her armpits and did a silly chicken strut.

She stopped and held up a finger. "You have to come to my Writers Group. It's at my house tomorrow night. You'll fit right in."

"Ah, I don't know. I don't have anything to share."

"Excellent. The rest of us share too much. There'll be wine and nibbles. Say you'll come."

"We'll see. I have so much estate stuff to do."

"And I have resources for you." Gretchen pulled out her cell phone. She said, "I found numbers for the two girls in our neighborhood. Bob said he talked to you about them. And I also have Sky's number. He sometimes helps me out with yard work. He's a good hand."

After numbers were shared to my phone, we continued down the trail. We craned necks to peer through the huckleberry bushes when we passed the back of Arkady's property, but we only saw part of his backyard. There was no sign of a maroon sedan, which, logically, would have been parked in his garage or on the drive at the front of his house.

"He's an architect?" I asked.

"Oh, better than that. He designs septic systems."

"That's better?"

Gretchen winked. "Professional skills with less stress than being an architect. The workday ends by five."

I could have picked Gretchen's mind for details on the Eliopoulous family as we wandered past the rear of the peaches-and-cream mansion, but I found I really wasn't that interested. Instead, we spoke about the returning geese honking overhead, and the fun of seeing turkey vultures riding wind currents as they circled high in the sky.

"We're forest bathing," Gretchen said. "Reviving our souls. Building strengths, connecting with the ecosystem. Are you feeling the empowerment?"

"I'm feeling that the knees of my jeans are wet after kneeling down to take pictures," I said. "It's surprising how little it bothers me after yesterday's soaking."

"See. Tougher already."

We walked a bit further, then reversed, with Gretchen continuing to act as travel guide.

My phone pinged once. I glanced at the text from my brother. He'd sent, "Glynnis here. Barky dog. Help?"

I decided not to respond just yet. I couldn't see having Ashlee's mother out to stay with me. The idea was depressing in the extreme. I hoped the credit union would approve my loan application. That would give us all some breathing space.

It would be better to call Kent with loan details than text now. I switched off my phone and took in a deep breath of fir-scented air.

Gretchen blessed me with a wink and a nod of approval.

We descended the trail spur that led to my family's backyard. I kept thinking of the olive-green farmhouse as 'my family's,' even as I was the sole resident. We traipsed around the house to the side door near the kitchen where there was a small covered porch with a bench and a rack to hold outside footwear.

A cardboard carton of eggs sat on the bench. The top of the carton was embossed with a Yo Mommas' Llamas logo. There was a lined indexing card next to the carton with a handwritten note.

I picked up the card and read it aloud to Gretchen. "Sorry to have kept you waiting at the mailbox yesterday. My apologies. Your neighbor, Arkady."

Gretchen's eyebrows rose. "How very interesting," she said.

CHAPTER SIX

Beware the barrenness of a busy life.

SOCRATES

Friday, May 1 - 11:00 a.m.

GRETCHEN DECLINED MY offer of coffee and a late-morning snack. "Books don't write themselves," she said. "I need fifteen hundred words to stay on schedule."

"Working title?" I asked.

"*Kind Kami's Camisole Adventure*." Gretchen's eyes sparkled as her words were delivered dead pan.

"No!"

"I'll change the title if you come to the Writers Group tomorrow night."

"How about changing it to *Gretchen's Basic Blackmail Challenge*?"

"Seven o'clock. Don't be late." Gretchen paused, then added, "I'm really glad you turned down the barn cats. Bob's been a bit down lately. He's got some health issues. Cats around his bird feeders would be an additional bummer."

"He seemed tired yesterday," I said. "What's up?"

"Old age." She paused before adding, "He knows he needs to start reducing his own collections, and he's struggling with it."

I couldn't find a response that didn't sound bitter, but managed, "It's tough."

Gretchen nodded and waved a goodbye.

Minutes later I was divested of my shoes and jacket. The wall clock in the kitchen showed it was almost eleven. I could get an hour of estate processing in before the high school kids had their lunch hour. Gretchen had suggested texting them. She'd said, "Friday noon is a great time to catch Sky, before he makes Saturday plans."

I trudged into the dining room and stared at the taxidermied jackalope sitting on the far end of the long table. I dusted, measured and photographed the thing. My next tasks would be to write a blurb, then upload the paragraph and photos to eBay.

It was depressing beyond words. Even if there were one or more teens to assist, would it go any faster?

There had to be a better way to handle the hundreds of items on the property, or at least identify and address the valuable things.

What if the process were reversed?

I didn't give myself time to hesitate. I left the dining room for my father's office where I went to the nearest of four tall filing cabinets.

Yanking the top drawer open, I grabbed a handful of folders and went back to the dining room. The first folder was labeled 'Appliances.' It held instruction manuals and receipts for a refrigerator and a dryer that had been replaced. There were also articles clipped from Consumer Reports, and a sheet of pros and cons for buying solar panels, written in my father's hand.

I was in a ruthless mindset, quickly dumping the lot into the recycle bin under the dining table.

The next folder was labeled, 'Appalachia, 2012.' It should have been in front of Appliances, but I knew my father's filing was often only loosely alphabetical. The folder held gold.

That is, it held receipts that could be turned to gold. There were notes from a trip my parents had taken from West Virginia south through eastern Kentucky, Tennessee and ending in northern Georgia. My mother's notes told me the redbud trees had been spectacular.

And the shopping had been delightful. I found an eye-popping receipt for "Artist-Signed Blue Ridge Pottery Plates" with the note "Keep for special occasions" also written by my mother. I knew then to look in the bottom shelf of the sideboard where holiday dishes resided.

Off I went like a kid on a scavenger hunt, to the massive sideboard in our formal entry way. There I found two dozen plates carefully packed into two cardboard boxes, each marked 'Blue Ridge.'

The computer helped me find more on 'Blue Ridge Pottery.' There were hundreds of postings, most selling for modest amounts, but the Artist-Signed pieces were in a different league.

My parent's purchase of three-hundred dollars of plates might be worth two thousand today.

I returned to the file and found a five-hundred-dollar receipt for an Appalachian dulcimer. My online research bogged down for a moment as my fingers kept finding error-prone ways to type 'Appalachia,' but I soon sorted that a dulcimer was a musical instrument, which meant it should be upstairs in the bedroom my mother called her 'music room.' It had a comfortable arm chair, a CD player and a nice reading lamp.

There were instruments in cases in the closet. I had thought it was only my brother's middle school trombone and a rather sad old guitar, but this receipt suggested there could be at least one more instrument, possibly of value. The file folder also had a trifold brochure listing the wood of the instrument, the maker's name and the year of construction.

File folder sleuthing took time. It was dirty work too, and yet this last half hour had me zero in on twenty-five hundred dollars of easily sellable items. I washed my hands and sent a text to the three teenagers. "Wish to hire help with estate paperwork. Good pay. Text or stop by after class. Your neighbor at 8674, the green farmhouse. Kami Schmidt."

I'd have to check in with Kent on what "good pay" was these days, but at least I now had the beginnings of a plan. Instead of roaming through the house trying to identify the high-end collectables, the teens could work through the filing cabinets, looking for receipts or references. The filing cabinets had to be cleaned out before the house changed hands, so it'd be a double win.

The teens should be on the lookout for items valued at more than a hundred dollars. I fetched thumb tacks and index cards from a kitchen drawer and returned to the dining room. I labeled one card, "ceramics/dishes" and another, "instruments" and tacked the cards to the wall, adding the receipts I'd found underneath.

It was a big wall. We'd need it.

Checking email along with eating a sandwich, I saw the credit union had approved my application! I called Kent.

"We have a home equity loan lined up," I said. "Which gives us some capital to work with. Could you and Ashlee come out together for a planning session?"

Before he could object, it was easy to add, "I know time off is hard, but we really need to be on the same page. There may be three teens to help me work through the file cabinets. Between the loan and identifying some big-ticket items, we can muddle through to getting the house on the market."

"That is fantastic," Kent said. "My God, that gives me hope!" He paused. "I think we could get there this afternoon. Duc is working after lunch. He'll be fine if I leave the shop for a bit. Let me give Ashlee a call. Maybe Glynnis can watch the girls."

"Glynnis arrived this morning?"

"Early."

There was a ton of weight behind the word. My heart went out to my brother. "How's the dog?" I asked.

"Barks. A lot. Gotta customer walking in. See you soon. Glad you put in for the loan."

I cleaned up my breakfast and lunch dishes before returning to the dining room table. The next folder was labeled 'Apples' and held descriptions of trees my parents had planted on the property. I made a new note card, labeling it 'Home Sales Details' and tacked it and the tree list to the wall.

The rest of the folder pile was simply tedious. I tossed perused paper into the recycling bin and fetched another pile of folders from my father's office.

My phone chirped with incoming texts. Sky would stop by after school. So would Cadence. My brother sent, "About 2:30. After Ami's nap."

I continued ferreting through the A folders. Air conditioning articles were an easy toss, knowing my parents had upgraded the house to a heat pump a decade before. This was followed by articles on Alabama, Albania, Acapulco and Growing Acacias. There was a thick folder on the Abominable Snowman with a note to also see the folders on Bigfoot and Sasquatch.

"He missed 'Yeti'," I grumbled.

I had some hope for treasure when opening a folder marked, 'Accessories,' but only found 2002 directions on how to add microphones to a home sound system.

At least this was still real progress. I thought about drafting a budget for how we'd use the loan money, then decided to wait to hear Kent's preferences.

With a sigh, I returned to the folders. After another hour of concentration, my eyes were drooping. I crossed my arms over a stack of folders and went to sleep.

Silly me, I didn't lock the doors.

CHAPTER SEVEN

---

*If you do not change direction, you may
end up where you are heading.*

Lao Tzu

Friday, May 1- 2:30 p.m.

I AWOKE TO a shriek and a shout. My sister-in-law was bellow-
ing, "I said, put that DOWN."

Rubbing my eyes was a mistake. My hands were gritty from
handling stacks of folders and their innards.

Eyes smarting, I winced more as a crashing sound came from
the kitchen. Moments later, my niece, Mai, came running into
the dining room, laughter on her face.

"Hey, sport!" I snatched her up and gave her a small toss up
into the air. She squealed and yelled, "Gan!" which I translated
as "Again."

"Oomph. You are heavier than you used to be." I swung her
around by her arms. She accepted this as a fun substitute.

Ashlee came in, sour faced and balancing baby Ami on her

55

hip. "Sorry, about a coffee cup in the kitchen," she said. "You've got a crease on your cheek. Looks like we woke you up."

"It's okay." I sat back down in a dining room chair and lifted Mai to my lap. Her bottom felt damp, and she was pungent with the sewer-smell of a loaded diaper. "I was sorting through some folders and blinked off."

"Must be nice," Ashlee sniffed. "Wish I had time for an afternoon snooze."

"Don't the girls have a nap?" Mai was wiggling in my lap now, saying something that sounded like "Down."

"Sometimes." Ashlee groaned. "Not today. Damn barking dog."

"I'm so sorry," I said.

"But you're not sorry enough to help me out."

"Ashlee, believe it or not, I'm working really hard out here." I had a flash of guilt as I thought of my long morning walk with Gretchen.

I said, "Sorting through all these things isn't exactly skittles and beer. It's depressing and exhausting."

"You have a house to yourself. No rent. No responsibilities. Why not take a thousand years to sort through some papers?" Ashlee sneered. "Sounds like a life of Riley to me."

"You'd be wrong."

"Anybody here?" My brother's voice came in from the kitchen.

"Daddddddda!" Mai's wriggling became a full body contortion.

I set her down, and she ran, thick little legs flashing, to the door just as Kent stepped in and grinned. "My little beauty! Come to see Aunt Kami?"

He swooped Mai up in a hug, then blinked. "Whoa. Stinkpot. You need a change."

"Yes, she does, and you can do it!" Ashlee flushed pink as she hugged baby Ami. "I should have changed Mai before I left the house, but we all know I'm the world's worst mother on top of being a terrible businesswoman."

Tears glinted, then spilled to roll down her cheeks. "Let's all just say it. I'm a stupid loser, and a total ball-and-chain."

"Ashlee." Kent carried Mai, damp as she was, on his hip and went to his wife, encircling her with his free arm. "If anyone's a rotten businessperson, it's me. Let's not kid ourselves."

Ashlee leaned into Kent and burst into a full rain of tears. "You had a plan," she sobbed. "I just torpedoed everything."

I sat there, watching my sister-in-law, with my mouth open. Several highly inappropriate thoughts went winging through my brain.

Agreeing with my brother that he didn't have a head for business wasn't a smart move. Saying that Ashlee wasn't the world's worst mother, because, hey, the Greek goddess Medea flat out *murdered* her kids? Well, that also didn't seem smart. Agreeing that Mai should have been changed earlier didn't sound wise either.

And commenting on the wisdom of buying five thousand dollars of essential oils on the store credit card? Nope. I wasn't going there.

Ashlee leaned into Kent and continued to weep.

This, at least, I understood. Despite our different paths to the destination, Ashlee and I were both on planet Overwhelmed earning zero respect for our efforts and having no launchpad standing by with a handy, dandy escape pod.

I grabbed up my pen and wrote furiously on the outside of a manila folder. This was it! My next Main Character would be female, and she needed to escape a doomed planet before it imploded. She'd be in her early thirties, and she'd be smart but not brilliant. Her super power would be resilience, and…

Mai's scream of "Down!" pulled me back. She was wiggling like a landed trout, but my brother wasn't letting her go.

"You can run around after you're changed," Kent told his

daughter. To Ashlee he said, "I'll do it, if you tell me where the diaper bag is. And we're going to be okay. Kami found a way to get a cash flow started."

Ashlee sniffed, wiping her face with her sleeve. "The diaper bag is in the car. I'm sorry, baby. I should have brought it in." She sniffed again. "It's raining. God give me strength, it's always raining."

This too, I recognized. Olympia has a long, cool spring with abundant showers that can seem endless. I stood up. "While Kent's changing Mai, why don't you sit down? Can I get you a cup of tea?"

Tears welled up again. "That'd be so nice," Ashlee wailed. "I was so awful to you and now you're making me a cup of tea."

It seemed a bit churlish to tell her that drowning a tea bag was a small price to pay for a story inspiration. I came up with a smile and a shrug. "I was bawling my eyes out after my oatmeal this morning. As hard as we are trying, we ought to at least get bonus points for effort."

I pulled out a dining room chair and motioned her to it. She sank down into the chair with the baby clutched to her chest and tears streaming down her face.

Ashlee was a bit more collected by the time I returned from the kitchen with cups of tea on a tray. I put a pile of cookies on a plate too.

Little Ami was nursing, a plump foot kicking into the air, as I set the tea cup and cookie plate down.

"Thank you," Ashlee said. "I really haven't been myself."

"Me either."

We drank tea to the sound of Ami's grunts and sighs.

Kent came in, carrying a giggling Mai like a football. He sat down at the table and plucked cookies off the plate for his daughter.

"Quick," he said. "This will only keep her still for a couple of minutes."

"You didn't tell Ashlee about the credit union?" I asked.

He shook his head. "Didn't have time. Go ahead."

Turning to my sister-in-law, I said, "We know this house will sell for about seven hundred thousand dollars. Maybe more if it's cleaned up. Your idea to identify valuable collectibles first before calling in an auction house was a great idea, but I am too slow at it."

Ashlee blinked. She clearly was not expecting to be told she'd had a great idea.

She sniffed, nodded and took another shaky sip of the herbal tea.

I could feel my confidence rising in the plan as I said, "If we can pull together, and hire some help, we might be able to get the house on the market in a month or so. We need help, but we are lacking a cash stream."

If there is a Goddess of Smooth Words, She was working with me now, sprinkling star dust on my use of 'we.'

Ashlee blessed me with a stronger nod of agreement.

I went on. "There's no mortgage on the place. Yesterday I applied for a thirty-thousand-dollar home equity loan with the credit union. When this property sells, we will get the sales price minus the real estate agents' fees and minus any of this loan that we've used."

"Got it." Ashlee exhaled. "It's not one of those scammy loans like we get text messages about for the shop."

"Right. This morning the loan was approved. But we need a plan. Kent and I don't have a great money management history."

"Nah. We do!" my brother corrected. "We have a great history of watching money flow out the door."

"You should have this house re-roofed," Ashlee said. "And painted. It looks so sad right now. Sad houses don't sell well."

"Re-roofed," Kent agreed, "But we might get away with having the house pressure washed and the windows professionally cleaned."

"There's the store rent," I said. "You need to catch up on that."

Kent exhaled. "It'd be a huge help. We should do more business as the weather warms up." He looked at Ashlee. "If we can have a good summer, then we might get into a situation where we can expand our offerings for the fall and winter."

To me, he said, "We've got Baskin Robbins on the west side, and Olympic Mountain Ice Cream has the upper end sewed up. We can't compete. We need to offer more food choices or sell the business. What we're doing isn't working."

"Either way," I said, "Getting you a strong summer is a smart move."

"Right."

"I'll keep working on unloading the essential oils," Ashlee said. "I am going to at least try to come out even."

"Is your mother any help there?" I asked.

Ashlee sniffed as Kent's shoulders came forward in a hunch. I didn't need the Twin Connection to sort out the answer was 'No.'

"She thinks she is," Ashlee managed. "She's sure telling me what to do."

"Is she sleeping on your sofa?"

"No. She's in Mai's new big girl bed," Ashlee sighed. "All of us are in our bed."

I looked at Mai, now flopping around her father's lap like a landed trout. "That has to stink."

"More ways than one," my brother agreed.

"That dog," Ashlee said, "is a mess. Mother says she is training him, but I'm not seeing it."

"What kind of dog is it?" I'm not sure why I asked. I know very little about dogs.

Kent said, "She calls Truffles a MinPin, which is a miniature pincher. He looks like a foot-high Doberman. Smooth coat. Hyperactive as hell."

"Truffles?" I asked. "Like the mushrooms?"

"I guess." Kent sighed. "Maybe it's one of the dogs that can find buried truffles? I'll be happy if she can just train it to quit yapping."

Kent rubbed his eyes. "Truffles barks at everything. I do mean everything."

Baby Ami let go of her mother's breast with a burp. Ashlee smoothly tilted the baby up while adjusting her clothes and smiling down at her daughter. "Topped off, little girl?" Ashlee cooed.

Ami beamed and thrust her legs out like plump little pistons.

"Ashlee," I said. "You have blessings. I have blessings. We both have challenges. Should we compare? I don't have a partner. I don't have a baby. Once this place sells, I won't have a home."

My sister-in-law froze, a miserable look replacing her maternal smiles.

"I'm so, so sorry," Ashlee said. Her body sagged as she shifted baby Ami. "I've been such a screw up, and it's embarrassing. I shouldn't have said what I did."

"Yep. No more using me as your punching bag." I crossed my arms and gave her a hard stare. "But I'll take your advice on what can help get this place shaped up. What else should we hire done?"

"Interior cleaning," my sister-in-law said. "Bathrooms and kitchens sell houses. Those spaces should sparkle." She stood up as she added, "I'll take the girls home. You and Kent can plan out expenses. You don't need me."

"I'm glad you came out," I said. "It's good to be on the same page."

"It is." Ashlee exhaled. "You're right. I was fantasizing about your life out here. I'd give anything to have five minutes in the bathroom alone." Her eyes produced a small sparkle as she said, "I don't want to put the girls in daycare, and I want to be a successful businesswoman. I am woman, hear me be conflicted."

I laughed. "The 70s classic? Man, that's ancient."

"My mom likes it. I'd write an update to the lyrics if I could find two neurons not too tired to fire." Ashlee nuzzled Ami's neck. "There we go, baby girl. Momma will make a fortune with her non-existent musical talents."

Her eyes flashed with humor. "Stinky singers in sweatpants being the in-thing these days."

"Kent," I said, "One of the budget items should be a salon day for Ashlee."

"What?" Ashlee had Ami on one hip and had been extending a hand to Mai. Now she stopped and stared at me.

"Do hair. Skin and…" I waggled my fingers.

"A manicure? Seriously? You think there's money for that?"

"You're about to sell thousands of dollars of product," I said. "Sad houses don't sell well," I quoted back to her.

Her eyes went to Kent.

"Hey," he said. "Why the hell not? I'll bet Glynnis will watch the girls for a few hours. She talks about investing in oneself all the time." He gave Mai a guiding push towards Ashlee. "And if Glynnis won't, we'll figure out something. Kami's right. You should catch a break. You've been working as hard as the rest of us. Heck, more so because we get coffee breaks and a chance to go to the toilet without company."

Ashlee's sweet smile about broke my heart. Her days were as mentally burdened as mine. Now she waggled her fingers and just about floated out of the room, gently shushing Mai when the little girl tried to reach for a fourth cookie.

"Thanks," my brother said.

"Not a problem." And it wasn't.

"I know a roofer," he said. "I think he was out here last year to give a quote, but things got postponed. I'll give him a call."

"Super." We sketched out a plan and agreed I'd transfer money for the store's back rent to his account.

My fingers itched to get back to the story notes I'd scribbled. I could feel the writer's river of story-building growing.

Which, of course, meant the doorbell chimed.

Get a good story idea budding and the whole world shows up on your doorstep. Never fails.

Chapter Eight

Friday, May 1 - 3:40 p.m.

I LEFT KENT at the table and went to answer the door, realizing that the afternoon was getting on. Any of the three teens might be on my doorstep, and I should figure out what to say, plus decide our payrate.

I opened the door to find Hollywood on the welcome mat.

A fantastically gorgeous young man stood inches away from my astonished face. He stood about six foot two and had impossibly broad shoulders. Luxurious dark hair swept across his forehead, providing a partial curtain for eyes as blue as lupines.

Of course, those glorious orbs were heavily fringed with dark eyelashes.

To round out the dazzling presence, there was a smile revealing perfectly straight, blazingly white teeth and a pair of giant hands holding out an egg carton.

"I'm Sky," the dreamboat said. "I'm here about the job? And I brought you some eggs."

It seemed rude to ignore the outstretched hands. It was the second dozen eggs to arrive in twenty-four hours, but I like eggs.

The Douglas squirrel chittered her warnings about this new arrival as I took the eggs and stammered, "I'm Kami."

I could hear my brother's footsteps coming down the hallway. I waved a hand and said, "And this is my brother, Kent."

Sky must have been nervous because he began speaking rapidly. "I've worked with computer files and advertising for our llama wool products. I'm reliable, and there's no commute, so I shouldn't be late. I'm earning money for college. I'd really like the job."

Kent was now at the door, exclaiming, "You're hired!" Kent clapped a hand on my shoulder and added, "We need the help, and you can make a difference."

He was right, of course, but I was feeling crowded. I'm a cynical little control freak who is deeply skeptical of fast, happy results. We hadn't discussed salary or hours, and these two were smiling like all was right with the world.

I didn't have a chance to regain control of things as a very tiny and lime green Smart Car arrived, bumping up the drive, before slowing to a stop next to our porch.

"Juno." Sky's voice was reverent as he breathed the name.

A leggy girl with a long cascade of light oaken hair emerged from the car. She had a broad, open face that broke into a wide smile as her eyes lit on Sky.

A short, dark-haired girl stepped out of the far side of the car and followed Juno.

Sky stood frozen as the girls came up the steps.

Juno spoke to me and the Sky-statue. "We just got out of

Student Council. We came as fast as we could. Sky, are you our competition for the job?" Juno asked, "Any interest in job sharing? We could work together!"

Everything about Juno was long. Her hair, her legs, her torso. Now she brought together two long oaken-brown eyebrows in a look of concern. "Are we too late? If you've hired Sky, I get it. He's amazing."

It was a good thing I'd taken the egg carton because Sky was doing a great imitation of a doorstop. When Juno flipped a hank of hair away from her face, I swear I could feel an ocean of hormones emanating from Sky to swamp the porch in a high tidal wave of awe and desire.

Kent spoke. "We're just doing introductions. I'm Kent and this is my sister, Kami."

"Juno." Her long fingers waggled a hello. "And this is Cadence."

Cadence stepped forward confidently and offered a handshake. Having omitted this social courtesy made Juno blush and shuffle.

I knew Kent hired teens to help in the ice cream shop, and now I saw his experience in play. His tone was light and welcoming as he described a house full of belongings, the need to separate the valuable from the mundane, and the challenge of finding the corresponding paperwork to add value to the collectibles.

"We could use all three of you," he said. "Pay is twenty dollars an hour. Scheduling is flexible, but we need to get a lot done, fast."

Juno brought her long eyebrows together again. "Estate processing means someone has passed away. I am so sorry for your loss."

A smidgen of the cynical tightness in my soul thawed a bit. A girl this beautiful could be an entitled princess or a mean thing. Juno, however, was showing herself to be enthusiastic, friendly, and above all, kind.

"Our parents," I said.

"Oh," Juno said. "That's so hard."

Cadence was all business. "Sorry for your loss. You need some help. I need the money. Can we start work now?"

Kent lifted an eyebrow my direction.

The Douglas squirrel went into overdrive with her warning calls. I ignored her.

"Sure," I said. "Come on in."

Kent stayed almost a half hour longer. I was grateful for his calm, clear instructions. The teens were to work in the dining area. They were not to handle the katanas. They could use the bathroom down the hall, Kent said.

"Wait," I interrupted. "That toilet has been gurgling. I'm not sure what's going on with it. There are bathrooms upstairs."

All three teens had laptops in their daypacks, a necessity I hadn't considered.

Although I had spent many summers as a camp counselor and had worked as a university teaching assistant, I hadn't actually hired workers before. There were details and then more details to cover.

Kent reviewed the basics of file security. I saw head nods and arms unfold as he laid out our preferences, naming pragmatic steps and inviting questions.

Sky still vibrated with a lashed-down intensity as he angled to be close to Juno. I suspected her shy smiles to him were hitting like hurricane slaps against a seawall.

If I put a pair of massively hormonal young people in my new novel, would they be relatable? Or a distraction?

I scribbled a note on my folder cover as Kent went over food stuffs. Breaks were fine, he said, but not chips eaten over paperwork.

A few minutes later, Kent waved a goodbye and headed back to town to relieve his shop assistant. Sky's brain began emerging from its hormone-induced fog as he opened his laptop to design a spreadsheet. I took the carton of eggs into the kitchen and returned with a small oil painting of a Fairy Slipper orchid that my mother had hung near the kitchen door.

"We can work this process two ways," I said to the teens. "First, there's working through the file folders, identifying items of value from receipts or supporting documents. When you find a good clue, check in with me, and I'll give you some ideas of where we might find that item." I told them about my success finding the Artist-Signed Blue Ridge pottery.

"I found the receipt, then located the box," I told them. "Next will be unpacking the box, and photographing and writing a description of each piece, to include measurements."

"I'm good at going through files," Juno said. "I've helped my father with that sort of thing."

"Photos are my thing," Sky said. "And I've written sales text before. My moms sell wool online."

"Research for me," Cadence said. "Definitely my strength."

"A different path," I explained, "is to notice an item, like this little oil painting, and then try to think where documentation or information could be filed. It might be under 'P' for 'painting' or 'O' for 'orchid' or something else, like the painter's name."

"Who is the painter?" Cadence asked. Her fingers were poised over her keyboard.

"If we're lucky, this is a Winslow Homer," I joked.

She typed a moment, then leaned back with a whistle. "An original Winslow Homer can be worth *millions*."

"I'm teasing," I said. "It's not a Winslow Homer. Unless we can decipher the artist's signature and find documentation in our files of its provenance, what we have is a nice little painting of a plant." I shook my head. "Don't get your hopes up. We're looking to find the things that might be worth a hundred dollars or more. I doubt there will be anything worth a great deal."

While three heads of gloriously thick teenager hair all bobbed in acknowledgement, I could still feel their excitement for being in on a hunt. To be paid to find treasure was a most excellent student gig.

"As you get something figured, please go ahead and make out a card and tack the card on the wall, with the receipt if there is one," I said. "That will give me a quick visual."

I made an executive decision. "Why don't you work on this for a bit? I've got things to do, but there's some frozen pizza that I can bake. We can have pizza about six and plan a course of action for the weekend."

Cadence raised a hand, "Would it be alright if I walked around to find items that could be researched?"

"Sure. Knock yourself out. Bring what you find here, and we'll start a To-Be-Researched pile."

"Any place I shouldn't go?" she asked.

"My bedroom upstairs," I replied. "Second door, down the hall. It's a mess, and there's not much in it besides my own stuff." I took a breath and added, "You can definitely work in my mother's music room upstairs. It has a wall of art, and there's knickknacks. You could grab a basket from the laundry room and bring down a few pieces that look promising."

We split up, and I returned to the kitchen to make lists of things that needed doing.

At six I carried in a stack of plates and napkins to serve pizza and found the dining area had been transformed into a war room. Sky's hair stood up like a cockatoo crest as he ran a hand through it while scrutinizing a photo on his laptop. "Not focused," he mumbled. "Damn."

It looked like a perfectly fine photo to me.

"Ready for some pizza?" I asked.

"Definitely." Sky stood up and stretched his impressive long frame. "Getting a good, focused shot can be hard," he said. "I'm getting better at it."

Cadence had a dozen small pieces of art spread out on the long buffet at the rear of the dining room. "Making progress," she said. "I think these four are from a local artist. I can ask my mom."

"Super," I told her. "That helps."

Juno had a greasy streak on one cheek and a giant stack of folders at her feet. "Your parents collected lots of interesting articles," she said. "I'm starting the Cs. And I found this, under *Currency*." She held up a certificate of authenticity for a Roman coin with a clipped-on receipt for four hundred and fifty-seven dollars.

"Super. They may have picked that up on their trip to Italy." I looked at the certificate. "From the Numismatic Guaranty Corporation. That sounds official. We need to keep eyes open for a coin, probably in a clear box or perhaps in a frame."

"Good find!" I waved at the stacks of things on the table. "Can you make a space? And this is dirty work. Washing up is a smart idea."

I very much enjoyed the pizza and brainstorming session that followed. The young people were into the mission.

They were eager to continue, but even with pizza I was running on fumes. "Can you come back tomorrow? About ten in the morning?"

Juno agreed. Sky said he had something to sort with his mothers, but he'd 'find a way' to make a schedule shift.

Then Cadence said, "Pretty sure my folks don't give a damn about where I spend the weekend. I'm in."

The teens helped clear the pizza plates and were moving out the front door when my brother called.

"That goddamned dog," Kent said. "Bit Mai. In the face."

Calypso
bulbosa

CHAPTER NINE

We need the tonic of wilderness.

HENRY DAVID THOREAU

Friday, May 1 - 7 p.m.

THERE'S NOTHING QUITE as deflating as capitulation. Although the farmhouse had five bedrooms and a fenced backyard, I had held firm against Kent's mother-in-law being a temporary roomie. I saw no upside to having Glynnis and her pet in my space, even if this was 'my' space for only the short term.

However, as Kent's furious story unfolded, I caved. A small house with adults busy preparing dinner had set the stage for a fast and disastrous meetup between an enthusiastic toddler and a wired little dog.

"Send Glynnis and the vampire hound out here," I said. "They can have the blue room."

"Thanks." I could hear Kent exhale in an effort to stay calm.

"How bad is the bite?" I asked. "Does Mai need stitches?"

"We got lucky there. The skin wasn't broken. Honestly, I can't totally fault the dog. It happened so fast. Mai ran at him. He tried to get away, but then she had him by the ear, and he snapped. More a warning snap than anything, I guess."

"And her face was right there," I said. "Kid face being the same height as dog mouth."

"Right. Caught her on the cheek. It's a bit bruised." Kent took another settling breath. "Christ, she screamed like she'd lost a limb."

"And Glynnis?" I asked, then added, "Scratch that question. If it'd been a good response, you wouldn't be calling me."

"Thanks, twin."

"Hey, I got a line of credit going if you need bail money."

"I don't think they set bail when there's a homicide charge," Kent grumbled. "I'm going to hang up now. I am going to tell Glynnis she and Truffles can have a bed with you, or she can get a motel, but she's out of here within the hour."

"Got it. Love you."

"Love you too." Kent clicked off.

I treated the kitchen walls to a pithy stream of curse words before glancing at the wall clock. Glynnis, being Glynnis, would take Kent's full hour to pack up. It'd take her another twenty minutes to drive out. I really should run upstairs to the blue bedroom to do some preparation. There was an attached bathroom that I never used. I had no memory on whether it was stocked with soap or toilet paper.

"Screw the shoulds," I muttered. There was over an hour of daylight left. I shrugged on a jacket, stuffed a headlamp and my phone in the pockets and headed for the woods.

My previous walks through the forest had always been with Gretchen and had been morning walks. Now I realized there were wonders to be found in the early evening. The light was different.

A gentle breeze carried the fragrance of firs and cedars. A tiny yellow violet gleamed from a shadowy nook. The perfection of the violet just a foot away from a tangled mass of last year's bracken ferns had me thinking of my neighborhood. The shiny violet looked as bright as Dr. Jaeger's house. The tangled mass of dead ferns surely represented my life.

I was getting better at scanning the forest floor as I walked. "Aha!" I spoke out loud as I spied a handsome mushroom. It's light, svelte stem and light brunette cap shone like an actress at the Oscars as it was front lit by a sunbeam. A sprinkling of ivory spots dotted the cap. There was even a full skirt hanging from the waist of the mushroom.

Kneeling, I marveled at the graceful beauty of this handsome mushroom. It was extraordinary. I started taking pictures, talking to the mushroom like a photographer on a fashion shoot. "Your left side is marvelous, darling," I crooned.

As absorbed as I was in the photography, my ears weren't completely off duty. I heard a cough and a snuffle. I managed to rock to my heels and shut up just as my neighbor, Delphina, came shuffling down the trail.

Delphina is a big woman. This day she wore a dark purple raincoat that contrasted with her cloud of red-brown hair. She carried a small basket and a walking stick.

"Out for mushrooms?" I called.

With a smile she came closer. "Collecting fern fiddleheads," she said. "And please don't eat that mushroom. It's *Amanita pantherinoides.*"

"It's poisonous?"

"Yes," she said. "It contains three or four different toxins. There are some recipes for getting high off of it, but I can't recommend any of them."

"No problem." I rose to my feet. "I was just admiring it."

"It has a European counterpart," Delphina said. "*Amanita pantherina.* Recent DNA work has shown the mushroom of the

Pacific Northwest is different enough to be its own species. *Amanitas* can be very complicated."

"You've studied them?" It was dawning on me how little I knew of this immediate neighbor. I knew she did book indexing work and had cats. Delphina's backyard fencing had a long overhang that kept the cats in. I could imagine Gretchen and Bob approved of the feature.

Beyond this, I knew little of Delphina.

"I'm no expert," Delphina said. "I belong to a local mushroom club that has monthly lectures. A professor came through with a long PowerPoint show. When I wasn't snoozing, I did pick up a few bits."

I smiled at her easy humor. "I'm a novelist," I told her. "This mushroom has the characteristics to make an interesting villain. Beautiful, complex and poisonous in several ways." I almost added, "Reminds me of my brother's mother-in-law" but that seemed like oversharing.

"Did you like the eggs?" she asked.

I blinked. The eggs that Sky had brought? Or was she referring to the earlier eggs left on the porch by our neighbor, Arkady?

"They're great," I said. "We are so lucky to have free-range eggs available. A dozen eggs is such a nice treat." There. I was grateful without being specific.

Delphina beamed. "Arkady was so worried that he had been rude to keep you waiting at the mailbox."

"No worries. I think he must have had an important call." I wasn't going to mention the shouting, but I was all ears if Delphina knew more.

Her easy smile slackened. She said, "He's having a bit of a rough week. He's not neurotypical, you know."

"I don't know him at all," I admitted. "I've been working on clearing out my parents' place, and I haven't been social. If anyone's been rude, it's been me. I have been very absorbed in stuff." I paused, then managed, "It was good of you to drop off a sympathy card. I have been meaning to tell you 'Thank you.' Time just got away from me."

"Your parents were wonderful to me," Delphina said. "Not everyone welcomes a fat, old cat lady as a neighbor."

I blinked. I could see how Delphina might have such a label, but those words would have to come from someone terribly mean.

"Somebody doesn't like your cats?" I asked.

"Ms. Fancy Pants Eloise Eliopoulous for one," Delphina said. "When I asked her for a donation to the Feline Friends Fur Babies fundraiser, she told me I should be concerned about unborn babies, and the whole idea of fur babies is silly."

"Your babies are your babies," I said. "Did she really do body shaming too?"

Delphina's eyes lit with the shine of anger and the easy curve of her mouth moved downward. "She didn't have to say the words. You can tell."

I knew what she meant. I asked, "How does she get along with Ivy?"

Delphina snorted. "I haven't been present with both of them, but one can imagine." She pulled in her chin and looked at me. "I hope you won't take on a feral cat colony. To do a colony right is significant work."

"Not happening," I assured her. "We're working through my parents' belongings, and then the house goes on the market."

"Good. I mean, good that you aren't adding a feral cat colony."

"Why doesn't Ivy have the cats at her place?"

"Too close to the traffic on our county road. She's hoping for a place at the bottom of the cul-de-sac," Delphina answered.

"Yo Mommas' Llamas couldn't take cats. Not with their chickens," I said. "Gretchen and Bob are birders. I can't see Dr. Jaeger and stray cats combining."

"Which leaves your place – and your place has outbuildings."

"I see the allure, but I'm not a cat house host. I just can't." I looked down the trail with some longing. "Honestly, I'd like to keep going and not come back. I'm about to have my brother's mother-in-law for a visit. I might as well warn you. Her name is Glynnis, and she's coming with a yappy dog."

"What breed is the dog?" Delphina's eyes shone bright with interest.

"A miniature pincher, I think."

"The MinPin are fast, athletic dogs," Delphina said. "They don't do well with small children."

"Wow. You know about the breed?"

"I do book indexing for a living. I know so much trivia I'm banned from the trivia night at the Cozy Corners Bar and Grill."

I laughed. "This dog is named Truffles, and he's banished from my brother's house for snapping at one of his kids."

"Truffles? Is he trained to hunt mushrooms?" Delphina frowned. "It's not a breed I associate with truffle hunting. The MinPin is a toy dog. Truffle hunters are more often hunting dogs, like retrievers, spaniels or pointers."

"I think his owner has high hopes and no experience." Glynnis did not strike me as a doggy sort.

"MinPins are excellent agility dogs," Delphina spoke with an encouraging smile, even as she added, "They require training from confident, experienced hands."

"We can count on Glynnis to be confident," My tone bordered on sour. "Experienced or even somewhat competent remains to be seen."

"Oh, dear," Delphina said.

"My sentiments, exactly."

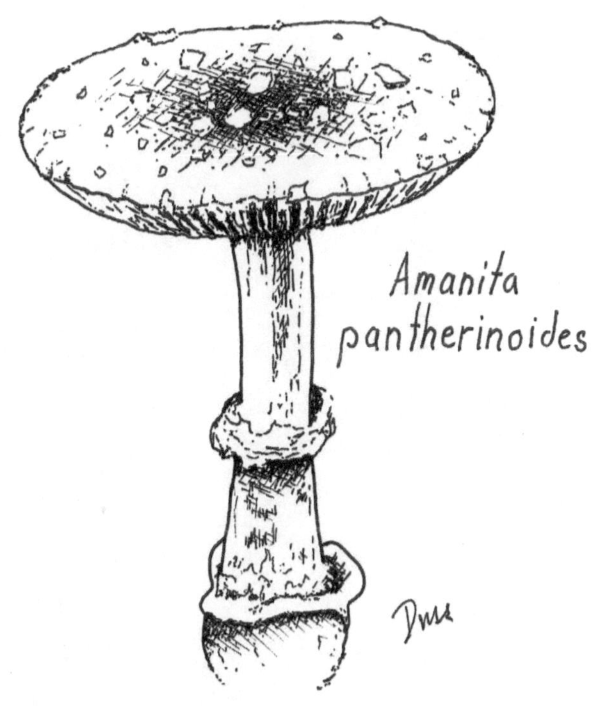

Amanita
pantherinoides

Chapter Ten

A friend is another self.

Zeno of Elea

Friday, May 1 – 8 p.m.

DELPHINA INVITED ME to accompany her in the hunt for fern fiddleheads. "It's really the end of the fiddlehead season," she said. "I've had a major project, and I didn't get out much in April. Now the job is finished, but the ferns are almost all unfurled."

"Do you collect different kinds of ferns?" This seemed like a safe question. I knew, from Gretchen, that there were several species of ferns in our woods. At the moment the particulars were gone from my brain. I knew the giant sword ferns, and that was it.

"Lady ferns are nice," Delphina said. "They like moist spots, so we often find them with horsetails. You can eat the horsetails too, if you get them early. Of course, there you want the reproductive shoots, not the sterile ones."

"Okay." I had nothing to contribute. Total bupkis.

"In 2002 I built an index for a foraging handbook," Delphina said. "Horsetails are high in silica. They also contains quercetin, which can help stabilize mast cells, reducing inflammation. Unfortunately, tea made from horsetails contains alkaloids, so you have to take it in moderation."

"You learned all this in 2002, and it's still in your brain?" I exhaled, fluttering my lips in a buzz. "I can't even remember if there's toilet paper left in the blue bathroom – which may be a problem when Glynnis arrives."

"Remembering supply levels uses a different part of the brain," Delphina explained, "Because supply levels change. If horsetail tea contains alkaloids in 2002, it still will have alkaloids when you make it today."

"Do you have a photographic memory?" I asked.

She shook her head. "Photographic memory is a myth. It is far more likely that my work has enlarged parts of my brain. Studies of London taxi drivers have shown that ongoing cognitive exercises and stress expand and plump up neural connections."

Delphina stopped to examine a fern clump near a big log. "Alas, building one area can mean another area is neglected. In my case, socialization skills have stalled somewhat, and I didn't have a childhood that gave me many. I have a hard time making friends."

"I hear you." I kicked a branch off the trail. "I'm lucky. I have a twin. Grade school would have been a total nightmare without him. I'm reasonably bright, but not athletic." I kicked another branch. "And I had awful skin in high school."

"Definite kiss of death," Delphina agreed.

We walked the trail in pleasant companionship until we were the Eliopoulous home. There we found a second *Amanita pantherinoides.* We were now in the faded light of gloaming. I didn't try to photograph the mushroom, but its gracious elegance did make me smile.

"This mushroom is making me think of Glynnis," I said. "Robust, elegant and damned if it's not poisonous. I'm starting a new novel, and it is so tempting to make a Glynnis-like character into the villain."

"Does Glynnis have the characteristics of a compelling villain?" Delphina asked. "There is a list for that."

"Seriously?" We were now walking on the gravel at the edge of the main road. I stopped with a crunch. "I released my first book this last winter, and one comment was my bad guy was too predictable."

I sighed. "The reviewer said, 'A cardboard villain who is twirling his moustache at every opportunity.' That hurt."

"Ouch. I can see that it would."

We reached the head of Grand Fir Lane and turned down the road, heading home. Delphina said, "A compelling villain should have core beliefs they hold with complete conviction."

"Like Glynnis believes a Multi-Level Marketing opportunity is a good thing."

"That level of certainty, yes. Does she have the power to persuade others?"

"Oh, my God. Glynnis could convince a cobbler to buy shoes."

"Is there such a thing as a cobbler anymore?" Delphina asked. "Shoe repair, yes, but aren't most shoes made in factory lines instead of by cobblers?"

"Scratch the analogy. Or is it a metaphor?" I snorted. "Let's just go with a 'Yes' in the ability to persuade."

"Is her goal directly opposed to the goal of the hero?"

"Hmm. In real life, no. She wants her daughter, Ashlee, to do well. Ashlee is my sister-in-law. I actually want Ashlee and my brother and their kids to do well too."

"We're mixing reality with fiction. In your story, your character can have whatever goal you choose."

We reached the head of Delphina's drive.

"This has been a fascinating conversation," I said. "It's been a lovely break, and you've given me some things to think about."

"Perhaps we could go again sometime?" Delphina's intonation was careful.

"Absolutely. Can I get your number?" I pulled out my phone, and we traded contact digits. I felt a bit bad that I hadn't reached out to her months ago when I had first arrived to care for my parents. I had a memory of a plate of cookies she'd left with a note and having zero energy to follow up with words of appreciation.

I tried to make amends now. "I remember the cookies you brought over. I should have said 'Thank you.' Things were… just crazy."

"I don't make very good cookies," Delphina brushed aside my apology. "And not everyone likes sweets. That's why I suggested leaving eggs to Arkady, but he did worry you were vegan."

"Nope. Just socially inept at times."

With a smile, Delphina said goodnight.

Which left me sixty feet from my own driveway and the upcoming adventure of welcoming Glynnis and Truffles to my messy, temporary home.

A memory of Delphina's cookies surfaced. They had been almost burnt on the bottom and flat like cow pies. The cookie fail made me feel even worse about not acknowledging the offering. She had tried to be neighborly.

I could respond better with the eggs from Arkady and Sky. My mother had kept a box somewhere that held an assortment of saccharine note cards. Perhaps the teens would be willing to look for it.

Thank you notes. One more thing to remember to do.

Turning down our drive, I saw Glynnis, standing next to her Prius, holding a small, dark dog. I was surprised to see her in conversation with Eloise Eliopoulous, who was wearing an elegant cream-colored coat that provided a smooth backdrop for the flat pink box in her hands.

"Good evening," I called.

The women turned, each with a practiced, plastic smile.

"I was just saying how excited my daughter is to be working for you," Eloise said. "Cadence says your estate holds many interesting items."

"Estate is generous," I said easily. I didn't like how Glynnis came to attention at the word 'estate.'

I plowed on. "Unfortunately, most of the items are more interesting than valuable. For instance, I have a jackalope taxidermy piece sitting on the dining room table right now. It's utterly weird and very dusty."

"How fascinating. I can see why Cadence is having a lovely time working as your assistant," Eloise said. She held out the pink box, the top inscribed with the name of Olympia's premier bakery. "Cookies for you. I really appreciate you bringing down that clot of mail."

"Oh. Thanks" I took the box. "I appreciate the cookies, but it's really not necessary. I feel bad that I hadn't been checking the mail. I hope nothing was held up too long."

"That's the other reason for my visit." Eloise was only five-foot-two, but when she looked directly into my eyes, she seemed to grow a foot. "I wanted to make clear that *all is well.*"

She had to be referring to the overdue notice that I'd inadvertently opened.

"Great," I said. "Super. Looks like you met Glynnis. And her dog." I was almost babbling now. I wanted to change the topic because I really, really did not want to hear details about Eloise's overextended days, bank accounts or anything else.

"Yes. We had a lovely chat. So nice to see you again." With that she strode away, her too-warm-for-a-spring night-but-ever-so-glorious coat bouncing slightly as she moved.

"Do you know who that is?" Glynnis hissed.

"My neighbor in the corner house," I said. "The big peaches-and-cream place."

"Eloise Eliopoulous is on the Governor's Diamond Donor Committee!" Glynnis's voice held a definite touch of reverence. "I'd kill to sell to that crowd. You have *got* to chat her up for Ashlee."

"Don't go there," I said. "I don't know the woman. I take it this is Truffles?"

The light was going fast now, but the little dog in her arms didn't look like a child-eating monster. He was alert and carefully watching me. I don't know diddly squat about doggie IQ, but somehow this pooch seemed bright enough. Delphina had said the MinPins made good agility dogs.

My hopes for a doggy-hostess truce were shattered when the Douglas squirrel began chittering. It leapt to the front porch railing and sounded off, shaking with emotion as it sounded alarm after alarm.

Truffles went berserk. He leapt out of Glynnis's arms and charged the porch, barking in a shrill staccato.

Glynnis yelled, "Quiet! Shush! Quiet!" to zero effect. She ran after her dog, who danced away and kept barking.

The squirrel went up an octave and increased the pace of her calls.

Truffles matched the squirrel, taking the volume higher.

I went inside the house, carrying the box of bakery cookies, thinking I might just eat them all.

Chapter Eleven

*Between every two pine trees there is
a door leading to a new life.*

John Muir

Saturday, May 2 – crack of dawn

MY PHONE CHIRPED at six in the morning. "Gahhh." I rolled over, folding my pillow over my ears.

It was no use. My inner anxiety monsters fretted the call might be from Kent or from a friend with an emergency. I fumbled for the phone and brought it to my bleary eyes.

Gretchen's name popped up on the screen.

I swiped to answer, coughing up phlegm and croaking a "Hello."

"Good! You're up!" Gretchen's voice boomed into my ear.

"I am now." I flopped back onto the mattress. "Did you hear the barking barrage last night? I have roomies who moved in."

"Barking barrage. Excellent alliteration, but I missed it. We saw a Prius in your driveway when Bob and I drove to town for dinner. Who's staying over?"

"Glynnis, my brother's mother-in-law, and a very yappy dog named Truffles."

"Can he find us some truffles?"

"First on his list is finding and demolishing my Douglas squirrel, who is opinionated and fast."

"Bit frustrated, is Truffles?"

"Ye Gods. And, get this, Glynnis is an expert in multi-level-marketing. She sells makeup and essential oils. She convinced my sister-in-law, Ashlee, to buy a garage-sized lot of essential oils for five grand. My brother gave her the boot yesterday."

"Your brother is divorcing?"

"No. No. Sorry. Wrong 'her.' Kent booted Glynnis out after her dog bit one of the kids."

"Wow. And now you've got her and the pooch living with you?"

"For the moment." I yawned. "Like I needed more to deal with in my life."

"Well, I have happy news," Gretchen said. "I was out for a walk this morning and found the most wonderful thing."

"Okay." I yawned again. "What time did you get up?"

"About four-thirty. I'm an old woman. I hardly sleep. You have to see this."

"What is it?"

"Gold! Forest gold. I had my headlamp on, and it gleamed like a nugget on the forest floor. You have to see it for yourself."

"Flower, mushroom, tree, bird? What have you found now?"

"Be a sport. Just come with me so I can get my lecture out of my system."

"Give me half an hour, please. I need a shower and a cup of coffee."

"See you in a few." Gretchen clicked off.

A hot, steamy shower helped. When I emerged into the hallway, Truffles was waiting, dancing with a click, click of his nails on the hardwood floor.

He whined.

My brain did a mental rewind to the night before. I had semi-hosted Glynnis through a microwaved dinner of pad thai. She'd set some leftover noodles down for the dog, which he had devoured.

I had shown Glynnis the blue bedroom, and she'd been pleased to see the television. She'd shut the door about nine. I'd heard talk show laughter from her room when I went to bed at ten. I didn't remember seeing the dog then.

As a reasonably light sleeper, I think I would have noticed if Glynnis had walked by my bedroom to take the dog outside. Among other things, the stairs squeaked.

It was possible Truffles had not been outside for a whizz since he'd barked at the squirrel the previous evening.

Not good.

There was no sign of Glynnis now. The dark door to the blue bedroom was shut.

"Come on," I said. The dog and I clattered down the stairs. I took Truffles to the backdoor that opened to our backyard. Truffles ran down the steps and began to pee, creating a sizeable puddle.

The backdoor had a pet door with slider we'd never used, my parents not being pet people. I heaved and wiggled the insert until it slid free, revealing a yellowed plastic flap.

I stood inside, shut the door, and held the flap up with one hand. "Truffles! In here!" I called.

Truffles zipped up the steps and charged through the opening with no hesitation. He danced on the hardwood, eyes shining.

"Pretty good for a beginner," I told him.

Coffee was the next order of business. I set up the French press, started some toast and began to crack eggs.

Truffles high-stepped on the linoleum, interested.

I cracked three more eggs and added them to the skillet.

The dog and I ate eggs and toast. I drank coffee.

At seven fifteen, Gretchen came striding up the driveway. I snagged my jacket and told Truffles, "You stay here."

By the time I joined Gretchen on the drive, Truffles had shot out the back door's pet flap, found footholds in the chain link and was scrambling over the top of the fence.

He joined us a moment later with his hind end wiggling. He didn't bark.

"Damn. That's impressive," Gretchen said. "Is he going on the walk with us?"

"Apparently." I looked down at the little dog, amazed by his spunkiness. "Do you know of a path that goes past an eagle or a big owl who wants a dog-sized breakfast?"

With a snort, Gretchen led the way to the woods. We hiked past the big row of rhododendrons and turned north, taking us behind Delphina's place.

I pointed to the elegant *Amanita* mushroom. "Delphina says it's poisonous. It reminds me of Glynnis."

"There's more to the system than meets the eye," Gretchen said. "There is an underground mycelium – like a root system – working its way to new territory. When it gets to a rock, it doesn't have to choose left or right – it can move both ways to seek new opportunities."

"That sounds like Glynnis." Truffles trotted along, keeping up easily. I shook my head. "I don't get why Glynnis has a dog. She doesn't seem to particularly like this guy."

"Hmm. There's a story hook in there. Wonder what it is." Gretchen raised an eyebrow as she spoke.

I smirked. "Way ahead of you. Glynnis is already an assist to my writing. I need a villain, and she's giving me ideas."

"Excellent. And we are here." Gretchen used her walking stick to point at what looked like a yellow pine cone sticking out of the earth. "Isn't it gorgeous?"

"Looks like a baby pineapple."

"*Kopsiopsis hookeri*," Gretchen announced. "Vancouver groundcone. This is the first one I've found."

"Oh, goody?"

"Don't be a grump," Gretchen said. "This is fascinating biology. The Vancouver groundcone is a parasite on the salal plant. It taps into the salal roots with a root of its own and sucks out nutrients. This fruiting body is lemon yellow today, but it will change to dark purple over the next week or so. Which is a delightful mystery. Why those colors?"

Truffles snuffled in the fir needle duff. Now he raised his head, slowly stiffening. I could sense he was about to bust out in his incredibly penetrating staccato barks. I crouched and put my hands out, one on his chest and the other on his back. He looked at me.

I stood up, folding him to my chest with a sudden thought of spaghetti sauce. I took a sniff. Oregano. Truffles smelled like oregano. There were additional elements to his smell, as if he'd been shampooed with multiple products.

"Quiet," I told him. "The neighborhood's still asleep."

"Perhaps not." Gretchen's eyes were sparkling as she smiled. She jerked her head towards Delphina's house. We were uphill from her backyard, partially hidden by trees, huckleberry bushes, and high salal. We watched as Arkady and Delphina stood on her back porch and passionately kissed, entwining arms around wide waists.

The two seemed to sizzle in the morning light. They modeled a most ardent passion as hands ran up and down bodies and mouths parted, smiled, joined, then melded.

"My, my. We live in such a neighborly neighborhood," I whispered.

Gretchen snorted, and we turned to quietly move down the trail, my hand over Truffles' snout.

We didn't speak until we were back to my family's driveway, where we both burst out laughing.

"I thought we were getting an early start to the day," I wheezed. "But they looked like they've been awake for a while."

"All night?" Gretchen bent over, gasping. "I'm having to rethink my assessment of Delphina. I thought she was quiet and bookish. Wonder if they swung from the chandelier?"

"Stop it." I giggled. "It's bad enough when I have you and Bob in my head."

"You think I can do acrobatics at my age?" Gretchen giggled. "You're the one who actually has a chandelier."

She was right. My mother had an enormous light fixture installed in the dining room that now was a decade past due for a cleaning.

"My size could be an issue," I said. "We'd have to upgrade to huge anchor bolts to hold the light fixture in."

That sent us both off into another round of laughter.

"Goodness." Gretchen wiped her eyes. "I have to scoot home. I have some thoughts I need to capture for my next book."

"The working title is *Indexing Arkady*?" I asked innocently.

"No. That's too close to the mark." Gretchen sobered. "They are both sweet people. I'm glad they are finding some happiness."

I set Truffles down. He shook and looked up at me, waiting for directions.

My driveway guard Douglas squirrel ran out to the end of a branch and began its alarm call. Truffles hammered back with a barrage of barks.

"Now my work day begins," I shouted.

"Don't forget you're coming to the Writers Group tonight. Bring your new story idea."

"I'm still working up a villain."

"The best villains are the ones where you can see yourself in the role. Don't worry," Gretchen called over her shoulder. "Inspiration will come."

An upstairs window slid open at Dr. Jaeger's house. The doctor yelled, "Shut that mutt up, or I'll call the police!"

"Villain inspiration is everywhere," Gretchen's right eye came down in a bold wink.

I grabbed Truffles, held his squirming body close and carried him inside.

Chapter Twelve

Every crowd has a silver lining.

P.T. Barnum

Saturday, May 2 – 9:00 a.m.

GLYNNIS WAS UP. She was in my kitchen, seated on one of the dinette benches, smoking a cigarette as she held a cup of coffee.

"Please don't smoke." I made the statement flat and unwelcoming.

She sighed and tossed the lit cigarette into the coffee dregs where it hissed out. "Sorry," she said. "I'm glad you brought Truffles back. I've got a pitch session at ten."

"A pitch?"

"It's a Zoom meeting with pet spa owners in Arizona. I'll be demonstrating German chamomile and Roman chamomile for dog therapy. If I get a good vibe going, I'll pitch the Helichrysum. That's one of our most expensive oils. One twenty for five milliliters."

"A hundred and twenty dollars for a few droppers full?" I blinked. "Wow. Who pays that?"

"All sorts of people," Glynnis smiled. "But I can't do the peppermint oil or the *Eucalyptus radiata*. Small dogs can't handle them." She sighed. "I should have picked a bigger dog."

"Truffles is your essential oils model?" It was a disturbing thought.

"Right. He's cute, but I could have made a better choice." Glynnis shook her head. "Dark dogs don't video well. He's got great eyes, but if the light's not right, you can't even see them."

"That's true for animal shelters," I said slowly. "Black dogs can have a hard time being adopted."

"Shelters need better lighting." Glynnis stood and carried the coffee mug to the sink. I noticed she didn't clean out the cigarette butt.

"Why are you doing this pet stuff?" I asked. "Aren't there enough people around to buy your products?"

"People will pay for their pets before they will buy for themselves." Glynnis crossed her arms and glared at me. "This is how I make my rent. It'd help my morning if you wouldn't give off such a judgmental aura."

"It'd help my morning if you would walk and feed your dog," I parroted her tone precisely, adding, "What happens to Truffles when you are done selling pet oils?"

"None of your beeswax." She took a breath and held up a hand. "Sorry. Believe it or not, I am really upset that Truffles snapped at Mai. I know Kent is furious with me, and I get it. I'll do this pitch today and see where we are. I'm not going to toss Truffles into a dumpster. They have animal shelters here too, you know."

She squatted down and chirped at Truffles. He ran over and wagged his tail as she stroked his head. "Multi-Level Marketing is hard work," she said. "And sometimes I over-do it with a sales technique."

Glynnis stood up and looked at me. "But I'm my own boss. I get some dignity with this. No one is patting my ass, telling me to work a double shift, or saying my time is worth seven dollars an hour."

I reined in the grumpy observations that were flooding into my brain and acknowledged that Glynnis had done a good job as a single parent. Her daughter is a good person. Ashlee wasn't ever going to be a buddy for me, but, despite her outburst yesterday, she was loyal to Kent, a devoted mother, and she was often generous and kind.

Glynnis sold stuff for a living. She didn't steal. I squirmed. She did hook others on the Multi-Level Marketing path. Truffles was a tool for her, not a companion.

Mixed good and evil in the same being. Not evil. Downsides that could be perceived as evil. Story treasure! "Be right back." I bolted from the room.

I ran to the dining room and found the manila folder that held my story ideas. Picking up a pen, I added, "Villain has personal standards even as she undertakes evil actions." Interesting. I had apparently decided my villain would be a 'she.'

Glynnis stuck her head into the dining room. "You could help Ashlee," she said. "Clean this place up and host your writer friends to a party. Artistic sorts are fabulous buyers. Jasmine could inspire a romance writer. So could a rose oil. Jatamansi is good for anxiety. Aren't all writers full of anxiety?"

"Don't you have a pitch session?" I did not want to discuss writer's anxiety. Not now. I was picturing my villain. A senior woman. Graceful like the *Amanita* mushroom. Poisonous. Light brown hair. Her name was… something sophisticated. Monique? Audette?

Glynnis kept talking. "I'd like to set up in the little office down the hall. Lighting is good with the curtains open."

"No!" I stopped my scribbling. "That's my father's office."

Glynnis raised an eyebrow. "I would just sit at the desk and face the window. I wouldn't move anything."

My heart squeezed. My father had died in January. At some point the whole office needed to be cleaned out. Eventually this entire house would belong to someone else.

"Alright," I capitulated. "The teens will be here at ten."

"They need to be quiet," Glynnis said.

"They need to do their work," I countered. "I'll meet you partway. Let's move some file folders out of the office now for the teens to process."

"Can you do that? I've got to grab a shower and get my broadcast face on."

Grumbling, I agreed. I grabbed a plastic bin from the pantry closet and went down the hall to my father's office. Truffles followed along, nails tapping on the hardwood floor.

Pushing open the door to the office, I could see why Glynnis wanted to work in this space. The handsome mahogany desk faced a broad window overlooking the backyard. Morning light streamed in.

My father's beloved berry red shade repeated across the wall shelves, in ceramics, in a painting, in a book cover. It all came together to create a charming, but currently dusty, space.

I went to the row of filing cabinets lining the left wall and pulled open a drawer. Did it matter what the teens started on? I decided it didn't. All the folders needed a review. I pulled out handfuls of folders and filled the bin.

Truffles trotted after me as I traipsed back to the dining room with a full load of file folders.

We did two more trips, emptying the first two drawers of the four-drawer filing cabinet.

There were a lot of files remaining.

Kent called, jumping into his news without a word of greeting. "Jay, my roofer pal, is booked through to September."

"Bummer. Think all the roofers are booked out?"

"Jay says so, but get this. He's had a cancellation. Not only that, he gave a quote to Mom and Dad early last year. He still has the paperwork, so he knows the job. His crew can come out on Monday to do a tear off. Then they'd roof on Tuesday. One catch."

"Which is?"

"We'd get the product the canceling customer ordered. Ashlee looked at a sample on-line. She says it'll be fine."

"Hey, saves me from having to make a choice." It all sounded great to my ears. "Go for it." I clicked off just as Truffles stiffened and began to bark. The wall clock said 9:45. "Somebody's early," I said to the dog. "Quiet."

Truffles ignored me and kept barking as he did a stiff walk towards the kitchen.

"We're going to work on this." I scooped him up and put a hand around his muzzle. He squirmed, then surrendered, his alert eyes signaling it was a temporary peace.

I let go of his snout to open the kitchen door. Truffles whined, but didn't bark. "Good dog," I told him.

Juno was walking up the drive with two people I took to be her parents. My new employee did not look happy.

"Hi," I called. "I'm Kami Schmidt."

"My parents, Briar and Thorne," Juno said, looking more miserable by the moment. She really hunched up when she saw Cadence and Sky coming up the drive behind her.

Briar and Thorne were lean people in jeans and flannel shirts. Thorne was tall, balding and easily three inches over six feet. I could see where Juno got her height. Briar's hair was darker than her daughter's and threaded with gray and silver. Thorne gave his wife a gentle smile as she leaned in to speak.

"We wanted to come tell you about a great opportunity," Briar said.

I squelched a mean thought about introducing her to Glynnis so the two women could bounce their sales pitches off each other. I didn't need a great opportunity. I didn't need essential oils. I needed less stuff in my life, including any manner of 'great opportunity.' Still, there was no reason to be nasty. Not yet.

"Come on in," I invited. "You can see Juno's work space, and I can give you a few minutes before we get going. There's a lot to be done." There. Whatever the hell Briar wanted could get squeezed into a short time frame.

The whole crowd followed me through the kitchen into the dining room. I set Truffles down, telling him, "Go sniff everyone, but be quiet."

I was rather pleased when he did just that.

Sky's gorgeous blue eyes looked troubled as he glanced at Juno. He kept to the perimeter of the room even as Cadence plopped her daypack down on the dining table and extracted her laptop.

Juno looked at the floor, hands clasped and still.

"These boxes of folders are one half of just one of my father's filing cabinets," I said. "It'd be great if you guys can get through this lot this morning. There's a… guest in the office who has a business meeting starting in a few minutes. We need to be quiet, please, until the meeting is finished."

I turned to Briar. "You said you had an opportunity?"

Glynnis walked into the room at this moment before Briar spoke. All heads turned towards her.

"My guest, Glynnis," I said. Glynnis looked fabulous in a bright blue dress. She wore far more makeup than I ever would, including false eyelashes and a lip gloss applied with a heavy hand.

"I need my Truffles," she chirped. "But I'd love to hear about your opportunity."

"Wonderful." Briar's smile was bright. "One of America's greatest advocates for animal welfare is coming to Olympia this week. Flint Heroux will be staying with us!"

Juno stared at the floor as if a pit forming at her feet would be most welcome. I felt for her. Her mother's crusade was not hers.

"He'll be an organizer of events?" I asked.

"Oh, yes. We'll be doing outreach on multiple levels to promote veganism. There will be a rally and a march culminating in speeches at the State Capital building."

Briar's chest expanded as she lifted her arms with abundant enthusiasm. "Flint is so empowering! It was his passion that inspired us to take on the names Briar and Thorne. He does an amazing job of opening eyes to animal suffering and the importance of moving to a plant-based diet. It is our individual choices that are going to save the world."

Glynnis snorted and added an eyeroll. "Vegetarian I get, sorta. But veganism? And a parade with speeches? Bet there're donations to be collected. Honey, you're being played."

Briar's eyes went flat as a snake as she inhaled to respond.

"Glynnis, stop!" I ordered. "You have a business meeting. My workers are here to get work done. Nobody has time for a brawl this morning."

I snapped my fingers to Truffles, who edged closer. I picked him up and shoved him into Glynnis's front. "Take him and go."

With a swish of her dress, head held high, Glynnis left the dining room, fancy heels clacking.

"So sorry," I turned to Briar. "She's my brother's mother-in-law and is only staying a few more days."

"You are so kind to be tolerant of *that*," Thorne said. Beside him, his wife sniffed, then nodded in agreement.

"I'm doing my best." I worked to keep my tone easy. "What was it you were wanting?"

"A donation," Briar said, her voice shaking. "From your estate."

CHAPTER THIRTEEN

Understanding a question is half an answer.

SOCRATES

Saturday, May 2 – 10:00 a.m.

I DID ANOTHER pretty good imitation of a Koi goldfish with an open mouth that moved without verbalizing

"You don't have to donate!" Juno said.

"Of course, there's nothing compelled," Thorne said. "We're just making an inquiry."

The words 'compelled' and 'inquiry' had my writer's antennae quivering. I dredged up the knowledge that Juno's dad was an attorney for a nonprofit. Big words, small salary. Do-gooding with a vengeance. It all fit.

My heart went out to Juno. She hated what her parents were doing.

"I knew your mother," Briar was saying. "She'd be thrilled to support a good cause like this."

Given that my mother's signature holiday dish was a bacon-larded pot roast, I had my doubts that Mom would have been a big supporter of the vegan crusade, although Mom had, indeed, been a generous donor to many groups. I knew because I was finding it impossible to get off their mailing lists.

My eye landed on the dusty jackalope head still sitting at the far end of the dining room table. Salvation.

"The word 'estate' is misleading," I said. "I am wading through multiple collections of small value. There're nesting dolls, there's ashtrays, there's an occasional collectible coin – but there's a ton of stuff like this head." I pointed at the jackalope. "Which will fetch somewhere between one and two hundred dollars on eBay. This is the sort of thing I have to donate."

Briar's face was priceless. A dead bunny head with dead deer antlers was not the donation she had been envisioning.

"I also have a fiduciary responsibility," I continued. Thorne wasn't the only one who could drop in a thousand-dollar word.

With a nod to the stacks of file folders, I said, "We're only in the documentation phase now. My brother and I would have to identify a suitable donation, agree on its value, and make sure any donation was in compliance with my parents' wills, a chief component of which is funding college accounts for my two nieces."

I was on a roll, choosing to not mention the part of the will that left me lots of latitude to make decisions about items. "I'm not adverse to making a donation, but you'll have to let me get back to you on that. It might be a month out. Or more."

Thorne put a hand on his wife's shoulder. This seemed to be a signal to retire from the field. Briar gave her husband a small nod and let him lead.

"Thank you for hearing us," he said. "We'll leave a card with you and let you get on with your day."

Juno's face was solemn as her father handed me a business card and her mother gave her a goodbye hug. There was no light in the girl's face as her parents departed.

When the kitchen door shut behind the parental pair, I turned to the teens. "Let's get going. There's work to do!"

"I can quit if you want me to," Juno offered. "I am so sorry about this morning."

Sky looked stricken at the notion. Cadence sat still, waiting for my decision.

"Please don't quit," I said. "We have mountains to get through. I really need your help." My fingers itched. I wanted to scrawl *internecine conflict detracts MC* on my storyline. I did just that once the teens got started on the file folders, adding *foreign emissaries add potential conflict. Dietary or political issues? Both?*

Glynnis's voice could be heard through the wall. At one point she said, "Yes, we do have a lavender, and it is less expensive," in a tone that indicated only an uncaring, knuckle-dragging Neanderthal would choose the less spendy path.

The teens worked fast, opening folders, scanning contents, and tacking discovered receipts to the wall. It was as if Sky and Cadence were giving coverage for Juno's embarrassment by abundant action.

Which delighted me. Progress, especially fast progress, was a balm to my heart.

I stepped out to the front porch and took in a deep breath of clean, May air. The sky shone blue above with just a hint of wispy clouds on the horizon. I called Kent. The ice cream store opened at ten, but he had few customers in the early morning. He picked up right away.

"Briar and Thorne want a donation." I told him about my visitors. "The great Flint Heroux is coming to Olympia and will be staying on our humble road. We are requested to support his mission to end all animal industries."

I sighed. "Poor Juno. She just about died of embarrassment."

"I should have warned you that teen workers come with teen parents," Kent laughed. "Employer tip: if anything happens, like somebody bruises a pinkie, you call the parents ASAP. You'll be talking to them anyway, so might as well be pro-active and get it over with."

"Got it. Anything else?"

"Your's is a short-term gig like a babysitting job. Pay them cash. Or Venmo. Pay up every day or couple of days. Keeps them coming back." Then he added, "I think we should give the vegans something."

"Really? You're going vegan?"

"Nope. I run an ice cream store. I'm kinda pro-dairy. But we have to be changing our ways. Our planet needs less meat eating, and the loonies who are way on the left make the general left look sane and reasonable."

"Point taken. Do we have anything pro-vegan to donate?"

"I've heard of this Flint guy. He's a gifted entertainer. Does music, poetry, and," Kent's voice went on a long, meaningful drawl. "Puppets."

"The Indonesian stick puppets!" I smiled. "We could donate those. That's brilliant. I think they're in a trunk in the music room." I tried to recall what else might be in with the puppets. "There's also batik fabric and maybe a gong?"

"Give him the whole damn trunk," Kent said. "Hey, gotta go. Ashlee's calling."

I liked the idea of parting with an entire trunk's worth of stuff, but it was best to take a look through the trunk first. I checked in with the teens, who were still going at things fast and hard.

After answering a question from Cadence and approving a choice of Juno's, I tiptoed down the hall past my father's office where Glynnis was still going strong with her sales pitch.

The stairs squeaked as I ascended. Truffles barked.

I kept going.

A few minutes later I was sneezing. The trunk of Indonesian goods had been stored under a day bed, and the lid was fuzzy with dust.

The contents of the trunk, however, were delightful. There

were half a dozen Indonesian stick puppets, two handsome gongs, yards of colorful batik and a small xylophone-looking thing labeled "Slenthem."

I took photos, sent them to Kent and returned to the teens.

"We have something for your parents," I said to Juno. "There's a trunk upstairs with cool stuff from Indonesia. My brother thinks it'll make a good donation, and it helps our clearance work too."

Juno nodded, cautiously positive.

I wanted to reassure her. "When Glynnis is finished in the office, we'll look for an instruments file. Or an Indonesia file. There're two gongs and a thing called a slenthem."

Cadence looked up. "I found that receipt a minute ago. It was under 'Bali.' It's on the wall."

"Excellent." I went to the wall and found the receipt. "Three hundred dollars in 2014. That means it's a nice instrument. Nothing like a Stradivarius violin though."

"Your folks might have a Stradivarius?" Cadence asked. "Wow."

"No. That was a joke," I said. "Honestly, tourist collectibles tend to decline in value. If we go to eBay, we may find a comparable instrument on sale for fifty bucks. We won't know until we look."

Cadence's fingers were flying across the keyboard even as I was speaking. "Full range," she said. "For xylophones we go from twenty-two dollars to four thousand."

I showed Cadence photos of the slenthem, and she smiled. "That helps. Let me work on it."

There was, ever so briefly, a moment of buoyancy. These young people were so smart and working so hard.

Then my day changed.

Truffles came trotting into the room as my phone chirped. I answered the call, to hear Kent say, "Ashlee's freaking out. It's supposed to freeze tonight."

"Bummer. Kinda late in the season, but we get May frosts. Does she have some geraniums out already?"

"No. She has twenty-thousand dollars-bought-for-five-thousand-dollars of essential oils in an uninsulated garage. I can't just toss in a heat lamp. I've already called four hardware stores. They're sold out."

"Hang on." I looked at Cadence. "Would you bring up a weather forecast, please?"

Cadence's fingers flew, and she blinked. "Whoa. Twenty-eight degrees tonight. That's icy." She added, "It hasn't been that cold in Olympia in May since 1996."

Sky said, "I should go check in with my moms. We'll have to get the chickens ready."

I nodded, saying, "Go. My sister-in-law has a garage full of essential oils that aren't supposed to freeze. Can you come back if they don't need you? My life may be crazy with finding indoor space for her product line."

Sky nodded and headed out the door as I returned to my brother. "Give me an idea of the volume here. How much stuff? Can I move it here in my Mazda?"

"It's in so many boxes. I think it'd take you a lot of trips." He sighed. "I can't get away to help you load."

"It's okay. I can do it." Tears prickled as I said this. I did not need essential oil storage added to the house full of belongings.

"It'd just be for a couple of days." Kent voice had an edge of tension.

"I know," I reassured my twin. "You sell ice cream. I got this."

Glynnis entered the dining room with a frown on her face. I tapped off the phone, not wanting to hear another anti-vegan word to be coming out of her mouth.

"I just used the bathroom," Glynnis said. "The toilet gurgled a lot when I flushed, and now there's water all over the floor."

CHAPTER FOURTEEN

Saturday, May 2 – 11:15 a.m.

I RAN DOWN the hall, skidding to a stop in front of the small bathroom. A four-foot-wide lake greeted me.

Stepping carefully, I was able to grab two hand towels and toss them onto the flood. This also gave me a place to put a foot so I could reach the toilet turn-off valve. The toilet gave an ominous burp as I cranked off the water.

"It was just pee," Glynnis whined. "It wasn't me that clogged it."

"Right." I eased back to the door and recalled the wisdom of a camp director from my long-ago-camp counselor days. *Save your strength. Never do something yourself that you can get a kid to do for you.*

"Glynnis, do me a favor," I said. "Go make a sign that says this bathroom is out of order and tape it to the door."

"Won't the tape take off the finish?"

I worked to quell an inner shriek of rage and frustration. "Tape the note to the doorknob. Or feel free to design another solution. I need to work on getting some plumbing advice or the whole water system could implode. We might both need hotel rooms tonight."

That was a bit of a reach, but it got me a head nod and her departure.

Gretchen had said our neighbor Arkady was a septic system designer. He had to know something about gurgling toilets. Even if it wasn't much, it would be more than I knew.

Moving to the kitchen, I called Delphina and used an innocent tone to ask if she knew anyone who knew anything about backed up toilets. She quickly gave me Arkady's number. She ended with, "Tell him I said 'hello'."

Right-o. If she didn't want to mention a morning snogging session, then who was I to do so? I tried, and failed, to not be bitter at how much better her day had begun.

Arkady answered on the first ring. He started a bit gruff, then warmed up as I thanked him for the eggs and mentioned Delphina.

"I've got this toilet that just leaked a lake onto the floor," I told him. "I know you're not a plumber, but I don't know what I should do. I tried plunging it the other day, and that didn't seem to help."

"Downstairs toilet?" he barked.

"Yes."

"Good. You call Hector." He rattled off a number and repeated it more slowly when I failed to capture it the first time. "You may have roots in the line. He can take care of that. You may have a full septic system. When did you last have the tanks pumped?"

I stammered. "This is my parents' place. I'm sure there's a note in a file somewhere. Short answer is I have no idea."

"It was pumped when your parents purchased the place. Washington law requires it."

"Fourteen years ago." That seemed about right.

"If that was the last pumping, you're about a decade past due," Arkady said. "It'd be great if you can find the house records."

"I'll look." I was past tears at this point. I thanked him and dialed Hector, who picked up right away.

"This is Kami Schmidt," I began. "My neighbor, Arkady, suggested I call. We have a gurgling toilet that is leaking onto the floor."

"Ah. Arkady gave you my private number. He must like you. Your name again?"

"Kami Schmidt. I live a couple doors down from Arkady."

"Kami Schmidt? The author? You wrote *Aliens from Babylon*?"

My knees went weak. "That's me! You've read my book?" Long-dormant hormones surged through my body. Hector was clearly a highly-intelligent man, a tradesman with a successful business. We'd make beautiful babies. They'd have dark hair and Hector's long limbs. I clung to the phone like a life line.

"I really liked the part about calculating the rocket thrust," Hector said. "So many people get the math wrong."

We'd have a dozen babies. He'd be the perfect father. He would be plumber-cum-nanny as I wrote my way to a Nebula prize.

"My wife said…"

I didn't quite catch what Hector's wife said. The fact that there was a wife was enough to bring me back to reality. I didn't just have my balloon punctured, with the words 'my wife', my fantasy was annihilated.

Still, it was a nice mini-vacation while it lasted.

"I'd have to charge you Saturday rates," Hector was saying. "But I could be there in half an hour. You lucked out. My wife is at the garden center, and I am okay with being gone when she gets back with her holes-to-dig list."

"Great. I'd appreciate it. See you in a bit. Bye."

Truffles was curled up at my feet. His ears alerted at the word,

"Bye" and he stood up, cocking his head. He'd been through the pet door once, but that was unlikely to be enough training for him to be self-sufficient in using it.

"Glynnis!" I yelled.

She came out of the dining room. "Yeah?"

"Does Truffles need to go out?"

Her shoulders slumped. "Probably. I'm in my good shoes. Can't you take him?"

"I'm kinda busy. It's supposed to freeze hard tonight. Ashlee's product line needs to be moved out here."

Glynnis inhaled, leaned against the wall and moaned.

"You okay?" I hated to ask, because clearly, she wasn't doing great.

"I don't want to see those boxes again. It's so depressing." Glynnis took both hands and tapped under her eyes in an attempt to keep tears from rutting her makeup.

"You were the owner of that lot?" I was back to making a goldfish mouth. "I thought you were a connection to an opportunity. But you set your own daughter up with your leftovers?"

"She's young. She can do it." Straightening up, Glynnis grumbled, "After all I've done for her, the least she can do is help me get to Hawaii."

"What's in Hawaii?"

"Warmth. No damned rain from October to June. Condo sales. I can do condo sales or time shares and build a retirement. I just have to get out from under the essential oils first."

My mind leapt into story-telling mode as I could picture my villain having a reason to be villainous. My fingers itched to scratch ideas on my story-line folder. My evil-doer would be awful, but understandable. She was shaping up and filling in rapidly. I could so see a moment of entitlement or a weariness of life descending into justifications for all sorts of bad behavior.

At the same time, would my villain unload trouble onto her own daughter?

I pulled back from my mental plot and character building. Real life troubles came first.

"Ashlee's stuff will be no good if it's frozen into popsicles," I reminded her. A few ripe profanities were rising on my tongue, but I could see Juno and Cadence in the dining room, quiet and listening.

I went with, "Is there anything you can do to help?"

"I'll put Truffles out back," Glynnis said with a sigh. She pushed off the wall and straightened up. "And I'll give him a bowl of water. Then I need to do follow up emails from this morning."

"Where's your product ship from?" I didn't want to think about more boxes being somewhere vulnerable, but it was better to know than to be surprised.

"This pet line is out of the national office," Glynnis said. "I just have to connect the clients with the shipping section."

She looked at me. "Don't go making me the bad guy. Ashlee is chomping at the bit to do something to help out. She's smart. She's got a good product line. I'm happy to get her started, but it's not like I saddled her with dead bunnies with antlers."

I could feel my jaw drop. I wanted to leap in and defend my parents, but to what end? One more round of me doing the imitation goldfish mouth, and I said nothing. I just shut my mouth and glared.

Squaring her shoulders, Glynnis said, "I'll get enough orders in today to pay for my plane ticket, so there is that." She stalked off down the hall, chirping to Truffles to 'Come.'

It took a moment of deep breathing to get my blood pressure down from boiling to merely simmering. It was time to check on my new employees. Putting my head into the dining room doorway, I called, "Ready for a tea and cookie break?" I was craving chocolate, but one of Eloise's bakery-made sugar-frosted cookies would do.

It was the right question to ask. I was blessed with wide smiles and a chorus of "Yes."

Cadence and Juno joined me in the kitchen with some successes to report. There were four more collectible coin receipts and an information sheet from the credit union about a member's life insurance policy for a thousand dollars. I'd have to follow up on that one after tracking down account numbers, but it was a solid clue to a nice hidden dab of money.

We were finishing the tea when Sky drove a battered blue pickup up the driveway. The door panel proclaimed 'Yo Mommas' Llamas' in a curly font over a silhouette of a llama.

Sky came in the door beaming. "The chicken shed is ready with heat lamps. My moms said I could use the truck to help bring your sister-in-law's boxes over."

I almost sagged with relief. "That is awesome. Absolutely fabulous." I paused. "It may take a couple of trips."

Juno spoke up. "I could go with Sky. Two of us could load things faster."

Delight dawned on Sky's face. There was no way I could rain on that look of joy. "Sure," I said. "Cadence, what works for you? Box moving or more file folders?"

"I'll stick with the file folders," Cadence said. "I don't like getting sweaty."

"Let's do this!" Sky held out a hand. Juno blushed and took it.

The two practically ran out of the kitchen to the truck.

"They're sweet," Cadence said.

I had to agree.

A moment later Sky was taking the truck bouncing down the drive, in reverse.

Too late I saw that Dr. Jaeger was driving in from the left, headed to his own home. My shouted, "No!" was not fast or loud enough to help.

Fortunately, the doctor had excellent reflexes and a well-maintained BMW. He managed to swing the car to the right and find space to stop, leaving a double line of tread skids in the gravel and grass.

Sky put the truck into drive, turned the vehicle and rolled down his window to yell "Sorry!" before driving off.

Dr. Jaeger jerked the BMW back to the left and drove to his house, throwing a dirty look my way as he drove.

In the backyard the Douglas squirrel chittered, and Truffles began to bark.

Chapter Fifteen

<hr>

Don't call the doctor after the funeral.

Japanese Proverb

<hr>

Saturday, May 2 - noon

HECTOR ARRIVED IN a white work truck. He was a lean, ropey-muscled man of about sixty, and he walked up to the kitchen door holding a copy of my novel.

I refrained from kissing him.

I did smile. A lot.

"I thought maybe you could sign it?" he asked. "It's not every day I get to meet a famous author."

"Hardly famous." Jesus, this man was adorable. "I can do one better," I told him. "I've got some copies upstairs. Let me sign one of those for you. On the house. That way you can have a shelf copy and a reading copy."

"Oh, man. That'd be great!"

A few minutes later he was looking at the bathroom floor and shaking his head. "You have a partial blockage. I can take care of that for you. My concern is you also have a long-time leak with water that's gone under the tile and has soaked the subfloor. It's not clean water either. It's toilet water."

"What do we do?" I was afraid of the answer.

"Today I can work on the blockage. I can also yank the toilet. It's older and stained, and it'd be hard to clean it up. I suggest replacing it."

"Okay." That didn't sound too bad.

"But you have the septic tank issue. If it hasn't been pumped in a while, that should be done. And you have a flooring issue. You need to take up the tile, get the subfloor clean and dry, then have someone come in to re-tile. You can do that yourself if you want to save some bucks."

"I can't even frost a birthday cake. Home repair is beyond me."

"Get a contractor in. Make sure it's someone insured and bonded." Hector paused. "This time of year is busy. It may take a few weeks."

I blinked back tears. "Sounds expensive too."

"Check with your homeowner's insurance. It may be covered." He added, "This could be worse. Water didn't get out to your hardwood floor. That would have been a real mess."

"Right. Just gotta find the right file for the insurance information." I sighed. "This is my late parents' house. We're working to get it on the market. I'm having fits figuring out where things are."

"I hear you. One of my cousins is a realtor. Marta Moreno."

"I've seen her signs around. Moreno and Sons."

Hector smiled. "That's her. One of her sons is a Hector. Check them out. They might be a good fit. Marta has a list of contractors she recommends."

I left Hector to his work and checked on Cadence, who was back at work in the dining room.

Cadence held back her dark hair with one hand as she spoke, her green eyes sparkling with intelligence and purpose.

"The Slenthem is one instrument in an Indonesian gamalan orchestra," she reported. "By itself, it's more a tourist item than a big asset."

"That's helpful," I told her. "I'm now also on the hunt for a folder that holds home insurance information. The downstairs bathroom is totally out of commission and needs new flooring. I'm hoping it's covered by an insurance policy. Of course, I have no idea where the policy might be."

"Is it okay for me to go into the office and look under 'I'?" Cadence asked.

"Absolutely. Glynnis is done. Knock yourself out."

Cadence stood up, swallowed hard, then said, "Restroom. Back in a minute." I watched as she bolted out of the dining room, then heard her charging up the stairs.

Could the cookies have given her food poisoning? That didn't seem likely.

I decided I'd hang about until she returned, just to make sure she was okay. I used the moment to call Sky's home. One of his mothers picked up. "Thank you for loaning the truck," I said.

"Not a problem. Sky texted that he almost creamed Dr. Jaeger's sportscar."

"I wasn't going to mention that," I admitted.

"Hey, no blood, no foul. Kids find boundaries by plowing through them. He said they were through loading and will be heading back. He can take Jaeger some eggs and get his ears blistered. I hope we'll be good after that."

I wasn't sure which parent I had, but I found I was liking her a great deal.

My next call was to Juno's parents. There was no answer, so I left a message. "We have a trunk of items collected from Indonesia. It consists of some performance items, including several very elegant stick puppets. You are welcome to it, but please plan to take the entire trunk."

It was a small victory. A five-foot trunk of stuff out the door was a win I'd take.

Cadence returned, looking pale.

"You alright?" I asked.

"Definitely. I had bad chicken salad for a late-night snack." Cadence shrugged. "I thought I was ready for cookies, but maybe not. I should have checked the expiration date on the chicken." Her eyes flashed. "I ate alone, as usual. No need to worry about my family."

"I'm so sorry."

She shrugged again.

I didn't like her wan look, so made an offer. "It's lunch time. I've got some vegetarian broth and crackers. Would that help?"

"That'd be great. I'll go look for the insurance file."

I heated a cup of broth for Cadence, but decided to do more for the rest of my employees. I melted butter in a large skillet and made grilled cheese sandwiches. I had a tray of sandwiches warming in the oven when Sky and Juno pulled up with a truck full of boxes. I set out a bowl of chips and another of sweet pickles.

Juno didn't object to the cheese and butter. "My parents are vegan," she said. "I'm not." With a most excellent eyeroll, she added, "Counting the days here until college."

Hector declined to join us, saying he was almost finished with his work.

I sat down with the teens and had lunch. Miracles of miracles, Cadence had found a homeowner's policy in a folder actually labeled "Insurance." Sky reported it would take another three trips to move all the boxes.

"Good grief. Where will we store them?" I sagged against the kitchen bench's upholstered back.

"Your living room is big," Juno suggested. "We could shove furniture against the wall."

My brain thought *Any Port in a Storm* as my mouth said,

"Fine. Just leave me a walkway through, please." I thought a moment. "I need to get you guys paid today. Cash or Venmo?"

"Cash for me," Cadence said. "Today would be super."

Juno and Sky opted for Venmo.

"I need to make a trip to town," I told the trio. "There's a trunk upstairs in the music room that needs to be dropped off to Juno's place. We're donating it. Could you take it in the truck?"

Juno started to object, but I cut her off. "Your folks can raise some dollars with the contents. My brother suggested it, and it'll be one less thing to eBay."

Glynnis walked in the kitchen, scoping out the lunch. She'd changed out of her business outfit and now wore black stirrup pants and an oversized pink sweater.

The teens stood up to get on with afternoon tasks. I invited Glynnis into the dinette booth for a sandwich. She loaded a plate with sandwich, chips and pickles and added zero words of thanks.

"You'd do Ashlee some good if you'd sell to the Writers Group," she said around a mouthful of melted cheese. "Artistic sorts are fabulous buyers. Especially writers. You guys are so damn anxious. I swear, if a top novelist says she writes in pink plaid pajamas, you can count on a run of pink PJs."

I hated that she might be right. Feeling pugnacious, I argued, "Most writers are strapped for cash."

"Dropping sixty-five dollars for a bottle of oregano oil is cheaper than a trip to a therapist," Glynnis swallowed and added, "And you don't have to play phone tag for days to get an appointment."

I decided to ignore her. Hector was moving his gear back to his vehicle, passing Sky and Juno as they unloaded boxes. I ran upstairs and fetched a copy of my book, lamenting my missed opportunities to distribute advanced copies to potential reviewers. I'd just run out of energy. Maybe a free copy to an avid fan would make up for that slip-up.

Signing "To Hector," and my signature in front of a grinning reader was a delight. I handed the book over, and he handed me a bill. "Rotten trade," he said.

"My life," I responded. "Thanks for coming out on a Saturday."

A few minutes later Hector was gone, Sky and Juno were heaving the Indonesian trunk into the farm truck. Glynnis disappeared to the upstairs, having taken no cleanup actions in the kitchen.

"We're going to have a conversation with Glynnis about being a thoughtful roomie," I told Truffles. I was taking a minute to stretch my legs before driving into town. Truffles had met me at the kitchen door when I stopped for my jacket. Now we were on the trail behind the house, the dog snuffling through the needle duff as I took in a few sunbeams.

I was surprised at how strongly the woods called to me. I felt a need to be among the trees – I'd never had an addiction, but now I was wondering if this was what an addiction felt like. I could feel myself growing agitated when away and calmed when I was here.

An olive-green slug slid along the trail's edge, his long body moving with surprising grace. To my amusement, a cluster of fir needles poked up from the slime at the tail of the slug, like a miniature peacock's fan of feathers.

"Regal fellow," I murmured as I put my hand on the trail to estimate his length. Eight inches. A very big slug.

I continued to speak to the slug. "Are you another hermaphrodite, and I should be using a collective word? What are your preferred pronouns?"

Gretchen had instructed me in the use of the iNaturalist app. I now knelt down to photograph the slug and clumsily tapped my way through the app to make use of the photo recognition software. "Pacific Banana slug, *Ariolimax columbianus*," I read. "Second largest slug on the planet. Changes color with diet."

Truffles snuffled in the needle duff as I continued to read. "Able to mate with themselves. That has to come in handy."

With a sigh, I tapped the phone off and awkwardly stood, carrying fir needles up on the damp knees of my pants. "Fir needles are cuter on the slug," I grumbled.

As I bent over to brush off the fir needles, a brisk breeze came funneling up my back.

Yellow violets at my feet proclaimed it was spring. The breeze held a reminder of the long Pacific Northwest winter.

"Come on, May days," I muttered as I zipped up my jacket. I still needed to get cash for the teens, read the homeowner's insurance policy, find a contractor and… I didn't want to think about it.

I sent a text to Gretchen. "Swamped. Not sure I can make it tonight."

My phone rang almost immediately.

"You have to come," Gretchen said. "There'll be wine, nibbles and interesting people to talk to."

"I'm worn down," I said. "I'm running on fumes."

"We'll be discussing fears," Gretchen urged, like that was a treat.

"Like fear of clowns or spiders?"

"Yes, but the whole arc of being scared. Having a great villain isn't enough. It's a better story when you incorporate fears."

She was right, of course.

"I'll see. Maybe I can catch a nap later." I clicked off, whistled to Truffles and returned to the farmhouse. I put the dog in the fenced backyard and checked on Cadence, who was into the Ds, which was amazing progress.

"I'm going to run into town," I told her. "And we'll get you paid. Be back soon."

"No probs," she said. Her color was better.

A few minutes later I was backing my Mazda down the drive when I saw Truffles scale the fence. A four-foot chain link fence did nothing to keep him in. He simply placed paws in the Vs of the fencing squares and kept going up.

"No! No!" I moaned. "Stay home!"

Truffles reached the top bar and scrambled over, leaping to the ground, then racing to my car. I braked, terrified he would dash under a rolling wheel.

I opened the car door. Truffles jumped in, crossed my lap and sat down in the passenger seat. He looked up with his dark, bright eyes shining.

"Looks like you're going to the credit union," I told him. "Boring. Joke's on you."

Truffles turned to put his paws on the passenger side armrest. He looked out the window and wiggled his rear.

"I could call you a stupid dog," I told his backside, "But I'm not sure you're the one who's stupid."

Ariolimax
columbianus

Chapter Sixteen

It is the same life whether we spend it crying or laughing.

Japanese Proverb

Saturday, May 2 – 4 p.m.

PAYING SMILING TEENS made my day. They had worked hard, all of them. The living room was stacked with boxes and the recycle bin in the dining room had been filled and emptied three times.

"I'm not sure about tomorrow," Sky hesitated before adding, "I need to check in with my parents."

"Understood," I said. "If you'll each send me a text in the morning as to your availability this next week, then I'll make a plan from there. I know senior year is super busy."

"It was crazy in the fall," Cadence admitted. "But I've got nothing going until my mother tries to ship me off to Whitworth in August."

"Whitworth" was spoken with no joy.

Juno slipped an arm around Cadence. "I'm headed to Antioch," Juno said. "Not my choice either."

"You didn't choose your colleges?" I shut my lips to avoid another round of making a goldfish mouth.

"Hey, I got to choose between Whitworth and Liberty University," Cadence said. "Bitter? Nah. Not me."

I began to see why Cadence wanted to be paid in cash. I couldn't picture this smart, sarcastic young woman sitting in a student chapel or prayer circle. However, May to August is a long time. It's long enough to build a stash and do something other than attend a conservative, Christian college.

"Antioch's not so bad," Sky said. "It's a good school."

"I suppose." Juno did not look excited.

"Where are you going?" I asked Sky.

"Oregon State," Sky smiled. "Forestry." At least he looked happy.

The trio left around four, with Cadence and Juno walking and talking as they left the farmhouse. Sky took an extra moment to secure a moving dolly in the bed of the truck before backing the vehicle down the drive with some care.

I surveyed the towers of boxes in the living room. There wasn't just essential oils. There were also vitamin supplements, ceramic diffusers, T-shirts, tote bags, makeup, and grow-your-own herb sets complete with lights. I could have saved the teens some work if I'd specified only the oils and other temperature-sensitive products. Too late now.

Truffles followed me as I reviewed the collection. He hopped up on the sofa with me when I stretched out. A few minutes later I was napping, his body snuggled next to mine.

A vivid dream of falling katanas came to me. When the shower of falling swords let up, there was a villain who arrived and departed, face obscured by a swirling black cloak. A dog barked, warning me to watch out as the villain moved closer, seeming to be ready to reveal a face.

A bell chimed.

I came awake, realizing that Truffles was gone. He was in the front hallway, barking, as the doorbell rang.

"Bleah." I struggled to sit up, calling, "Coming!" The towers of boxes were disorienting. I stood up, took a breath and headed for the hallway, bleary-eyed and fog-brained.

As I emerged into the front hall, Glynnis appeared to my left, chirping to Truffles with a "Here, baby." He ignored her and kept barking.

Our front door has sidelight windows. I leaned to the left and could see a lanky man on the doorstep. I ignored Truffles, shushed him and opened the door.

"Ahhh." My sleep-fogged brain felt like a lawnmower that wouldn't start. The man had dark, hooded eyes and a mesmerizing face. The deep 'crow's feet' wrinkles which would have been considered a flaw on a woman, made him look wise and kind. Strong cheek creases and a left-side dimple reminded me of the cowboys in tobacco ads. His nose was strong with a touch of a hook.

"Hello. I'm Flint Heroux. I wanted to thank you for your donation."

My subconscious reined in my libido, and I realized he was actually older than he presented. He wasn't forty-five. He was more likely sixty.

A sexy, handsome sixty.

"Your support is so welcomed and so needed." Flint smiled broadly and nodded to Glynnis who was now on my left, holding Truffles.

"You said you're Flint He- ro?" Glynnis dragged the last name out with a cold, hard tone. "You the vegan guru?"

"Guru?" Flint smiled, his dimple deepening. "I am more an

imperfect warrior." The smile broadened. "May I come in?" he asked.

Glynnis stepped right, bumping me with her shoulder so I took a staggering step to the side. "Sorry," Glynnis said. "Kami has an important meeting shortly. I was just coming to remind her so she's ready. Good of you to stop by. Thanks." With that she slammed the front door and locked it.

"To the kitchen," she whispered, leading the way from the front door.

I followed her. "What was that about?" I asked. I wasn't upset she'd taken over – just confused.

"Honey, the vegans that were here in your kitchen yesterday spoke like that man is God's gift to the world, which right there tells you he's a player. Then he shows up, as gorgeous as sunshine, and he knows it. Anytime a man's 'Hello' makes your panties wet, you'd best hold onto your wallet."

"You should know," I grumbled.

"Yes. I do."

"Do you know him?"

"I know his type," Glynnis flashed me a smile. "Ashlee is a good-looking gal because she sure had a good-looking sperm donor." She set Truffles down in the kitchen.

"Too much information." Truffles came to me, a worried look on his face. I gave Truffles an ear scratch while I tried to get my thinking neurons firing faster.

"What's for dinner?" Glynnis opened the refrigerator. "We're out of the pad thai."

"Do I look like a short-order cook?"

"Hey, I'll help. I'm trying to get you to your Writers Group."

"So you can sell them some essential oils?"

"I just saved your ass from donating your life to Mr. Charismatic. Cut me a break."

She had a point.

"We've got lots of eggs," I said.

By a quarter of seven, we'd eaten omelets and cleaned up the kitchen. I found I did feel chirpy enough to get to Gretchen's Writers Group.

"Can you keep Truffles with you?" I asked Glynnis. "He can climb the back fence in a heartbeat."

"Sure. We'll watch some shows."

I added gloves, a sweater to my jeans and flannel shirt, then shrugged on a jacket and stuffed a headlamp into one pocket. Truffles perked up, then put his head down when I told him, "Stay. Stay home."

The gravel drive was already taking on the shine of a frost. I was glad I'd refrained from buying potted geraniums to perk up the front porch. People who had bought early annuals had to be worried about this night.

I enjoyed the stroll to Gretchen's, taking in the evening light and a darting bat as I walked up her long drive. The Douglas firs behind her cabin made a dark green lace against the navy-blue twilight sky.

I was intrigued by how different the home styles were in my neighborhood. The Eliopoulous place was definitely upscale and pseudo-Victorian palatial. The llama farmhouse was one story but sizeable. The vegans, along with Arkady and Delphina, had smaller one-story ranch-style homes, while Dr. Jaeger and I had two-story colonial-style farmhouses, with Dr. Jaeger's place being far showier.

Gretchen, and our neighbor Bob had heavy-timbered cabins. Gretchen even had a chainsaw sculpture of a bear out front.

The driveways were long enough that the neighborhood's mishmash of styles wasn't obvious.

There were a number of cars parked in front of Gretchen's home. I let myself into the cabin and immediately saw and heard my people.

"The best scare scenes are unexpected," said a tall woman in a lovely, but holed, cashmere pullover. The burgundy of the sweater didn't suit her. The merlot in her wine glass seemed to suit her completely as she re-filled the glass near to the brim.

"Oh, I agree," came from a round man with dark-rimmed eyeglasses. "Think of Hansel and Gretel," he said. "Lost in the woods, they find a gingerbread house. It *should* be a safe haven. Brilliant twist there."

Gretchen waved me in and pressed a wine glass in my hand as she said, "I like layering fears. You know, pairing Fear of Shame with Claustrophobia."

"I'm not sure I want to live in your head," I muttered into the wine.

"I heard that," Gretchen said. "Wait until we get going. We'll totally terrify you." She lowered her voice and murmured, "Bob is here. He's not feeling so great. Ivy is here too. Keep the conversation off cats, will you?"

Bob waved to me from the kitchen. He was in his Bob uniform of long sleeved, tie-dyed shirt, fleece vest and field pants. A few minutes later he showed up at my elbow and handed me a small plate with a napkin and a trio of skewered olives.

He leaned in to speak with a whisper. "Do you like crab puffs?"

"My favorite. Seriously." I'm sure hope dawned on my face. "There are some?"

"I have a tray to go in the oven after a bit. We'll have them out at the end of the lecture." He gave me a wink. "I'll make sure to set aside a few for you. The privilege of being a neighbor."

"Wow, I'm glad I came over."

"Me too. Gretchen is worried about you."

"I'm worried about me too," I said. "My life is a mess."

"Been there." Bob clapped a hand on my shoulder, gave a me a tiny squeeze and moved on to speak to another guest.

Gretchen called our group to order. A tall man in an ill-fitting corduroy jacket and wrinkled khaki slacks stood near a white board on a tripod. With an easy grace, he made four columns with a marker and labeled them: Mutilation, Humiliation, Rejection and Extinction.

He capped the marker and said, "Our four basic food groups. Welcome to *Fear and the Writer*. Tonight, we are going to look at what is scary, in the hopes we can tap fears in creative ways to entice and enthrall our readers."

With a dramatic pause, he pointed to the white board. "I submit the notion that our fears consistently fall into one of these four groups. Like a nutritionist planning a school lunch, we writers can pick and choose from these categories to make a full plate."

"You left off 'Loss of Control' like, ah, drowning," Ms. Burgundy Sweater said.

The scribe raised a finger. "I'm thinking that would fit under Extinction." He smiled. "Let's see what fits where. Suggestions and questions?"

"Where do spiders fit in?" Ivy asked.

"Mutilation," our speaker said. "We could be disfigured by the bite of the spider. Or we could put spiders under Extinction if it was a deadly spider."

"Humiliation," I offered. "If our character acts like an idiot when seeing the spider."

"Good one," the speaker said.

"Chainsaws have to be Mutilation," Bob said. "And Extinction."

"Are you finding that you are drawn to the fears that are greatest within you?" our lecturer asked.

"For sure." A stylish young woman spoke from a spot in a deep armchair. "I've always been afraid of being lost in the woods. It's a form of rejection, I think, to be separated from my community."

"The woods have their own communities," I objected. "There are so many intertwining lives. I've been walking with Gretchen in recent weeks, and she's constantly pointing out connections."

"The woods are frightening to one, but not to another. An excellent point," our leader said. To me, he asked, "Would you be afraid to go out in the woods in the dark of night?"

I thought for a moment. "I would be afraid of bumping into other people. I wouldn't be afraid of the mushrooms, the plants or the wildlife."

"Not even a bear or a cougar?"

That made me squirm. "You have a point," I admitted. "If I really thought there was a bear or a mountain lion, I'd be thinking Extinction or Mutilation for sure."

"But you would be more afraid of a person?"

"Absolutely."

"More afraid of a person you knew or more afraid of a stranger?" The lecturer raised an eyebrow. "Or does that depend?"

"Interesting to think about," I answered. "I could be afraid of a stranger. I could really, really be afraid of someone I knew, depending on what their backstory was."

"Which brings us to details." With a smile, the lecturer turned to another in the group and invited comment.

I leaned back in my chair, accepted a small plate of cheese and crackers and nodded when the wine-refilling author came around. I was glad to be here. Contemplating abstractions was a huge improvement on dealing with realities.

CHAPTER SEVENTEEN

*This is the law: blood spilt upon the
ground cries out for more.*

AESCHYLUS

Saturday, May 2 – 9 p.m.

I ENJOYED MYSELF thoroughly. I never did catch the lecturer's
name. It didn't matter. He was skilled at inviting in new voices
and at redirecting when discussion stalled.

The official part of the Writers Group ended after about
ninety minutes.

Bob was true to his word. I heard the oven timer 'ding,' and
he soon showed up to hand me a second small plate, this one with
crab puffs. They were divine.

The party went on, voices rising and falling as observations
were shared and plotting paths explored.

At one point, I ferried my wine glass and cheese plate to the
kitchen, only to be cornered by Ivy.

"I saw the trunk of stick puppets you donated," she said. "They are wonderful!"

"Good. I hope Flint can make use of them."

"Absolutely. Are you coming to the protest tomorrow?"

"No. I have a house full of stuff to sort." I paused, not wanting to know, then wanting to know. "Where are you protesting?" I asked.

"Capital campus grounds. There should be a thousand of us." Ivy hoisted her wine glass. "Flint will be the keynote speaker. He's incredible. I think we'll make national news."

I refrained from saying 'I'd rather have a root canal than scream for an egg-free life.' I managed to smile and say, "Looks like you'll have a sunny day. I hope it goes well."

That wasn't good enough for Ivy. Her voice rose with an insistency. "This is really important. Far, far more important than sorting belongings." She paused, then said, "I am so sorry about your parents. Wouldn't they be proud of you if they knew you were taking up a truly *meaningful* cause?"

I set my cheese plate down in the sink and flexed my fingers to control my rising anger. My parents had always been proud of their children. I resented, like hell, anyone using that love as a tool to further their personal agenda.

With a saintliness that would have astonished and amused my mother, I said, "I'm so pleased you are finding satisfaction in your work protecting cats and addressing the challenges of animal industries. Alas, I really do have some very challenging family obligations right now."

"Let me show you," Ivy responded, blowing right past my well-laid refusal. She tapped furiously on her cell phone. "Here. YouTube. This is Flint speaking at a Florida rally in January."

"Florida in January," I murmured. "How divine."

Ivy has the hide of a rhino, I'll give her that. She tapped up the volume and shoved the phone under my nose. I heard Flint compare himself to Nelson Mandela, Mother Teresa, Joan of Arc and Jesus Christ.

He interspersed clips from slaughter houses with appeals for action. I could see the video clip had been played millions of times and had a hefty 'like' number.

"How much does he rake in?" I asked. "From the YouTube ads and the GoFundMe actions?"

"This isn't about the money!" Ivy all but hissed. "Look, he also spoke in Jamaica in February." She stabbed at the phone and brought up another video clip.

The other writers were gathering coats and saying their Good Nights. Bob was smiling, chatting to the woman in the burgundy sweater near the door. His face was a healthy pink now, and his actions animated. I inhaled, pasted a smile on and congratulated myself for keeping Ivy from invading Bob's evening.

"Jamaica looks so inviting," I said. "And what a crowd!" There. Positive voice tone managed.

"The animal industries there are unspeakable." Ivy began describing a Jamaican butcher shop that sounded like... a local butcher shop.

Gretchen came to my rescue just as my knees were starting to pop from the strain of standing over Ivy's cell phone photo collection. "Oh, Ivy. Give Kami a break. She's had an exhausting day!"

Ivy still had a lot to say, but Gretchen cut her off. "Out you go. Thank you for coming. I need Kami's attention on a small item. You go on. You need your rest to be ready for that rally tomorrow." With that Gretchen put her hand on Ivy's forearm and actually pulled her to the front door.

I found a kitchen chair and plopped down. "Thank you," I mouthed as Gretchen came back into the kitchen.

"Sorry you got sandbagged." Gretchen looked cheerful, but a bit worn. "Thank you for listening to her. That kept the others from being cornered. It was nice for Bob to have a cat-free evening."

"Why have her if she's such a pill?"

"To be neighborly. Also, you don't temper the passionate without listening to them."

"What are you converting Ivy to? Puppies and goat cheese?"

Gretchen threw back her head and laughed. "That would be lovely. I'll be happy if I can get that lot to ease up. It's all very hard on Juno." She flapped a hand at me. "Just stay a minute. I don't need anything. I just wanted Ivy out the door first so you could have a quiet walk home."

"You are a dear friend and may have prevented a murder. Ivy suggested my parents would be proud of me if I joined her cause."

We chatted about the evening as Gretchen washed wine glasses.

Bob came into the kitchen carrying a stack of cheese plates. He set them on the counter, kissed Gretchen on the cheek and waggled his fingers at me before putting on a heavy coat and slipping out the back door.

"Good night," I called. "Sleep tight."

"Bob's working on his memoir," Gretchen said. "I'm not sure tonight's topic was particularly helpful to him, but I'm glad he came." She sniffed, then added, "I mean that. I'm glad he was here."

"He's been looking a bit peaked," I said. "What's up with that?"

Gretchen put her sponge down, leaned against the kitchen counter and crossed her arms. "For your ears only," she said.

"Okay."

"Bob has a recurrence of a prostate cancer. He's not in a good way."

"I'm so very sorry." And I was.

"Everything is really hard for him right now," Gretchen told me. "He gets frustrated easily. I really appreciate you listening to Ivy."

"What does Ivy write about?" I helped clean off the leftovers of a canapés tray by loading my mouth with a stuffed mushroom cap.

"She contributes to a feral cat rescue blog," Gretchen said. "And she told me about a line of cozies she'd like to write. The heroine will live in a travel trailer and move about the country, rescuing cats and people. In that order, I believe."

"Probably sell a million," I grumped. "Cats and travel ought to sell briskly."

"How's your story coming?" Gretchen paused in the cleanup to give me her full attention.

"Bits. Little Sparks." I squirmed in the kitchen chair. "I get these flashes that I have to write down. It's hard to say if they will connect."

"Ooh. You may have a trilogy or series cooking."

"That is a terrifying thought."

"Lucrative," Gretchen corrected. "Think on it."

"Alright. Time to put my muse to bed." I stood up with a yawn.

Gretchen enfolded me in a quick hug at her front door. "Be careful out there. It's slick."

"Got my gloves and headlamp. I'll be fine."

When Gretchen opened the front door we heard Truffles off in the distance, barking a rat-tat-tat staccato like a machine gun, as if he was fending off an invasion.

"Damn. I told Glynnis to keep him in!" I went down the steps rapidly as Gretchen called, "Good luck!"

As soon as I was on the gravel, I turned on my headlamp and hustled down the drive. Being Saturday, Dr. Jaeger was unlikely to have early surgery hours in the morning, but I couldn't imagine he was happy about hearing Truffles' yapping.

I hoped the doctor was wearing excellent quality noise-cancelling headphones.

It didn't occur to me to be frightened of bears, cougars or people. Arms swinging, I sped-walked out of Gretchen's drive and headed for our farmhouse.

To my surprise, Truffles suddenly took it up a notch. He must have spotted my light across the level gravel of the cul-de-sac.

The headlamp elastic was too tight. I shoved it up, feeling the band catch in my hair. At almost the same moment, the bright front light from our farmhouse flipped on. I could see Truffles standing out on our lawn, rigid and hammering his warning.

Glynnis opened the front door and came down the steps, calling to the dog. As usual, he ignored her.

I was looking at Truffles and cursing Glynnis for being so slow. I could see them in the yard light even as the beam from my headlamp bounced up and down with each step.

Until I tripped.

I was halfway across the bottom of the cul-de-sac, in front of Dr. Jaeger's place when I tripped on a semi-hard form on the ground.

It took a moment for me to understand that there was someone sprawled out on the gravel.

"Sorry!" I scrambled back, mortified. "You okay?"

There was no answer.

Glynnis called, "You alright?" She had Truffles in her arms and now had his mouth held shut.

Dr. Jaeger's porch light came on and his front door opened.

"I'm okay," I yelled. "Somebody's passed out." I grabbed my headlamp and pulled the light down, illuminating the person sprawled on the gravel, who was facedown and very still.

I recognized the lean body and thick brown hair even as the black duffle coat was new to me.

It was Flint Heroux.

I gave his shoulder a strong shove, rolling Flint to his back. A deep, gaping wound split the front of his skull like a dark canyon. I could see a rim of white bone on the canyon's edge and brain matter speckled up into the hair.

I scrambled to my feet, chest heaving. I tried to call to Glynnis and only came up with breathless squeaks. I flapped my hands, finally managing a croaking, "Help."

Dr. Jaeger loomed into sight. He looked down at the body.

"What the hell happened?" he barked.

"I don't know. I fell over him." I got that far, then turned and lost an entire evening's worth of merlot, cheese, crackers and crab puffs.

Chapter Eighteen

A hidden fire is discovered by its smoke.

Spanish proverb

Saturday, May 2 – 10:30 p.m.

I FINISHED RETCHING, wiped my mouth and wobbled as my breath came in fast gulps. Afraid of falling or even fainting, I knelt down on the gravel, the icy rocks biting into my knees. I pulled out my cell phone and tried to punch the emergency call, but my gloves weren't cell phone friendly.

Swearing, I pulled one glove off with my teeth and tried again. My hands were shaking. Between the hand holding the phone shaking and the hand with the extended finger shaking, I was doing an awful job of connecting.

Dr. Jaeger stepped next to me and put his hand out. "You're in shock," he said. "Let me."

I surrendered the phone. I didn't want to. It was bad enough to find a body and vomit. I felt like a complete wimp. I couldn't even manage a call for help.

My headlamp light flickered over Flint's still body as my head bobbed with a nose wiping. There were more important things to think about than my dashed inner Wonder Woman. I stayed down, kneeling in the gravel.

Dr. Jaeger had a brisk, dominating voice. Once before in my life I'd had occasion to call the emergency number, and I remembered being intimidated by the operator's casual handling of my concerns. That was not happening now. Dr. Jaeger stated there was a body, definitely dead, and he needed an investigating team. They were not to waste his time with a preliminary drive-by assessment.

I struggled to stand just as Glynnis arrived, wearing a bathrobe and carrying Truffles.

Dr. Jaeger intercepted her, saying, "We have a body. Police have been notified. I will take Ms. Schmidt to my place and give her a hot drink. She will need to speak with the officers. There's nothing you can do here. I suggest you return to your house, lock the door, and we'll give you an update when we know something."

He paused, then said, "And keep the dog with you. Quietly, if possible."

Glynnis shot me a questioning look.

"I think it might be Flint," I said. "Please go home. We need to not muck up anything."

Her eyes huge, Glynnis gave me a nod, adjusted her hold on Truffles and went back to our house.

"Come on," Dr. Jaeger ordered. "Let's get you inside before you faint. I damn sure don't want to carry you."

That prickly bit of pissiness was a great stopper to my wobbliness. I found myself marching down his drive with my nose in the air. I'm a big gal, but he didn't need to make it sound like moving me would take a forklift.

Once inside, he directed me to an armchair next to a lovely fireplace, complete with burning logs.

"I'll be back with a hot drink," he said.

Dr. Jaeger disappeared. I heard a tea kettle being filled, a whoosh of a gas burner going on and a muttering as he went through a couple cabinets, including one, "goddamnit."

Perhaps the doctor wasn't completely cool and collected.

Returning with a steaming mug and a small plate of cookies, Dr. Jaeger set the plate down on a small side table and handed me the mug.

"Lemon tea with honey," he said. "For a minute I thought I was going to have to give you chamomile."

"What's wrong with chamomile?" I asked, blowing on the hot tea.

"Chamomile can produce an allergic reaction in some. It can be sleep inducing. It's also known to boomerang and impede sleep. You'll want to be alert and biochemically stable when you speak with the authorities."

I thought he might sit with me. Wrong. The man had no bedside manner, at least not for wandering writers who fell over bodies late at night. He said, "I am going to set up a light for the officers. Stay here." With that, he left.

The tea did help. I ate the cookies too. I watched Dr. Jaeger through the front picture window as he ran an electrical cord out from his garage and then made a second trip, bringing a work light on a stand. The light went on, casting long shadows.

Thankfully, a large rhododendron blocked my view of the body.

That worked for me.

I was finally warm enough to take off my coat when I saw flashing lights come down the road. An ambulance and sheriff's car were here.

The proper thing to do would be sit in the armchair until the sheriff's deputies came in to collect details.

But I was bored. And I needed to pee.

I convinced myself it was good manners to return the mug

and cookie plate to the kitchen. I behaved myself and didn't open any cabinets or drawers.

Dr. Jaeger had splendid taste – or his decorator did. There was a deep farmhouse sink, fabulous sink taps, about an acre of upscale granite countertops, and cabinetry with exquisite crown molding.

The little washroom off the kitchen was also first rate, with fabric-covered walls and a handsome soap dispenser. Even the toilet paper had a silky finish.

It was a bit depressing to see how fancy a farmhouse could look when an owner put time and money into fixtures and maintenance. I didn't begrudge my parents' love of travel and collecting, I just wished they had put more effort into organization and upkeep.

As I returned to the armchair next to the fire, it occurred to me that I should get a photo of Dr. Jaeger's place for advertising our farmhouse. "Sell a dream of what our place could be," I grumbled. "I'm starting to sound like Glynnis."

I managed a sweetly innocent face when Dr. Jaeger came back in. I saw no need to tell him of my small walkabout.

He went to a sideboard and poured himself a splash of whiskey. He didn't offer me any.

"No thanks, I'm fine," I said.

"You were in shock. We don't give shock victims alcohol." With that he flung himself in the armchair on the opposite side of the fireplace.

"What do you know about this Flint fellow?" he asked. He held up a hand. "I know you will have to tell what you know to the deputies. I'm asking as a neighbor who is trying to assess my exposure."

I wasn't sure what he meant by 'exposure.' Was he concerned someone would sue him for dead body landscaping?

Dr. Jaeger's face looked grim and tired. I decided to go easy on him.

"I met him extremely briefly earlier today." I explained about

Juno helping to sort through filing cabinets worth of material, followed by her parents' interest in obtaining a donation.

There were so many details crowding my thoughts. I struggled to stay focused and brief. "Juno's parents were hosting Flint for a week of protests against animal industries. His last name is something like Hero. Apparently, he's famous."

I took a breath to finish the basics. "I spoke with my brother. We had items that we could donate. I sent a trunk of things over with the teens. They were making trips into town to fetch boxes of… well, never mind. Things from my brother's place."

"Then Flint showed up on the doorstep this afternoon," I continued. "He said 'Thanks for the donation,' and Glynnis, the gal who is staying with me, shoved me aside and shut the door." I inhaled. It was hard to convey who Glynnis was and why she acted as she did.

I went with, "Glynnis has a lot of experience with multi-level-marketing work. She said Flint is a 'player.' By that I think she means he's a hustler. She was afraid he'd get his hooks in me." I snorted. "I've got a whole house of clutter and knickknacks. Maybe I should have given him a wholesale deal."

"Glynnis sounds smarter than you are," Dr. Jaeger said.

"Hey!"

He sighed. "Perhaps I should have said, 'more experienced with charismatic salespeople.' Is that better?"

"Yes." I glared at him.

"It's good news," Dr. Jaeger said. "If he's a charismatic man obtaining donations, then there will be outsiders who hate him."

"People he's fleeced?"

Dr. Jaeger nodded. "Or those who love the people he fleeced."

"Do you know Ivy? The woman who lives in the little caravan?"

"Yes," Dr. Jaeger said. "Scruffy sort in low-quality folk-wear outfits."

"I'm glad you're in medicine," I said. "Diplomacy is not for you."

That earned me a wintery smile. "Indeed," Dr. Jaeger agreed. "What about Ms. Ivy?"

"She showed me two YouTube clips of Flint. They have millions of views. And she said there will be a thousand people at a protest tomorrow where Flint was scheduled to speak."

"He's known to many." Dr. Jaeger sipped his whiskey, eyes narrowed as he mulled my details. "What exactly did he get from you?"

"Ivy told us Flint incorporated puppets and music into his programs. We had a trunk of things my parents had collected from Indonesia that included several stick puppets. They are almost two feet tall and very intricate. There was also batik fabric and a small xylophone instrument."

"A gamelan." Dr. Jaeger spoke with his usual confidence.

"Specifically, it was a Slenthem. I believe the term 'gamelan' refers to an ensemble of instruments." It was good to lecture even if I was certain Dr. Jaeger had more than a few IQ points on me.

Dr. Jaeger pulled on the whiskey. "A puppet master. If he enjoyed being a puppet master, perhaps someone objected?"

My fingers itched for a pen and paper. A comeuppance for a puppet master would be a great twist for my villain's path.

With a long reach, Dr. Jaeger picked up a slender computer tablet in an elegant case. He opened the computer and tapped and scrolled for several minutes.

"Mr. Flint Heroux is known for his animal liberation activities," he read. "He has been accused of staging breakouts so it will look like the animals have found a weak link in the facility. This technique has led to hundreds of sheep loose on a road in the U.K., pigs wandering about in South Carolina, and cows finding fences down at a Montana slaughterhouse."

"That would piss people off," I said. Then I sat up, horrified. "The llamas! Any chance he let the Yo Mommas' Llamas out?"

"Well. Fuck. That could be a problem." Dr. Jaeger stood up. "I'll go speak with the officers."

I had my phone out, hands now steady. "I have a phone number for the farm."

"It's late. It's past eleven."

"Sky's probably up playing video games. And if he isn't, the family will still want to know if the llamas have been liberated."

CHAPTER NINETEEN

There are men who walk through woods and see no trees.

MONGOLIAN PROVERB

Saturday, May 2 – 11:30 p.m.

ONCE AGAIN, I wasn't sure which Llama Momma I'd reached. It didn't matter. She was awake, brief and pragmatic.

"We'll go do a nose count right now. Thanks."

And she was off the phone.

I sat in Dr. Jaeger's living room, looking out the picture window at the flashing lights of the ambulance and sheriff's cars as people went one way and another. I was tired, and I wanted to go home.

Why not? I was past the shakes of falling over a man bludgeoned to death. I could answer questions in my own living room. I pulled on my coat and went to the front door.

I'm not sure why I quietly eased the door open. My plan was to speak with an official of some sort so they would know where I was. Yet ease it open is what I did.

"Delphina!"

I heard Dr. Jaeger's voice from the edge of the front lawn. I could pick out his silhouette as he held a phone to his ear.

"Delphina!" he said. "It's Gary. Please pick up. It's important. There's been a death."

Dr. Jaeger knew Delphina? And they were on a first name basis?

Apparently, she responded to his plea and picked up because he spoke again. "I know I'm an idiot. I am so, so sorry, my darling. I hope you can forgive me one day."

Holy shit. I swallowed, hard. It was the tone of voice that I'd dreamed of hearing from my ex-husband. Not that I would have forgiven him. I just wanted to be desperately missed.

I wanted to know Delphina's secret sauce for attracting men. Not that Arkady or Dr. Jaeger were my type.

Perhaps I could acquire cats. Or learn indexing.

Dr. Jaeger turned away. I could only catch an occasional word. It sounded like he was telling Delphina about Flint's violent end and asking her to lock up her home.

I eased the front door shut, took a few steps back into the entry way and made a stomping approach to the front door. This time I flung the door open and called, "Hey, deputy?"

Jaeger disappeared into the shadows.

A few minutes later I was escorted to my front steps by a cold young deputy in an inadequate jacket. I unearthed a front door key from under a ceramic frog, thinking we really should find a better hiding spot given Flint's brutal death.

The deputy shrugged off my thanks and left for more interesting work than watching me shut and lock my door.

Truffles came trotting into the hall, rear end wiggling. I followed him to the crammed living room where Glynnis lay on the sofa, snoring, with a fireplace poker resting on her chest.

"Hey." I woke her. I told her that Flint had been killed with a blow to the head. Beyond that I knew nothing. Glynnis nodded and took herself off to bed.

I didn't dare go to bed myself. I knew an official would want to speak with me at some point. I puttered in the kitchen, then scribbled notes on my story line while sitting in the dining room.

It was all terribly unsettling. I felt agitated and off.

Of course, I felt off. I wasn't accustomed to seeing brains.

My home was a mess. The dining room was an ocean of files and bins to go to recycling. The living room a fire trap of boxes of oil. I had a dog at my heels and a roommate who would sell my back teeth if there was a profit to be made.

And yet there was *something more* hovering at the edge of my thoughts.

Physics. It was something mathematical.

I discounted the feeling, suspecting my psyche merely longed for the safety of university life.

A senior detective rapped on the door at midnight. Truffles raced to the door and let off a single bark before I silenced him with a stern "Quiet!"

The interview was brief. More questions would be coming soon. I did learn the llamas were all accounted for. No down fences, no shaggy escapees.

The detective wasn't chatty beyond that. He produced a card and left.

I trudged up the stairs, Truffles at my side when I realized one contributing piece to my agitation. I turned and softly stepped back down the stairs to do a quick visual sweep.

I did not see the small oil painting of the Fairy Slipper.

It wasn't propped on the dining room table next to the chair where Cadence had been sitting. It wasn't stacked on one of the file piles.

It wasn't hanging on the wall in the kitchen.

It was gone.

My subsequent sleep that night was dreamless, deep and terribly short. I was awake by five. I punched the pillow, rearranged the quilts, went for a pee, and tried counting backwards from two hundred by sevens.

At five forty-five I called Gretchen.

She answered at the first ring. "Kami? Are you alright?"

"Not hardly. Did you hear the commotion last night?"

"No. I went to bed after you left."

"I was on my merry little way home when I tripped over the body of Flint Heroux."

"Who?"

"A guy named Flint. He's a charismatic vegan leader who has been staying with Briar and Thorne. He was supposed to lead an animal rights protest at the Capital today."

"My God. Are you okay?

Truffles peeked out from under the covers, his dark eyes seeking me. He settled as I stroked his head.

"Sorta. Truffles is going to need to go out. Why don't we go for a walk in the woods?"

"You, Kami Schmidt, are calling me to take a walk in the woods at dawn on a freezing morning?" Gretchen snorted. "I'll be damned."

"Hey. You're the one who said forest bathing could be addictive."

"Get your long johns on. I'll be over."

And she was.

We climbed the incline to the trail, moist breath making clouds in the cold. Truffles bounded ahead, his small dark body whipping through frost-tipped grass.

"Think he needs a coat?" I asked.

"No." Gretchen stumped along with her walking stick and raised an eyebrow.

"Right. You want to hear about last night."

"Yes."

I told her. I talked about falling over Flint, hanging out with

Dr. Jaeger, overhearing the "my darling" call to Delphina, and I told her about the missing oil painting.

"Do you think Flint took the painting?" Gretchen asked.

"I doubt it. I'm thinking more likely it's Glynnis." I paused. "Or one of the teens."

Her eyes narrowed. "Which teen?"

"I don't know." I kicked a stick into the greenery beside the trail and Truffles went after it.

"Bullshit. Which one is giving you the queasies?"

"Cadence. She stayed behind. She went charging to the bathroom, then told me it was food poisoning."

"Anything else?"

"She was quick to say she'd like cash."

"You're wondering if she has a little problem and needs an abortion?" Gretchen's tone wasn't critical. That's one of the things I liked about her. Life's messiness didn't surprise her.

"I have no idea," I admitted. "I get the clear message that life is not warm and cozy at home. If she is expecting, she's not going to have buckets of family support."

"How much is the painting worth?"

I shook my head. "Again, I have no idea. I made a joke that it'd be great if it was painted by Winslow Homer. Cadence looked him up and knows his stuff is incredibly valuable – but the painting is not a Winslow Homer. We found a squiggle on the back that reads Mary something. Cadence was going to look into that further."

We were nearing the county road where there was often traffic. I called to Truffles, and he came charging out of the undergrowth.

"How appropriate." Gretchen pointed with a jerk of her chin. "That's a patch of Vanilla Leaf."

"It's not Trilliums?"

"Nope. Here's a Trillium." She pointed to a tri-leafed plant with a robust three-petaled white flower. "Vanilla Leaf has three leaves too, but they're bigger leaves and the flowers are these little things on a stalk." Gretchen picked a sample and inhaled. "The dried leaves smell like vanilla. Its other common name is 'Sweet-after-death.' Want to collect some?"

My stomach gave a gurgle, as if it wasn't sure if I should eat or bring up a barf of bile.

I said, "I'd rather have breakfast."

Gretchen was agreeable to turning around. We reversed course and returned down the trail, rapidly warming as the morning sun filtered through the trees. Gretchen pointed out the previously golden Vancouver ground cone that was now streaked with purple.

"Why does it do that?" she murmured. "There must be some advantage."

"My mother favored purple as she grew older," I said. "Went well with her white hair."

"I doubt a ground cone has a fashion sense." Gretchen frowned. "Who else might have taken your painting? And why the hell do I care?"

She sent a fir cone skittering down the trail with a tap of her walking stick before answering her own question. "Because I don't want to think about someone dying a few yards from my home."

"It's more like a hundred yards," I said. "The attacker had to be a stranger. Some Montana cowboy whose herd escaped because of Flint's shenanigans."

"If it had been a cowboy, we'd have heard shots," Gretchen said. "Are you sure it wasn't a local?"

"It couldn't have been one of us," I argued. "Eloise is too short."

"And we never see her husband," Gretchen agreed. "Bob's a pacifist. Arkady was probably snuggling with Delphina."

"Dr. Jaeger can't possibly be that good of an actor." I felt confident on this. "He was rattled. He was a snob, but a rattled snob."

"Yo Mommas' Llamas are out. If the llamas were okay, Sky wouldn't have a beef," Gretchen said. She paused, then asked, "Can you have a beef with a vegan?"

We came to a halt.

"Sky wouldn't like it if Flint was making moves on Juno," I noted. "And Juno wants out from veganism."

"She's a few summer weeks away from shipping out to college," Gretchen tapped the earth to emphasize the point. "What teen doesn't want freedom from the rules of the household? Having something to rebel against keeps kids from being homesick that first semester on campus. I refuse to believe that sweet girl bashed anyone."

"That leaves us Briar, Thorne and Ivy," I mused.

"Right," Gretchen snorted. "Only if they caught Flint with a bacon double cheeseburger."

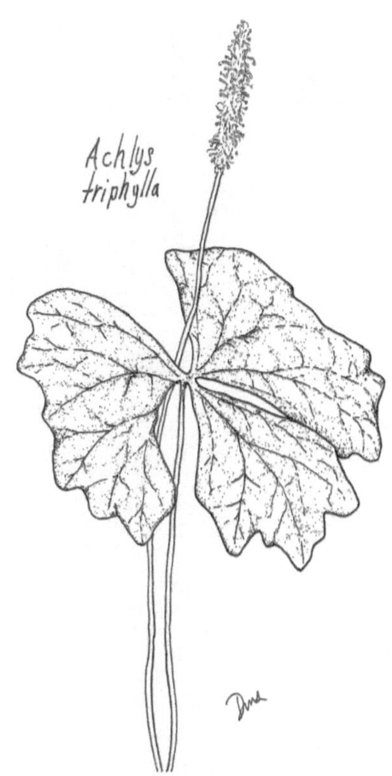

CHAPTER TWENTY

———————————

Too much of a good thing can be wonderful.

Mae West

———————————

Sunday, May 3 – 8 a.m.

"TOO MUCH OF a good thing is…" I was looking into the refrigerator and seeing eggs, cheese and green onion. "A recipe for high cholesterol and a heart attack. That's just what we need to round out the week."

We were back home, where I found myself talking to Truffles. Gretchen had declined breakfast, saying, "I want to check on Bob," before she strode off with her walking stick in the direction of his drive, skirting a lake's worth of barricades and "Do Not Cross" caution tape that surrounded a discolored bit of gravel.

Truffles and I needed to eat. Giving in to the limitations of the refrigerator contents, I made cheesy scrambled eggs, skipping the green onion for Truffles' share.

I made a to-do list as I ate. Grocery shopping was a must.

The morning light streamed into the kitchen, bright with May promise. It lit a kitchen full of grime and smudges. The windows were streaked. The baseboards held so much dust they looked as if they'd been coated with a velvet flocking spray.

The floor was sticky too.

Now the light caught cobwebs connecting the kitchen curtains and the overhead light fixture to the ceiling.

"Cleaning" went on the list. Adding "More Decluttering" made my eyes prickle with tears. Spending a few minutes in Dr. Jaeger's kitchen had me realizing how far things had deteriorated here. I should have done an extra five minutes of cleaning now and then.

"Cut yourself an eff-ing break, Kami," I scolded myself.

Truffles gave a single high-pitched bark, cocking his head in the direction of the kitchen door.

Someone was there.

"Good dog," I praised Truffles. "You're getting a handle on this alarm stuff."

I opened the door and was nearly bowled over from behind as Truffles charged forward to greet Juno and Cadence.

Juno looked like death warmed over. Her glorious hair was unbrushed, her clothes looked slept in. Her eyes were red-rimmed and swollen.

Cadence had a worried look on her face, but her greenish-tint was gone. She said, "I'm hoping you have work for us today." Her eyes on me, she added, "It's good for us to be out of the house."

"Right. Come on in." I could well imagine Briar and Thorne were shattered by the death of their famous guest.

"Let's have a cup of tea first." I directed the young women to the kitchen dinette where they silently slid into the booth. Recalling what Dr. Jaeger had said about unexpected allergies, I rooted in the kitchen cabinets until I came up with a box of assorted herbal teas.

I put a kettle on and soon had mugs of hot water, spoons,

honey and a choice of tea bags. Cadence went for mint. Juno chose a lemon balm. I stared at the options with a spinning brain before finally picking something floral.

"You look a little better," I said to Cadence. "Food poisoning defeated?

"Yeah. I'm good." She exhaled. "My mom's unhinged. We're supposed to be a safe neighborhood. She's been on the phone to the sheriff and all three county commissioners this morning."

"Oh, goody."

My snide remark had Cadence snort a bubble in her tea.

"I've never seen my parents so flipped out." Juno dragged a hand under her nose. "And now… Sky…" She burst into tears.

"What's with Sky?"

"The llamas stayed in last night," Cadence's voice was tight and high. "But someone opened the doors to the chicken coops. The birds were slaughtered."

"Jay-sus. All of them?"

Before she could answer there was a rapid rapping on the kitchen door. We turned and could see a disheveled Sky through the window of the door. He pounded on the door frame. Truffles began barking as the rapping continued.

"Juno!" came through the door. "Juno!"

"Truffles, be quiet, for Pete's sake." I slid off the dinette bench, stomped across the kitchen and flung the door open. Truffles surged forward and squirted between my legs to leap up on Sky's legs, tongue lolling.

Sky's chest was heaving. I could tell he'd been crying. He looked down at Truffles, looked up at me, then knelt to sweep the little dog to his chest as tears streamed down his face. "I'm glad you're okay, little guy."

Truffles wagged his hind end with enthusiasm and licked Sky's face.

"We're having tea," I said. "Will you join us?"

Sky struggled to his feet with a nod, wiping his nose on the sleeve of his jacket. He shuffled into the kitchen where Juno was crying with great hiccupping sobs. He went to her, knelt down and reached out to hug her.

"I'm so sorry," she wailed. "I am so, so sorry."

"It's not your fault," he responded. "It was a surplus killing times three. It's not your fault."

Juno's long hair fell over his shoulders as they wept together.

"What's a surplus killing? I asked.

Cadence shrugged and started typing on her phone. "A killing of multiple prey animals in one session," she read. "Also goes by the name 'henhouse syndrome.' A predator is in a space with easy prey, so it kills and keeps killing. It kills more than it can eat."

Sky lifted himself from the floor onto the dinette bench next to Juno where he encircled her in his long arms. After the hug, he turned to me and explained, "We have three hen enclosures and three roost houses. We think people came, opened the gates, then the hen house doors. After the people left, one or more predators came in."

"It was sabotage? No chance of human error?" I didn't think so, but I had to ask.

"No." Sky shook his head with certainty. "We have had the same routine since I was eight years old. You put down the evening mash. The birds come running in. You shut the hen door by letting down the string as you sing, 'Good Night, Ladies, Good Night Ladies. We're going to leave you now.' We count the birds, step out the people door and latch it."

He rubbed his nose again. "The only thing different about last night was the heat lamps. We had them on. Which means a predator had great light for killing."

"What kind of predator?" Cadence asked. "And how did it get into all three houses?"

I poured hot water into a mug and handed it to Sky so he

could fix himself a hot drink. He grabbed the first tea bag in the box and ripped into it. I had to hand it to the kid. He was not fussy.

"Monika, my blonde mom, thinks it was either a short-tailed weasel or a mink. Xiulen, my dark-haired mom, thinks it could have been a fox or a pair of foxes." Upending the honey for a long squirt, Sky said, "We can see the origin of the expression, don't let the fox guard the henhouse."

He sighed. "It had to be a person who opened the hen doors. They can't be opened from the outside. We found slices in the enclosure fencing that looks like someone used a pair of wire cutters. They had to have come into each hen house, and then they had to walk through to the hoist pulley to open the bird door."

"All the birds were killed?" My hand went to my mouth. It had to be a horrific sight.

"Sixty-three birds decapitated," Sky confirmed. "Which is why Monika thinks it was a weasel or mink. Apparently, head decapitation is a standard surplus kill technique for mustelids." He heaved a sigh. "There's a tiny red Cochin and a shell-shocked black Australorp who survived."

"Flint was known for shenanigans where an animal escape was made to look serendipitous," I said. "This sounds clumsy. There's no way anyone would think that *three* henhouses were left open in error."

"Which is why Monika called Thorne this morning and said we would sue." Sky sighed. "She says Briar and Thorne can be charged with a Class C felony for cruelty to animals."

Juno wiped her eyes and hiccupped. "My dad is totally freaked. He said Monika was the one who should go to jail for animal cruelty."

"Wait," I interrupted. "Do we know that Briar and Thorne opened the doors?"

Sky looked beyond miserable. "We have a security camera.

Briar and Thorne came down the drive with Flint about eight thirty in the evening. About twenty minutes later, Briar and Thorne walked out again. They turned right, which would take them back to their place. The camera is on the drive, not on the hen enclosures."

"It could have been all Flint," I said.

Juno shook her head. "I was working on a scrapbook. I could tell they were excited. Flint had this shit-eating grin before they went out. My parents were all wound up. My dad got a headlamp out of the drawer, then Flint told him, "You won't need that." I asked them what was up. My mom said something like "We're looking at the stars."

She sniffed. "Eight-thirty in the evening is awfully early for stargazing. It's not even totally dark until nine."

I thought about my walk home. The Writers Group had shut down a bit after nine. I had stayed to delay Ivy, and then I had visited with Gretchen. It had been almost ten thirty and very dark when I left Gretchen's cabin.

"When did your parents come back to your house?" I asked.

Juno thought. "I'm not really sure. They weren't gone long. It was just my mom and dad who came back. They were smiling. Excited. My mom said she had a news item to send out. My dad had a conference call about the protest. I was tired and went to bed."

"We checked the llamas when Dr. Jaeger called," Sky said. "That was about eleven. Monika, went to check on the chickens, but the main doors were shut and everything was quiet. She didn't go into the coops to check the hen doors. We think the doors were open then, but the predators might not have shown up until a few hours later."

Juno turned her swollen face to Sky. "I promise I did not know what they were up to. I would have stopped them. I swear I would have."

"I know." With a heavy sigh, Sky said, "My moms are calling our place a crime scene. They have a call into the sheriff's office." He took a deep draught of the super-honeyed tea before adding, "And they've called a friend at Channel 32 News."

Chapter Twenty-One

A man reaps what he sows.

Galatians 6:7

Sunday, May 3 – 9 a.m.

I SAT DOWN with the teens, sliding onto the bench next to Cadence. "Juno's dad is an attorney. What happens," I asked, "if an attorney is charged with a Class C felony?"

"I have a pretty good idea," Cadence answered. "My dad has served on a review board before. If Thorne is convicted, there's a chance he could be disbarred."

Cadence swirled the tea in her mug. "Let's be honest. The review board would be filled with conservatives. They aren't going to be warm and fuzzy to a vegan who has changed his name to Thorne."

Juno sighed and added, "The whole universe of people coming to the protest at the Capital doesn't help. Too many are going to be wearing black. That doesn't make them anti-fa, but reality doesn't matter much these days."

Cadence wore a scowl of disgust. "I really don't get why it's bad to be anti-fa. Isn't it nauseating to be pro-fa? Who needs fascists?"

Juno leaned back into the bench, pushing her hair over her shoulder. "It's the righteousness. Everyone is screaming their point of view, and you're a traitor if you disagree. Like one buttered biscuit makes me evil?"

Cadence rolled her eyes. "At my house, the evil is working on a project with a guy who wears nail polish. You'd think he was a baby-eater."

"Better a baby-eater than a baby seal basher," Juno said. "Bet the population control groupies have recipes."

Sky rubbed her shoulder. "My moms can separate you from your parents. You are not them. You're you."

"I don't recognize my parents anymore." Juno frowned. "They've gone down the rabbit hole of unreal. Maybe I should start watching Fox news. I'll go extreme right, and they can stay bonkers left. We could balance out at the ballot box."

"Like that will happen." Cadence shrugged. "Too much adtech at work."

"Adtech?" I hated the cynical, weary tones of the young people. I also couldn't see flaws in their statements. Now I was at sea with this new word.

"Every story you see on-line comes with advertising," Cadence said. "Say that ad is selling denture cream. If it's a boring story, you'll see the denture cream advertisement once. But if you see a story that makes your blood boil, you'll interact with the site. Maybe you click a 'like' or a 'heart.' Maybe you post a comment. With me so far?"

I nodded.

"The algorithms on-line will now know what you 'grok' to. They'll serve you more of that sort of story. You'll see that denture cream ad a lot more times."

"Been there," I admitted. "Especially if you ever click on the denture cream ad by mistake."

"Yep. But the real money comes if they can get you to forward or share a story. Now that denture cream ad is going to your circle. Your friends get the message it's the brand of denture cream you're using."

"Thanks for that mental image." I saw her point.

Cadence grinned at me. "There's more. The denture cream marketing team will customize and make a Red-white-and-blue all-American denture cream for conservative sites and an organic mint denture cream for lefties."

Sky took up the lesson. "The denture cream ad goes farthest if you're truly pissed or worried, because you'll share the posting, and it will upset others, who will share it. Domino effect."

Cadence exhaled. "The truth is boring. We know we have to keep an eye on government spending and waste. Duh. It's a thing. It's better for the planet and our bodies if we eat less meat. True, but boring. Inspections and oversight matter. None of this sells many units of denture cream."

Her body hunched as she scowled. "But a government conspiracy to put you into poverty or threatens your kids? Now you're moving denture cream units."

Sky nodded. "So will video of a farm operation that's a horror show. The more the mission ramps you up, the more you want to engage. It's all engineered to make you go berserk."

Juno rested her head on Sky's shoulder. "So, the right way for me to balance my parents would be to become a barbeque chef who sells denture cream?"

"Do you like meat?" I asked.

"I am turned off even thinking about eating a mammal," she said. "I'm more of a fish and seafood person. I like cheese and ice cream too."

"You should have some of Bob's crab puffs. They're divine." I looked around the table. "How long have you three known each other?"

Cadence shrugged. "I've lived on the corner since preschool, but I didn't get to know Sky until middle school when we worked on a science fair project together. My parents weren't into the 'two moms' thing."

"The project thawed things a little," Sky said.

"What was it?" I asked.

"Taste testing pound cake. Do free-range eggs make a lighter, moister, prettier cake?" Sky smiled. "Which, of course, they do. It wasn't until we were at the science fair that Cadence told me she'd added an extra half teaspoon of vanilla to the free-range egg mix. You have to watch her. She'll put her thumb on the scale."

Cadence's sly smile confirmed this.

"We moved in when I was thirteen," Juno said. "I went to a private school and then went to Germany for a year abroad as a sophomore. I switched to Capital High last year. I knew these guys before that, but not well."

She smiled at Sky. "I remember last summer when you invited me over for a bonfire, and it got out of hand."

"My pyromania phase." Sky pinked up. "Impress the girl by burning down her parents' fence."

"They were impressed that you took responsibility."

"And they shipped you off to the San Juans for pottery camp the rest of the summer."

The two gazed into each other's eyes.

I coughed. "I need to make a run to the grocery store, but I'm glad to feed lunch to anyone here," I said. "How do you want to handle today?"

"I need to go home and help my moms bury the chickens," Sky said. "I told them I needed to find Juno first and make sure she was okay."

"We should burn the chickens." Juno's long fingers tapped the table with an angry insistency. "On a bier. With a memorial service."

"Burning feathers stink." Sky's nostrils flared and wrinkled. "That many birds will be nasty."

"Works for me." Juno's long eyebrows came down in an angry, straight line. "My parents should have a reminder of the deaths they caused."

"Let's go talk to my moms," Sky suggested. "We should document everything too."

Cadence leaned forward. "I'd rather hang out here. I want to know more about Flint Heroux. I can't believe that's his birth name."

"You are formidable," I told her. "I think that's an excellent idea."

Sky stood up. "We could check back later and hear what Cadence finds out."

"I'd like a mid-day meetup," I said. "Tuna sandwiches?"

Juno gave me a shy smile and asked, "With potato chips?"

"You bet. I'll get some potato chips." Junk food sounded healthy and loving. We all could use some potato chips.

Glynnis walked into the kitchen, bright in a pink pullover paired with black stirrup pants, her hair smooth and chic. She said, "If you're going to the store, can you pick up some doggy kibble?"

"Sure. What brand?"

Glynnis looked at me and shrugged. "Cheap?"

"Right."

She didn't like my tone. "Hey, somebody got killed last night. Practically on the door step. I've got other stuff on my mind." She exhaled. "I'm headed over to wrangle kids for Ashlee. She's scheduled an afternoon at a spa."

Glynnis sighed, looked at Juno and said, "I'm bummed, and you look like shit."

"Thanks." Juno smiled. "Appreciate the honesty."

"Honey, I was snotty to your parents because I really do not get the whole 'end farms and eat almonds' thing. Growing almonds takes water. Lots of it. It's all Loony Tunes as hell, but the important thing is that I want you to be careful."

"Me?" Juno's eyebrows went up. "You think someone is going to be after me because my family is vegan?"

"That guy who got his head bashed in was a player." Glynnis looked at me. "I told Kami that yesterday. I'll bet he didn't give two figs about what the hell people eat."

She reached down and rubbed Truffles ears. "I'm on the cool-hearted side of things. I see this little guy as a great sales tool. Kami sees him as more than that. Truffles is her buddy. Kami's a warm sort. But Flint? His sort is stone cold."

Glynnis straightened up. "I've sold essential oils for a long time. Some of it is good stuff. I've heard and seen enough to know there are people who really are helped." She moved to the stove and turned the fire on under the kettle. "But we also sell hundreds of gallons of hopes and dreams. I'm okay with that too."

Glynnis looked across to Juno and said, "Where I really make money is when I sign up a true believer as a salesperson. They can put their whole life into it. All day, every day. Doesn't matter if they aren't making rent. Doesn't matter if their kids are doing without. They get in a zone and can stay there for years."

The kettle began to whistle. Glynnis turned it off, chose a tea bag and arched an eyebrow. She continued, "You can't let on to the True Believers that you're just a sales engineer egging them on. They'll rip you to shreds. I'm not kidding. One of our top people got caught on video dissing her sales force as gullible idiots. The next night somebody met her in the parking lot with a baseball bat."

Glynnis shuddered. "Dental implants are expensive."

She saluted Cadence with her tea mug. "You guys are figuring stuff out. A lot of those vegans are True Believers. If someone who really, really cares about animal welfare figured out Flint was gaming them – and I think he was - then they could be really pissed off. You be careful."

Chapter Twenty-two

Oh, what a tangled web we weave,
when first we practice to deceive.

Sir Walter Scott

Sunday, May 3 – 11:30 a.m.

WHEN I RETURNED from the grocery store, I saw a Channel 32 Television truck on the road in front of the llama farm. I also saw a lone sheriff's sedan parked near the caution tape in front of Dr. Jaeger's drive.

Otherwise, the neighborhood was quiet.

I carried the groceries into the kitchen where Truffles greeted me with a wiggling body and dancing feet. The rear end went faster when I filled a cereal bowl with a deluxe dog kibble made of duck and brown rice. I set the bowl on the floor and enjoyed watching the little dog devour a late breakfast.

"We're going to get this feeding-the-dog thing figured out," I told him.

The Fairy Slipper painting was back on the wall.

I stared at it. Was someone playing mind games? Had it slipped behind a pile of clutter and been noticed and rehung? Had someone taken it and had remorse?

A connection to the murder seemed unlikely – unless it had been Glynnis who'd taken the picture. She was shrewd enough to want a squeaky-clean reputation during a murder investigation.

I put away the rest of the groceries and chopped onion and celery to make a tuna salad spread. My recipe calls for a mix of mustard, plain yoghurt and mayo. I poured the tuna water into Truffles' cereal bowl, and he lapped it up, finishing with a burp.

Cadence was in the dining room at work on her laptop. She looked up when I entered the room to say, "Found stuff on the Flint-ster."

"Oh? Tell me, please."

She hesitated. "There's a lot. Mind if I text Juno and Sky, and we meet up? I could tell everything just once."

"Sounds like a plan. Please tell them I will have sandwiches ready soon. Invite Sky's moms too." I left her with thumbs flying on her cell phone to take Truffles out back for a whizz. He loped out onto the grass warming under a bright blue sky. The Douglas firs and cedars of the woods loomed green and inviting just beyond the fence.

I wandered around our backyard, longing for a walk in the woods even as my stomach yearned for a sandwich.

"We'll go again after lunch," I promised Truffles. He ignored me and sniffed through the small and poorly weeded rockery at the rear of the yard. A Western Star flower plant bravely held up paired pink flowers. This was one of the few local plants Kent and I had learned in childhood as the flowers often appeared in twos.

"Early, I think." I was doing a better job of noticing the ecology of the woods. They were clues to a world that was mine if I'd just pay attention.

The Western Star Flower also reminded me that I should check in with my brother and give him an update. I decided to wait until after hearing what Cadence discovered.

I chirped to Truffles. He followed me back to the kitchen, strutting out in his high-stepping trot. I made a tray of sandwiches. Cadence came in and mixed a pitcher of lemonade. We set out apple slices, sweet pickles and a large bowl of potato chips, finishing just as Sky and Juno arrived, looking worn.

"My moms say thanks for the lunch invite," Sky said. "But they're not in a space to be social. There's too much to do."

"Grave or bier?" I asked, pointing them to the sink for a washup.

"Bier." Sky said. "We'll light it this afternoon. We also found tracks that look like our predators were short-tailed weasels — maybe a mating pair." He sighed. "Which puts us in a tricky position. We aren't licensed to trap local wildlife, but they sure could cause us problems if we get more birds."

"A problem for another day," I said. "Let's eat."

The teens mowed through the lunch. Cadence set down her lemonade glass and said, "As weird as it is, it gets weirder."

"What'd you find?" Juno's eyes were tired but alert.

"Well, for starters, you'll be happy to know I had a pleasant conversation with my mother." Cadence's tone was dry and light. "That happens about once in forever. I called her to say I was researching Flint, and that I was running up against a paywall for people locator services. She offered her credit card number and said to gather as much information as I could."

To me, Cadence said, "That's like the first time, ever, that she's been positive about my on-line research time."

"She wants to know as badly as the rest of us," Sky said. "Who was he?"

"Flint starts life as a Bobby, with a 'Y.' Not a Robert," Cadence said. "Bobby Johnson. He graduated high school in Missouri and did puppet shows for kids' birthday parties."

Cadence continued, "He moves to Denver, works in a bong shop, gets arrested for having marijuana. Charges were dropped. Then he shows up in L.A. where he changes his name to Stone Johnson and lands a few movie credits as a cowboy in westerns."

"Next, he's up in Eugene, Oregon. That's where he's back to doing puppet shows and is charged with possession of child pornography."

"Whoa." Juno blinked. "My parents did not know that, for sure."

"Charges dropped again."

"When was this?" I asked.

Cadence frowned. "Can't remember the exact year. It's on my laptop. About thirty years ago?" She reached for a potato chip and continued. "He moves to Corvallis, is there about a decade and then he's in northern California. That's when he becomes Flint Heroux."

She waved the potato chip and said, "He goes to work for a big vegan retreat center, as an arts and crafts director. He starts documenting animal industries, putting up YouTube videos, arranging animal escapes and asking for donations."

"Successful in the fundraising?" I asked.

"Big time." Cadence shrugged. "I spoke politely with my mom a second time in a single morning, which has to be a record, and she told me political operators can burn through a lot of cash, but passionate supporters will give a lot of cash too. She's treasurer for everything Republican in the county, so she should know."

Cadence popped the potato chip into her mouth and chewed, talking around the mouthful. "The vegan retreat was burned in a wildfire last fall. Flint took his stuff on the road to Florida and Jamaica. As far as I can tell, he was operating without a home base."

"Checking out a farmhouse near Olympia that is about to go on the market makes sense," I said. "If that's what he was doing."

"There's more. Let me go get my computer."

I stood up so Cadence could slide off the dinette bench. She murmured, "You may not like this next part."

"A cliff-hanger," I joked as I sat back down. "Writer's love them. Bring it on."

Juno was rapidly firing a text off. "I'm letting my parents know they had a pedophile in the house."

"Alleged," Sky said. "He was charged, not convicted."

"If it makes them feel guilty, I'm using it," she said.

"Is this about the chickens?" I asked. "Or about more than chickens?"

Juno paused. "I want my parents back. The ones who asked me what I wanted for dinner this week. The ones who asked me what I wanted to do when I grew up instead of telling me what I'm going to be doing. So, yes, it's about more than the chickens."

Cadence came back with her laptop. "I can't believe how fast this stuff is blowing up. There's lots of news stories, but here's a screen shot that may be important."

She turned the laptop to me. I could see a grainy image of a newspaper photo showing Flint in a poet's big-sleeved tunic with a puppet in each hand, grinning at the photographer. A long-haired woman in a dark Renaissance Fair gown stood next to him holding a turkey leg, mouth open as if she were about to take a large bite.

The tiny-font caption read "Puppets, food and more at the Oregon Renaissance Fair this weekend! Stone Johnson and Gretchen Moore are ready to serve up fun."

Once again, my mouth did the goldfish-look. I peered at the photo and used my fingers to enlarge the screenshot.

"I can't tell if that's our Gretchen," I said, at last. "I know she's been married and divorced a few times. She certainly isn't Gretchen Moore now."

A chime came from Sky's phone. "Breaking news after a commercial, Channel 32," he said.

"Come on. Let's see it on the big screen." I led the way to

the living room and its mountain ranges of boxes. The four of us squeezed onto the sofa. Truffles leapt up into my lap as I fumbled with the television remote.

"Our update on the hour takes us to Olympia," an anchorwoman said. "First to Dontel who is near the death site of animal activist Flint Heroux. Dontel, we understand there was also a slaughter of chickens?"

The screen switched to show a slim black man in a blue windbreaker holding a microphone. He stood next to a dark-haired woman in a faded red barn coat. The two stood in front of the Yo Mommas' Llamas sign.

"That's right. This is Xiolen Chen, owner of Yo Mommas' Llamas. Ms. Chen, will you describe for our viewers what has happened here?"

Sky leaned forward, his elbows on his knees. "I should be there. Monika should be the one speaking. She's blonde. God, we screwed this."

"Shh," Cadence said. "Too late now."

Xiolen spoke carefully, with a slight accent. "We are a small, local farm selling llama wool and free-range eggs. We bring our chickens in every night to secure sheds, with lights for cold nights. Last night our security camera recorded three people coming up our drive. This morning we found the doors open to all three of our hen houses. The birds are dead. We suspect the people of opening the hen houses, which let predators in to kill the birds."

"Did you recognize the intruders?" Dontel asked.

Xiolen hesitated. "We are working with authorities. They will decide."

"Was Flint Heroux one of the intruders?"

This time Xiolen's voice was firmer. "The authorities will announce if this is so."

Dontel was wrapping up. "I know this has been very challenging. One last question. How much have you lost?"

Xiolen straightened and looked into the camera. "There is a loss of dollars, and there is a greater loss of friends. We know our birds. Everyone is dear to us. They are family to us. Anyone who has a puppy or a kitten will know how sad we are to lose our companions."

"She did great," Juno said.

"Mom's still Asian." Sky flexed his fingers, then closed his fingers into fists. "People won't believe her."

Juno put her hand on his knee. "Your moms are shrewder than you think. Monika might have come across as an angry 'Karen.' No one who is vegan wants to be painted anti-Asian."

"She's right," Cadence said.

The view returned to the Seattle anchor, who produced a serious face. "Heartbreaking. Thank you, Dontel."

Briskly, she moved on. "And now to Olympia, where grief-stricken protesters are dedicating the day to their slain leader, Flint Heroux. What can you tell us, Teresa?"

Teresa was a brunette with fabulous dentition. She gripped her long microphone and looked into the camera. "As you can see, crowds are dense here at the Capital. We are seeing many, many weeping people. There are some who are announcing a fierce resolve to end animal industries in the name of Flint Heroux."

The reporter pivoted and extended the microphone to a tall man holding a sign that read "The best things in life are cruelty-free."

The man leaned around his poster board to yell, "They can kill us, but we will keep coming. The world has to change. We say NO! to death. Tonight, we rally at Flint's murder site. Everyone join us!"

His voice rose to a louder shout. "We will free the cattle! We will free the pigs! We will free the chickens! We won't let Flint's last mission be our last mission. Enslaving animals must stop."

There was a cut to a shot of a cheering crowd and another

announcement of a memorial gathering. Teresa extended her microphone to a young woman who said, "We'll be there tonight. We'll sing, we'll dance, we'll organize, and then we WILL seek revenge."

The news reporter kept a professional tone, asking, "What would revenge look like? Will you be destroying property?"

The young woman hesitated, then said, "We are dedicated to non-violence. We will seek justice and accountability."

Moments later the screen shot returned to the news anchor, who had a promise of warmer May days to come from the weather forecaster.

We all sat still. My mind recoiled at the idea of the crowd coming to Flint's death site, located, of course, just feet from my front door.

Sky cleared his throat with a rough cough. "It may not matter who Flint was," he said. "What may matter is who people *think* he was."

Lysimachia
latifolia

CHAPTER TWENTY-THREE

Truth uttered before its time is always dangerous

MENCIUS

Sunday, May 3 – 1:15 p.m.

"ARE THE LLAMAS in danger?" I asked.

Sky's face sagged. He dragged a hand under one eye. "Maybe not. Llamas are territorial. They're big enough to ram a stranger in the pen."

He groaned. "But we could have issues if the fences come down. We worry about our girls getting out on the road. Cars and llamas don't mix."

"All girls?" Cadence asked.

"Currently. We get offered free male llamas all the time, but we turn them down. You have to work with them daily, or they can be hard to handle. My moms are also really careful about the quality of wool we can get. We're not a rescue outfit."

He leaned back and stretched his long arms down the back of the sofa, worry creasing his handsome face. "If the protesters are town people, then they often don't understand how hard we work. Most people can't make llamas and free-range eggs pay out. Monika sells how-to articles, and Xiolen's finished wool is top quality. Even then, we're a skinny income operation."

Sky shook his head. "Small operations are really vulnerable to shitty actions."

Juno's phone jingled with a happy tune. She took the phone out of her back pocket and stabbed on the call. Her long eyebrows came down into a formidable line as she spoke. "No. I'm not coming to the protest. Mom, you created a crapfest hurt our neighbors. You need to fix this."

I wasn't close enough to hear what Briar said, but it wasn't what Juno wanted to hear.

Juno's voice rose as she spoke into the phone. "Remember when Sky's fire got away from him, and he burned our fencepost? He *took responsibility* and made things right. You said that was *the right thing to do.*"

And Juno was just getting started. "No. I'm not coming home. You need therapy. Dad needs therapy. Me finishing high school isn't why you're depressed. Quit dumping your shit on me. Try getting some Omega-3 fatty acids. For fuck's sake, look up Orthorexia!" She smashed the end call button and threw the phone across the room where it landed in the seat of an armchair.

"Or-thor what?" Cadence asked, her voice cheerful as her fingers were poised over her own phone.

"Orthorexia," Juno sniffed. "O-r- thor- like the god- e-x-i-a." Her voice trembled as she added, "Refers to an obsessive-compulsive eating disorder where everything has to be all clean, organic and perfect."

"I see." Cadence typed the word in and scanned an entry. "Interesting. Want to bunk at my place? I can offer an atmosphere of garden-variety Republican narrow-mindedness, complete with homophobia, sexism and a dash of white supremacy."

That amused Juno enough to earn a fleeting smile.

"You two can stay here." I surprised myself with that, but kept going. "There's a room upstairs with two twin beds."

For the first time since I'd met her, I saw Cadence light up with a genuine smile of delight. "Really?" She whistled. "And we could eat, like regular meals?"

"Sure. If you're not too particular. I have lots of pasta and bottles of sauce." I did a mental review of the grocery store run. "There's cans of black olives too."

"Sounds great. I'm in." Juno said. "Especially if the sauce has sugar added."

"Not a clue," I told her. "On sale."

Juno looked at Cadence. "Let's do it. Our own Senior Skip Week. We'll skip being at home."

"Works for me," Cadence agreed. "I need to go grab some clothes."

"Me, too." Juno stood up and retrieved her phone. "Now is a good time because my folks are leaving to go to the protest at the Capital."

Sky stood up too. "I need to go help my moms."

"We'll grab clothes and come over," Juno said. "I want to be there for the service."

Sky nodded, and the teens tromped out. I followed them to the kitchen, agreeing when Cadence asked to take along a second sandwich.

"Go for it. I'm glad you like my recipe."

"It's awesome tuna fish," she said. "Everything at your place tastes great."

My stomach swooped at her words. Weren't appetite and enjoyment of food more signs of pregnancy?

If I showed any signs of worry, Cadence didn't pick up on it. She was joking with Juno. "Bet Kami uses wild flavorings that scare right wingers. Stuff like salt and pepper."

Sky stopped and ferried plates to the sink. "You two go on," he said to Juno. "I got this."

"There's not that much," I protested. "Go."

"You're sure?" Sky did a second trip.

"Go! Help your moms."

"You're an awesome boss." Sky surprised me with a quick hug, then he left.

I appreciated the approval. I loaded the dishwasher and contemplated the afternoon. There were, of course, hundreds of things to do to declutter the house. I decided against all of them, choosing to find my file folder of scribbles and sat down to think.

A story arc is a struggle for me, even as the process helped my characters come to life. I reviewed. I wrote. I crossed things out. Many writers do this on a computer, but I found laying out a timeline on paper helped bring the story into focus faster.

I wrote notes for a solid hour, delighting in the process and managing to ignore estate management tasks completely.

My fingers were tiring when I heard, "Yoo-hoo! Anyone home?" from the kitchen door. Truffles scrambled up from a deep sleep and ran to the kitchen with his rat-tat-tat bark.

"Quiet" I yelled. Truffles ignored me. I went after him, catching him in the kitchen and putting a hand on his muzzle even as I acknowledged my guest.

Cadence's mother, the elegant Eloise, stood at the kitchen door, every dark hair in place over a well-groomed… everything.

I opened the door. "Come in. I've got the little stinker."

A smile flickered across Eloise's face. "Thank you," she said. "I'm not much of a pet person."

"Grab a seat, and I'll set him down. He's not a jumper."

Tiny Eloise stepped across the linoleum with a ballet dancer's grace. Today she wore a heavy pale blue Icelandic wool sweater over jeans that were definitely not from Costco.

The day had warmed up. I was wearing a T-shirt and jeans, and I was toasty enough.

Eloise took a seat on the dinette bench, accepted a snuffle from Truffles and agreed to my offer of a beverage.

"Herbal tea would be lovely," she said. "I'm having a hard time warming up today."

She stayed silent until I placed a mug in front of her and sat down myself.

"Cadence tells me she'd like to come stay with you during this Senior Skip week." Eloise sipped her tea.

I couldn't imagine this woman ever slurped anything. Not even raw oysters. Close up I could see a few fine strands of gray in her cap of dark hair. Strain lines peeked through expertly applied makeup.

This was not a woman at peace with herself or the world.

"Juno's going through a rough patch," I answered. "Cadence is being a good pal, and there's room here. Would you like a tour?" I leaned back in the booth and added, "The place is a mess. It's dusty and gross. We can run the bed linens through the wash, but it's a real bedroom. I'm glad to show you."

"No need," Eloise said. "I haven't the energy. I just wanted to check in with you and say 'Thank You' for having them."

My eyebrows shot up before I had a moment to calm my face.

"I know," Eloise smiled. "I have a reputation for everything being just so." Her perfectly arched dark eyebrow on the right elevated just a bit. "I think we can understand one another."

She sipped the tea, then said, "Cadence was our 'Whoops' baby. Our older two were ten and twelve when Cadence came along. We were forever parking her with a babysitter as our older two went through middle school and high school events. Then I had a stretch of breast cancer when Cadence was eight and again when she was thirteen."

"Ouch," I said.

"Indeed. And then my mind was on participating in current events." She sipped the tea. "One can grow hungry for adult topics."

Eloise's eyebrow went up again, "Cadence feels we've neglected her. She's not entirely incorrect." Eloise sighed. "Last summer I finally shed two jobs as treasurer, thinking Cadence and I could spend time together before she leaves for college. I'd forgotten how busy high school seniors are. College applications are such an all-consuming nightmare, and we had a few fierce disagreements over college choices."

Eloise looked down into the mug. "Then I learned the replacement treasurers were not up to the job. The woman who was handling the county Republican funds is overwhelmed and can't keep up. And the man handling our PAC, well, he had some not-terribly-original ideas about an expense account."

She rolled her eyes. "My own muddled mess to navigate."

"Embezzlement?"

"Let's just say one can find lovely wines to purchase in our area and leave it at that."

"I'm so sorry." I found that I was.

"Might as well unburden the entire load." Eloise's tone was light, like her daughter could be at a sarcastic moment, only Eloise's idea of an 'entire load' was likely to be immensely diplomatic.

My fingers itched. What a fun character I could add into my story. She'd be elegant, understated, and full of surprises.

A dash of awareness arrived, unbidden. I studied Eloise and asked, "You're ill again?"

"Yes. Which is one of the reasons I thought to toddle down here. It would be helpful to have Cadence away tonight and tomorrow morning – in a safe place." Her eyes darkened. "Which I thought our neighborhood was until that charlatan went and had himself murdered."

I couldn't help it. I burst out laughing. "Not a fan of Flint Heroux?" I asked.

"Cadence told me a bit of what she's found." Eloise's mouth tightened, then she smiled. "My daughter is a good researcher."

"Headed to Whitworth college?" I tilted my head as I spoke. I was curious to hear Eloise's response.

She produced a wintery smile. "Alas, I think not, although I do believe it is a school with strong merits. I suspect from your question that you don't value tradition as I do."

There was a chill in her words, giving me a distinct 'back off' message.

Eloise said, "Cadence also quietly applied to the Northwestern University journalism program and was accepted. She signed a letter of intent with Northwestern in April. She thinks her father and I are ignorant of this."

Eloise's smile reappeared as she added, "She could not possibly attend without our support. It's been good for her to become more money aware. Cadence needs to get on with telling us. She'll get a good head of steam going, and we'll have it out. Peter's rather pleased with her moxie. He already has Northwestern pullovers for us in a box in his closet."

"I've heard it's a good school," I said.

"Currently ranked number fourteen of all colleges nationally." Eloise spoke with a happy glint to her eyes. "It is not Ivy League, but it will suit Cadence."

I had no interest in discussing college rankings. "What's happening tomorrow?" I asked. "It's fine if Cadence stays here. I just want to understand."

"I'm having a biopsy tomorrow. It's at six in the morning. There's no way I can pretend it's a lunch meeting that ran over."

"I see." I did. "And the results?"

"Peter and I will meet with the oncologist early in the afternoon."

"That fast?"

"A perk of Peter's connections," Eloise admitted. "I need to know."

"Do you want Cadence with you?"

"No. I don't." Eloise stared into her mug. "She has never seen me fall to pieces. I don't intend for that to change."

"I'll keep her busy," I promised.

"Thank you. She'll want to eat abundantly, I'm afraid," Eloise stood up. "She's trying out for a role as Bridget Jones for summer theater and wants to be plump. I hope she doesn't eat you out of house and home."

"No worries. I've got pasta and sauce on hand."

"Perhaps we can send along a pizza later in the week," Eloise offered.

She firmed her lips in a well-bred motion of resolve. "I really have not been myself lately. I let some chicken salad hang about too long. Cadence tells me it made her quite ill, and now she has catching up to do in her plumping program. I do feel awful that she felt awful." She added a smile. "Thank you for the lovely cup of tea."

I escorted the elegant woman to the door, feeling like an idiot. Cadence wasn't pregnant. Or if she was, she had a heck of a cover story.

Any way you sliced it, I was a simple, dumb bunny in comparison to Cadence and Eloise. They were queens of complexity, each hiding secrets as they moved forward with their lives.

My previous villain had been too flat. I was going to fix that in this next story. No matter what, I'd write a villain who had more layers than a lasagna.

CHAPTER TWENTY-FOUR

Attention is the chisel of memory.

DUC DE LEVIS

Sunday, May 3 – 2:30 p.m.

I STOPPED IN the dining room to scribble more notes for my story, then pushed back from the table before I became lost in my writing. I had houseguests coming, and it'd be nice not to be a total failure as a hostess. Although Glynnis might say that ship had sailed long ago. I never did confirm she had toilet paper at her end of the hall.

With a sigh, I trudged upstairs, Truffles at my heels, to take a look at the bedroom next to mine. We called it, variously, 'the kids' room,' or 'the green room' because it had twin beds with green bedspreads. The wallpaper was the original 1970s stuff with giant yellow and moss-green psychedelic flowers, faded now, but still cheerful.

The cluttered lane between the beds held yoga mats, light dumbbell weights, and a pile of elastic therapy bands in several

195

weights and colors. There was also a stack of board games and boxes of jigsaw puzzles.

I blinked back tears as I recalled my mother's determination to stay fit enough to wear her favorite slacks. My father had been the board game king, happy to spend an afternoon playing himself in several roles if no one was available to give him a game.

Using a 'linen check' as an excuse, I flung myself onto one of the twin beds and gave way to a sudden cascade of tears. Truffles leaped onto the bed and curled himself next to me.

I wept. I howled. I sniffed, sat up, saw my mother's therapy bands, laid back down and cried some more. Finally, I wiped my very runny nose on a pillowcase.

The pillow was musty. So was the bedspread.

I turned onto my side to sniff the sheets. Musty.

And when it's musty to a post-cry stuffed nose, it is really musty.

"We're making progress," I told Truffles. "We have identified another space in the house as being a mess. We should start numbering and ranking them."

Truffles raised his head and licked my chin.

"Right. Break is over. Come on." I stood up, pushed the dog off the bed and started gathering up the bedspread and sheets. A few minutes later I staggered downstairs with a load of linens sacked on my back.

I started a load of wash, then texted Cadence and Juno. *Pillows musty. Bring yours?*

Speaking to Truffles, I observed, "They can move the weights and games when they get here. They're young and strong."

My phone chimed with an incoming text from Juno. *Will bring pillows. Be there about 4. Sky too. Want to work.*

I replied with a thumbs up.

The correct course of action would be to review the status of things in the dining room so I could use the teens' hours effectively.

I took a look into the dining room, saw the unending stacks of files and papers and whistled to Truffles.

"You need a walk," I said.

He seemed to agree, toenails clacking as his feet danced on the floor. His dancing increased pace in the kitchen where I cubed some cheese to use as dog treats. I gave him two, and loaded the rest into a baggy for my pocket.

We left by the kitchen door, heading to the back of our property. Truffles turned right on the trail as we usually went that direction, past Delphina's, Arkady's and the Eliopoulous's place.

This time I whistled to him and turned left. I held out a cheese bit. We would walk behind Dr. Jaeger's place and behind Bob's place. Gretchen said the trail narrowed to nothing behind her house. It was time I saw this for myself.

Summoned and cheesed-up, Truffles agreed.

I felt safe, mostly, as it was a lovely afternoon on a sunny day in May. I had a dog, not that Truffles was a manslayer, but his barking would at least warn of someone approaching.

Even so, Flint's death was real.

I checked the battery power on my phone. I could call for help – and I sourly realized this would mean a responding officer would know which half of the county to search for my remains, as response time was slow in our area.

Despite the sour thought, I walked on, pleased to be out of the house and moving.

I enjoyed the familiarity of the plants I was passing. Thanks to Gretchen, I now could tell a Douglas fir tree from a cedar. I recognized the evergreen huckleberry bushes, the Oregon grape and the salal of the undergrowth.

"Bonus points!" I crowed when spying another slow-moving Pacific sideband snail. I spoke to it as we passed by. "I hope your love life is going well today. It's better than mine, I'll bet."

There was only a narrow break in the foliage to see Dr. Jaeger's back porch. The evergreen huckleberry bushes grew thickly for almost fifty yards. I did stop for a peek, hoping to see Delphina working her charms on the surly surgeon.

Delphina's interactions with our two neighbors were definitely more interesting to contemplate than my stuff sorting.

No one was out in Jaeger's backyard, and Truffles now was far ahead on the trail.

Truffles doubled back when I whistled and pulled out the cheese baggy. I put Truffles into a sit and fed him more cheese cubes.

"We're heading into new territory," I told him. "Stick close."

I suspect it was the cheese cubes and not my instructions, but Truffles did stay closer to me as the trail narrowed.

We saw Bob.

He was on his knees with his cell phone out, braced against a tree trunk, as he photographed something to our right.

Bob's face lit up with a big grin as Truffles came near.

"Hello, little cutie," Bob said. "Aren't you a handsome dog?

Truffles' rear end went into wiggle overdrive at the warm words.

"Hey, Kami." Bob stayed on his knees, using one hand to pet Truffles with thumps that sounded like a melon testing. "Come see this Pacific Coralroot. It's a beauty."

Bob's color was better this morning, even as there were lines of strain on his face and the cheeriness came across as forced.

I followed his directions and knelt down beside him, seeing only salal and evergreen huckleberry.

Suddenly there was something remarkable in front of me. Three fuzzy-topped burgundy sticks emerged from the ground to knee height. I was astonished that such bright red colors blended into the green background so well.

With a closer look, I could see the fuzzy tops were actually tiny orchid flowers.

"Are they really orchids?" I marveled.

"Yep. They come out every year." Bob took another series of photos before rocking to his heels and standing up. "You're seeing one half of the relationship here. There is a mycelium underground for a mushroom, and the orchid is parasitic on the mycelium. In this spot we have orchids blooming in May, and we'll have mushrooms along here in October."

"That is so cool." I bent over to take photos for myself.

"Brace against the tree," Bob told me. "Better photo hygiene."

I did as he instructed, enjoying the sharpness of the images as the camera focused on the flower parts.

"What kind of mushroom does it have as a partner?" I asked. "Something edible?"

"Everybody wants to know about eating mushrooms." Bob shook his head. "Five million fungal species and most of them aren't dinner. Makes me crazy."

"Sorry. I don't know much about mushrooms."

"You and too many others." Bob pointed at the coralroot. "Talk about your open relationship. We know *Corallorhiza maculata* has at least six genotypes and pairs with at least six different kinds of *Russula* mushroom."

"Okay." With a shrug, I added, "Better orgies than murders."

Bob frowned. "You worried about being out here?" he asked.

"What? With my watchdog?" Truffles had found something disgusting in the needle duff and was rolling in it.

Bob's face was serious.

"I am hoping," I said, "that the person who attacked Flint Heroux was someone who had a personal vendetta. Cadence is working for me, and her research suggests Heroux had a controversial past."

"Really?" Bob crossed his arms and studied me. "What did she find?"

"He'd had at least one different name and a couple different careers. He was charged for a crime, but the charges were dropped."

"What were the charges?" Bob normally is a flirty, irreverent guy. This Bob was serious as a heart attack.

I fumbled in my pocket for another cheese cube for Truffles. "Marijuana, I think. He worked in a bong shop?" I used a rising inflection to show that I wasn't sure – which was correct. Cadence had laid out a history that spanned four decades. I couldn't even remember what I'd had for breakfast.

Eggs. Right. I wasn't going to be having so many eggs now the neighborhood hens were gone.

Bob uncrossed his arms. "Bet you're right," he said. "Somebody from ages ago had an axe to grind. Or maybe it was someone who had animals Flint messed with."

"You were out the door ahead of me. Did you see or hear anything?"

"No." Bob was emphatic. "I didn't go down the drive. There's a shortcut between Gretchen's place and mine. I went home that way."

"Ivy walked home ahead of me," I said. "But it's unlikely she would have seen where Flint was. The same is true for the people who drove to Gretchen's."

"Where was he?"

"Right against the rhododendrons that run across the front part of Jaeger's place," I told him. "In the shadows. I literally tripped over his body."

"That had to be scary."

"Let's just say I got to have your crab puffs twice. Down and up."

"Ohh." Bob made a face. "Let's change the subject. What happens next for you? Gretchen said you have a new story idea."

"I do. It's a wisp of a thing." I wasn't ready to share, so I redirected, saying, "I need to get the household sorted, and we need to get the house on the market."

"Can you get an auction house out?"

"We almost certainly will at some point." I heaved a deep sigh, causing Truffles to pop his head out of the nearby Vanilla Leaf patch. "We have documentation that isn't yet connected to items."

"Like receipts?"

"That and more. For example, we have several high-quality katanas. They are Japanese swords that are astonishingly beautiful. Somewhere, I am sure, there is information on each one that tells us the maker and the year of construction, which adds to the value of the sword. We need to check every file folder, and it's exhausting."

"Got it." Bob chirped to Truffles, who ran over for a head rub. "And you're probably running into all sorts of memories."

"My father was an incredible pack rat," I agreed. "He cut out magazine articles, saved instruction booklets… you name it, he kept it."

"Really? No spring cleaning now and then?"

I shook my head. "If he thought it was interesting, he held onto it."

"Sounds hard."

"Hey, if we don't get it on the market this summer, maybe we can make it a Halloween horror house. Complete with unsolved murder."

Bob flashed me his standard, cynical grin.

"Where do you go next?" he asked. "After the house is sold?"

"No clue," I answered. "But I have a sinking feeling Truffles is staying with me. I'm getting used to having him."

"Keep writing," he said. "You definitely should keep writing."

"Right. It'll keep me out of the bars."

"I mean it," Bob said.

"So do I."

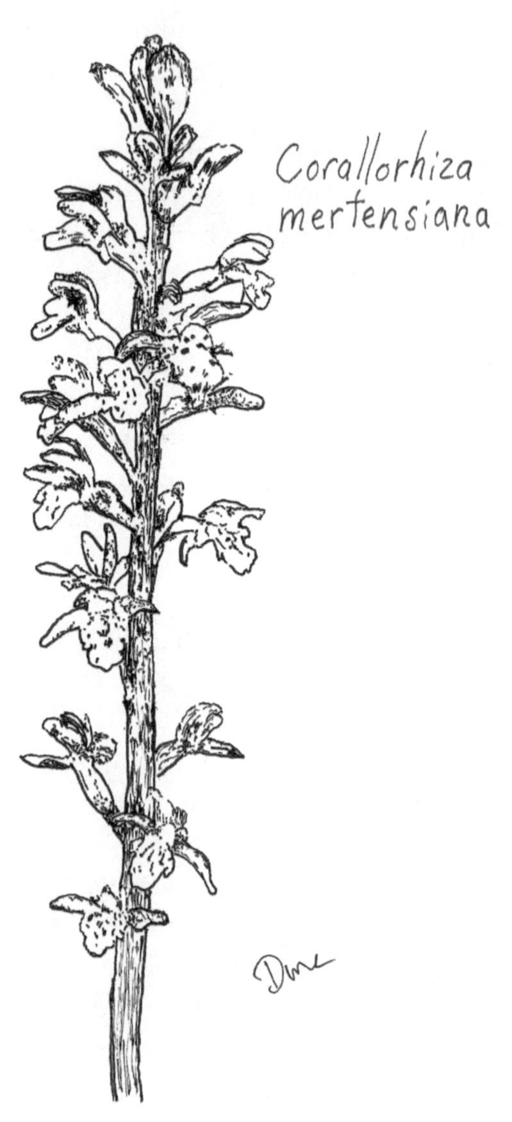
Corallorhiza
mertensiana

CHAPTER TWENTY-FIVE

*Just because you do not take an interest in politics
doesn't mean politics won't take an interest in you.*

PERICLES

Sunday, May 3 – 3:30 p.m.

BOB KEPT ME company. The trail ended at a jumble of stumps
and trailing blackberry to the rear of the llama farm. We could
see a funnel of smoke rising from the north side of the property.

"This lot was poorly cut and managed thirty years ago," Bob
said. "Now it's perfect hunting grounds for short-tailed weasels."

"Is it part of the llama farm?"

"No." Bob gestured to the east. "Belongs to the fellow who
runs the black Angus cattle." He grimaced. "The guy is armed to
the teeth and keeps rottweilers. And we wonder why the chickens
were the ones liberated."

"I should shut up," Bob grumbled. "I am in a mood, let me
tell you."

"Understandable." We watched Truffles scramble up a stump

and stand proud, like a woodland trophy dog. "Come on, Truffles," I called. "We need to get home."

To Bob, I said, "My helpers are coming over after the dead chicken service. I promised to feed them."

We fell in step, starting the trail back, when Bob's phone chortled with bird song.

"It's Gretchen." Bob motioned me to stop as he listened to her speak.

"Got it," he said. "Kami is with me. We're on the trail. I'll tell her." He clicked off the phone, saying, "Gretchen is watching the news. The protestors at the Capital are organizing a long night of mourning at the site of Flint's death. Speeches, dancing, crying, drum circles. The works. It will be big."

"Jay-sus. I was hoping it would sputter out." I kicked a fir cone off the trail with as much viciousness as I could muster. I finally rasped, "Dr. Jaeger will shit bricks."

That made Bob smile. "No kidding." His face sobered. "Want company going back to your house?"

"Not necessary. I've got Truffles, and it's not that far."

Bob knelt down, opened his arms, and Truffles ran to him. Bob gave Truffles a full body rub. "Atta boy. You bark at any bad guys, okay?"

We left Bob and headed back down the trail. I avoided thinking about the mob scene scheduled for the evening and concentrated on enjoying my improved ability to recognize things. The creamy-white blossoms of the Pacific Dogwood lit up the woods, and I even recognized the tat-tat-tat of a hairy woodpecker.

Truffles surged ahead with a bark. I ran after him when I realized he was charging two people coming down the trail.

Planting his feet about two feet from Delphina and Arkady, Truffles devolved into a barking banshee.

I scooped up the dog, put my hand on his muzzle and groused,

"Quiet!" even as part of my brain registered that Delphina was holding hands with Arkady.

Not only were they holding hands, Delphina was radiant with a sweet smile, even as Truffles acted as a complete doggie stinkpot.

Truffles wiggled and bucked.

I squeezed him closer and gave him a frown. "Stop this."

He surrendered, but kept a baleful eye on Arkady.

"Sorry. This is Truffles, who has not yet finished charm school."

"You're doing a great job with him," Delphina said. "You are firm and calm."

"For the moment," I said. "I was with Bob on the trail a minute ago. He had a call from our neighbor, Gretchen. People will be coming to our road this evening for a memorial to the man who was killed. Sounds like there will be drumming and speeches. I'm not sure what else."

"Oh, dear." Delphina's Madonna-like smile quivered and disappeared. "I know he was an activist."

"More than an activist, my heart." Arkady brought their hands to his lips and kissed her knuckles. "A charismatic leader."

"You knew him?" I asked.

"No. I only know what I read online this morning." Arkady's smile was serene.

"Y'all a bit high?" We're adults. I didn't see any reason to pussyfoot about.

Delphina blushed. "I'm pregnant."

"Wow. That's awesome. Congratulations." I put on a happy face and told the math part of my brain to be quiet. I would have pegged Delphina to be in her mid-forties. There were wiry gray strands in her cloud of brown hair and a bit of sag at her jawline.

Now she glowed with a radiance that had me dial back the age estimate. She looked lovely.

As if divining my math habits, Delphina winked. "I'm forty," she said. "I thought I'd only ever have kitty babies." She looked at Arkady. "Now I'll have a people baby, and Arkady will help me raise her."

"Congrats, Dad!" I said.

"Oh, I am not the father," Arkady said. "That is Gary."

I was back to making the goldfish mouth for a moment. "Dr. Jaeger?" I stuttered.

"The bio-Dad," Delphina confirmed. "He doesn't want to parent. I do. But, Arkady, you *are* going to be the father. You are my partner now. I would be lost without you."

I wish I had a photo of the look he gave her. I had no idea that such a rough, giant house of a man could look so tender and adoring.

Photo-taking was out because Truffles still required one hand to hold him close and another to keep his muzzle shut – and Truffles had had about enough of that. He began to squirm.

"I'm going to put him down. I don't think he'll bark."

Truffles didn't. He sniffed feet instead.

"Good dog," I told him.

"We just passed a cluster of *Harpaphe* on the trail," Delphina said. "They're poisonous, you know."

"A cluster of Har-pappies?"

"Yellow-spotted millipedes. They eat leaf litter." Delphina looked down at Truffles. "They carry hydrogen cyanide and smell like almonds. You don't want your pup to eat one."

"I didn't bring a leash." I sighed. "That will teach me. I'll have to carry him home."

"At least the millipedes have bright yellow markings," Arkady said. "You'll know when you reach the group."

And I did.

I carried Truffles another twenty feet beyond the millipedes and set him down. He sneezed and gave a full body shake.

"Hey, wasn't fun for me either."

I checked the time. Almost four. Kent closed the ice cream

shop at four on Sundays. If I kept an eye on the time, I might be able to get a call in to share the neighborhood events while he did shop cleanup.

Truffles stuck with me and scrambled up the kitchen steps to wait for me to open the door.

The little dog turned at the sound of Glynnis's Prius crunching on the gravel as the car came up the drive.

Glynnis exited the car with a groan. I waited for her as she trudged across to the steps.

I opened the door. Truffles darted in, and then I held the door for Glynnis. She thanked me with a silent, weary nod.

"Fancy a cuppa?" I asked as she came in.

"I'd take a beer," she said. "Or a whiskey." She dropped onto the kitchen dinette bench with a groan.

Truffles took pity on her. He trotted over to put his face at her knee.

Glynnis gave him a head pat, saying, "Dude, I get it. Another hour with Mai, and I would have bitten her myself."

I pulled two beers from the fridge, opened them and set the bottles on the table. If she wanted a glass, she could fetch her own.

In a moment of kindness that surely should polish my halo forever more, I also set out crackers, a cheese knife and unwrapped a circle of brie.

"How's the babysitting?" I asked.

Glynnis took a long pull from her beer, spread a thick cut of brie on a cracker, then spoke while chewing. "I have no idea how Ashlee does it. That Mai is a hellion."

"Seriously? I mean, wasn't Ashlee two years old at one point?"

"Ashlee was a quiet, sweet kid. Mai is a force of nature." Glynnis leaned back in the booth, her eyes starting to spark with a bit of life. "Must be your side of the family tree."

"Thanks, I think?"

Glynnis roused to take another pull from the beer bottle.

"She's smart as a whip. She hears 'No,' and you can just see her cock her head and start figuring out where the negotiation point might be. She'll be great as Secretary of State."

"You adore her."

"Yeah." Glynnis smiled. "I just don't think I'd survive raising her. Every muscle in my body has seen action today. Ashlee came home from her spa time and looks amazing. I'm glad you suggested it."

"Oh, shoot. I need to call Kent!" I called right then, and he picked up. I ran through the local events, starting with the murder of Flint, the death of the chicken flock, the two teens staying over, and the likelihood of a drum circle practically on our doorstep scheduled for the evening. I left out the visit by Eloise Eliopoulous and any mention of Delphina's popularity among the neighborhood's bachelors.

Glynnis listened in, which was fine by me. It brought her up to date and saved me time explaining things.

I also left off seeing the astonishingly beautiful Pacific coralroot, even though I considered it the bright spot in my day.

"Wow," Kent said when I finally ran down. He asked, "Do you feel safe out there?" I could feel him trying to sort out where he'd put me in his house.

"I think I'm fine," I said. "Truffles is here, and he's barky. Glynnis is here. Juno and Cadence are staying over. We're a full house."

"Lock the doors," he said. "All of them. You don't want some drum circle guy looking for the restroom."

"Got it."

"Call me. Anytime. I'm going home in a few minutes. I'll tell Ashlee what's been going on. I know she'll be fine if you need me to come over to be reinforcements."

"Thanks."

"Tonight's not supposed to be so cold," Kent said. "And there's a warming trend starting after about two in the morning. Ashlee and I are going to do some planning tonight for the essential oils. It may take a day or two before we're ready to get stuff shifted back to our garage."

"That's the least of my worries," I said. "I'll call the insurance agent in the morning and get going on fixing the downstairs bathroom."

"The fun never ends. Love you." With that, my twin hung up.

"Amazing." Glynnis shivered. "I thought this was a quiet road."

"Normally, it is." I was feeling better after the beer. Truffles now had his muzzle propped on my foot. I reached down to stroke his ears and made a decision.

"Glynnis, I've got so much work ahead to get this house cleaned out and on the market. The things that are saving my sanity are a new story idea, the teens, and my walks. Truffles and I make a good walking team."

"Whatever floats your boat," Glynnis said. "I'm holding it together to just get to Hawaii. If I can get a condo there and have Ashlee and the girls out a couple times a year, I'll be happy as a clam at high tide."

I refrained from pointing out the double servings of clichéd phrases. We writers always notice. We too often offer corrections. Besides, I had other fish to fry.

Yes. Ironic that.

"Mind if I keep Truffles?" I asked.

"Babycakes, he's all yours."

We clinked beer bottles to seal the deal.

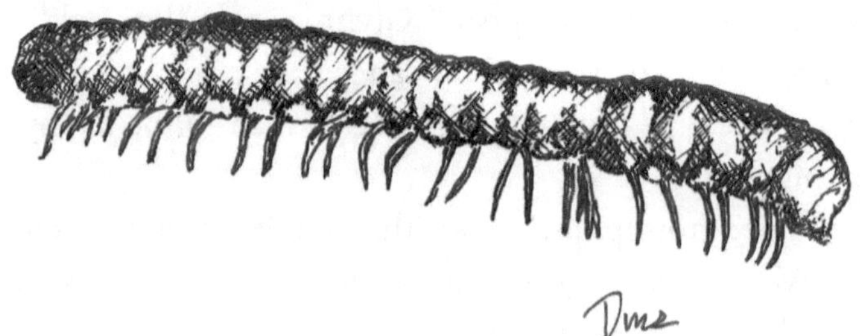
Harpaphe
haydeniana

Chapter Twenty-six

*The foundation of every state is the
education of its youth.*

Diogenes

Sunday, May 3 – 4:20 p.m.

OUR STRANGELY COMPANIONABLE time came to an end when Juno burst through the kitchen door, Cadence closely following. Both young women carried pillows, a daypack and a stuffed duffle bag.

"We're here," Juno announced. "I'm petitioning for emancipation." With a big gulp of air, she broke into tears.

"Whoa, whoa." I stood up, staggering slightly as my thighs hit the table edge. I reached to give her an awkward hug. "Sit down. We'll trade news."

I motioned to Glynnis to scoot over so the two young women could sit together. Juno and Cadence dropped their loads and slid onto the bench seat in front of my beer bottle.

"A beer sounds great," Cadence said.

"It is. Your lemonade is coming right up." I went to get them glasses and added ice cubes. I found napkins too.

Maybe I could replace Martha Stewart as a professional hostess.

"I thought you were eighteen already," I said to Juno.

"College financial aid doesn't count you as independent until you are twenty-four," Cadence told me. "You can petition for independent status if your parents have abandoned you or are abusive."

"Juno," I asked, "Is it that bad?"

"You tell me." Juno pulled a wadded-up paper out of her jeans pocket and shoved it across the table.

I flattened the paper and placed it so Glynnis could read it too.

Dearest Juno,

We are wrestling to find a way forward. We know our neighbors are suffering, but are we responsible? Would those hens have died if there were not animal industries?

We are hurt and astonished by your accusation that we have an eating disorder. We only want the best for you and our family.

The vegan path is the best hope for our planet. We cannot continue to abuse and consume other sentient species. We know change is hard, but we are committed to living an honorable, thoughtful life.

We hope you will enjoy a night or two with your friends and will return to your loving parents. We can arrange for you to see a therapist, if that sounds helpful.

With profound love,

Briar and Thorne

"It's not even 'Mom and Dad'," Juno sobbed. "They are total nutcases."

"The thieving, rotten rat bastards," Glynnis said, dead pan.

Juno dragged a shaking hand under her nose. "That's harsh."

"Kiddo, your parents are ding-dong fruit loopy," Glynnis said. "It doesn't sound like they are abandoning you."

Cadence's eyes narrowed. "The other day you were telling me that veganism was a bunch of dummies with an eggplant fetish. Now you are on their side?"

It occurred to me that Cadence would make one heck of a prosecuting attorney.

Glynnis shrugged her off. "You can be ding-y as a doorbell and not be a case of parental abandonment. Not if they can show you're mostly healthy."

She continued, "I know this financial emancipation stuff." Glynnis pointed a finger at the note. "When Ashlee wanted to go to college, I looked into every angle we could play. For her to be independent, she could join the military, get married, or stand in court and say I was an unfit parent. The options totally stink."

Her eyebrows went up, and her face brightened. "If both parents are incarcerated, the student can submit a request. Maybe you'll catch a break that way."

"That's horrible," Juno wailed.

"Yep. That's my point. Parents are on the hook for college dollars unless the kid is in a really awful situation – like in the Marines."

"What'd you do?" I asked.

"Worked my heinie off." Glynnis hoisted her beer bottle in a self-salute.

I sensed there was more. "Come on, Glynnis," I prompted. "Lots of people work hard. They get mired into student debt, even with parents helping. Give us specifics."

She puffed out her cheeks, then nodded. "Okay. It's ugly, but you girls need to hear this. I work in Multiple Level Marketing. You don't make money selling product. Everyone is told that the way to make it rich is to sell product. That's complete bullshit."

The young women sat still and listened.

Glynnis continued, "The way you make money is to *sign up sales people* who do more and more sales. You get a skim for every item they sell."

With an inhale, she added, "The two best places to meet potential sales people are gatherings of military spouses and Sunday school classes for evangelicals. You get *motivated people-pleasers* both places."

Cadence slit her eyes back to very narrow. "So, you prowled those places?"

"Prowled. I like that word." Glynnis grinned. "Short answer is 'Hell, yes.' I'd get a staff sergeant as a boyfriend. A sergeant boyfriend is the ticket to company parties. And I join his mega-church. It takes three or four months to get strong enough connections going, then another three or four months to get sign-ups. At nine months or so, I've tapped out what's possible. Then I moved on to another boyfriend in a different unit and join a different mega-church."

"My God, you're like a shark!" Juno's long eyebrows were up in high slants.

"Hey! It's a living!" Glynnis scowled. "I wasn't taking handouts."

"I meant ecologically," Juno said. "A shark has to move and eat constantly."

"She's right, Glynnis," I teased. "I had you down as a deadly mushroom, but a slender shark, sliding through the waters? Sounds about right."

A smile tugged at her lips. "You have a point."

Cadence leaned forward. "Don't you feel bad about being a predator? I mean, it sounds like most of your salespeople were women, and women with kids. Is it right to lead them to sell when you know they'll never make a profit?"

"Welcome to the College of the Real World," Glynnis said. Her tone was surprisingly soft. "Who is the real bad guy? Seems to me that colleges are the leeches."

I could join her there. "The Boards of Regents at colleges who build dazzling campuses and make ballplayers into Campus Gods by loading everyday students and families with insane levels of debt."

"Yep. You and Kent went through on your parents' dime," Glynnis said. "How many of your friends had no student loans?"

I shook my head. "I can think of one."

Glynnis looked at Juno. "Here's the piece it is healthy to know: you can look up average earnings for sales people of Multi-Level Marketing outfits on the internet. Most sales people net about a dollar a year."

"One dollar?" Juno gasped.

"One dollar," Glynnis confirmed. "But people hear 'You're special. Other people make it rich, so you can too.' They drive right past the flashing red lights and sign up because they like the dream."

"It's not just women," Cadence said slowly. "Alaska Gold Rush. A hundred thousand men rushed to Alaska, and only a couple hundred struck it rich." She looked at Juno. "From my Washington history middle school report on the port of Seattle. Even the mayor quit his job – only he made bucks shipping passengers north instead of actual mining."

"Yep." Glynnis nodded. "You're getting it. Dreams can be a big payday – for others."

Juno reached for her parents' note. She folded and creased it into a small square. "I didn't like Flint," she said. "He weirded me out. I think he was feeding on my parents' dream of saving animals."

"Yep." Glynnis repeated. "You are definitely getting it. And get this, too. Just because your parents have a dream or a way of being, it doesn't mean you have to have the same one."

"Have you said that to Ashlee?" I asked.

"She's hearing me by having a life experience," Glynnis admitted. "I sandbagged her with my leftover products. I have to get out from under it, and she was interested."

"The stuff Sky and I moved is really yours?" Juno's eyebrows were coming down into that fierce line I was coming to love.

"Nope. It now belongs to Ashlee." Glynnis drained her beer and set the bottle down with a thump. "Don't be so judgy-wudgy. She was asking me about getting started as an MLM recruiter. I could see the stars in her eyes, and she should know better. I don't want her doing MLM. She's heard me say that for years. I figured the best way to get her to back off was for her to have the experience of selling 20K of stuff. And I gave her a huge family discount."

She glared at Juno. "Parenting isn't easy. We can screw things up. You don't have to take it. You have to decide what is right for you."

"I'm trying." Juno licked her lips, and spoke with a rush. "I'm not going to go to Antioch. It's not a good fit for me now."

I felt like I was watching her swim free of an undertow.

Glynnis gave a fierce nod. "Right on. What is something that does fit you?"

"I want to go to OSU." With a deep, quavering swallow, Juno went for what must have felt like a wild idea. "Sky will be there. He's going to study forestry. I want to major in lichenology."

"How are you going to pay for it?" Glynnis asked. "Are you dinking around until you're twenty-four for financial emancipation? That's six years of waiting tables. Or are you going to suck it up and talk to your parents?"

"They don't listen to me!" Juno wailed.

"Do the therapy," Cadence said. "Say you'll go if they go with you."

Glynnis gave another nod of approval. "They want *you* to listen. You want *them* to listen. You say you'll listen, but you get it to benefit you because you're focused on what you want. You have a clear vision of where you want to land. Now you're talking."

"*The Art of War* by Sun Tzu," Cadence said. "Changing an Enemy to become a Neutral will save you time, blood and treasure."

"Good advice." Glynnis looked at Juno. "Think military. You have a goal. You decide your tactics, and then you execute your mission."

"Jesus." My head swiveled between Cadence and Glynnis. "You guys are scary."

Juno sniffed. "What would you do, Kami?"

I thought a moment. "I'd pay attention to our two in-house predators here. They are scary, but they get their way a lot." I managed a snort of laughter. "Things become clear in bits. I just asked Glynnis if I could have Truffles. Why I want a dog, I have no idea. But it feels right for Truffles to be with me, and I'm going for it."

"It's too late to apply to OSU for this fall," Juno pointed out.

"You don't know that until you read the website carefully," Cadence said. "They may have a wait list you can get on. Or go for winter admission."

Juno's long eyebrows went up. "Winter admission. That feels right."

CHAPTER TWENTY-SEVEN

*My center is giving way, my right is
retreating, situation excellent.
I am attacking.*

FERDINAND FOCH

Sunday, May 3 – 5:20 p.m.

I WATCHED CADENCE as I spoke the words, "You go, girl." I
was curious if she'd speak about her plan to attend Northwestern,
but Cadence only tucked a dark curl behind one ear and gave
Juno a sideways hug.

"We may have a crazy evening." I told the young women
about the protesters coming to celebrate Flint's life. "I'm not
totally sure what we have coming. It could be a drum circle, or it
could be an ugly mob."

"You should print off a *Beware of Dog* sign and post it out
front," Glynnis said. "And Kent said we should lock the doors."
She pointed at the kitchen door. "That one too."

"You're right. But I keep hoping it won't be too bad. The bedrooms face the backyard, and I think I can find earplugs for us."

"We should be fine," Cadence said. Juno nodded.

"I have the sheets in the wash," I said. "And there's some things you could shift from the bedroom to the garage."

"Thanks." Juno looked a bit better. "I hope we're not too much trouble."

"It's good to have a full house." I paused. "What happens in the morning? Are you off to school?" This earned me wary looks.

"Hey, I just need to know if I'm contributing to delinquency," I said. "Let's not have me be ignorant."

"I want to go to class tomorrow," Juno admitted. "I may be the only senior there this week, but I need to get a transcript ordered for OSU, and I should talk to a guidance counselor."

"I'll go with you," Cadence offered. "I've got yearbook distribution to do."

"Whoa. No car." Juno sagged. "I don't know if I can use the Smartcar. I didn't think to grab the key fob."

"Can you take the school bus?" I asked.

Two sets of incredulous eyes came my way.

"No." Cadence shook her head. "Rural school bus routes are crazy early. The bus stops by my house at 6:05 in the morning. It's insane." She looked at Juno. "I can make the argument to my mom that it's my turn to drive. I'll bet we can use her Mercedes."

"Ah." My mouth stuttered as my brain sent an alarm. "Your mom stopped by," I said. "She was checking me out. She mentioned she had a… breakfast meeting tomorrow."

"Great. Man, she didn't waste a second," Cadence groused. "The minute I'm out of the way, she adds in more meetings."

I didn't know what to say, but I felt a need to protect Eloise's biopsy time. I went with, "I'm working from home tomorrow. You can take my Mazda."

As soon as that fell out of my mouth, I wanted it back. The idea of teens driving my car gave me goosebumps of horror.

"Wow. Thanks," Juno said. "We'll be careful. I promise."

Cadence blinked. "Great. Thanks."

At least I'd surprised her out of her habitual mode of sarcasm.

If I had surprised Cadence, she returned the favor with her next words. "I forgot to tell you – I figured out the artist for the little flower painting."

"You did?" My eyes went to the painting on the kitchen wall. "I noticed it was gone for a day."

"I took it over to Delphina," Cadence said. "I should have asked, but you were busy."

"What did Delphina say?"

"She's reading the signature as Marianne North?" Cadence had her nose scrunched as she recalled the name. "Let me check."

Cadence scrolled through her phone and began to read. "Marianne North created eight hundred botanical paintings between 1871 and 1885. She was independently wealthy, visited seventeen countries and then donated funds to the Royal Botanic Gardens at Kew in London for a gallery to host her works. She began her world travels at age forty, after the death of her parents."

A snort emerged as Cadence read, "She was not fond of conventional society."

"She came to Olympia?" Glynnis asked. "And painted here?"

"No." Cadence looked up from her phone. "She traveled to Japan, but Fairy Slippers are rare there. Delphina had access to an art site, and we looked up Fairy Slippers on iNaturalist too. Delphina thinks the Fairy Slipper painting was done in northern California, which was another place the little old lady visited."

"Hey, forty years old isn't exactly 'old lady' to everybody," I said.

Glynnis wasn't wasting time with history. "What is it worth?"

"If we can find documentation, and it really is a Marianne

North painting, you might be looking at two grand. Maybe twice that."

"You know, Kami," Glynnis said. "You've got a lot of stuff to go through. Maybe I could help out a little too."

"For you, I'd pay minimum wage, no commission."

Glynnis shrugged. "Ugh. No thanks. Worth a try."

Cadence wiggled her fingers with a half hand-raise. "Delphina also said we do have this species here in our woods, and it often has a fungal partner."

"Really?" I leaned back in the dinette seat. "Bob was just showing me this really incredible orchid called the Pacific Coralroot. It's out now, and it's feeding on the mycelium of a fall mushroom."

"*Russula*," Juno said. "Pacific Coralroot is in a relationship with *Russula* mushrooms. Coralroots in spring show you where *Russulas* will be in the fall."

"Right." I nodded my head, working to cement the names in my memory banks. "So, the Fairy Slipper also partners with another fall mushroom?"

"Not the same pattern," Cadence said. "According to Delphina, the growing conditions for Fairy Slippers are also good for morel mushrooms. If you find a Fairy Slipper out in the woods this spring, you should look for morels nearby. Morels are late spring mushrooms."

"Morels?" Glynnis straightened up, eyes gleaming. "Aren't those expensive mushrooms?"

"Oh, very." I kept a straight face. "You can walk Truffles before bedtime and see if you find some."

"Ha Ha." Glynnis shook her head. "Your dog now."

"Why is he called Truffles?" Juno asked. "Can he hunt mushrooms?"

Glynnis shrugged. "Truffles was the name on his card at the animal shelter. I thought he was named for chocolates."

"Probably so," I agreed. "Delphina said Miniature Pinchers

aren't known for mushroom hunting." Just as I was speaking, Truffles came trotting into the kitchen with a sock dangling from his mouth.

"Hey!" I shouted. "That's from the laundry basket!" I leaned over from the dinette bench and grabbed one end of the sock, sending Truffles into a delighted game of tug-of-war.

I dropped my end. "Argh! Dog! It's stretched out now." I stood up and glowered as Truffles paraded around the kitchen with his stinky, purloined treasure. He had a high-stepping gait like a carriage horse which he employed now to strut his success.

"Time to get back to work," I announced. "I'm going to ignore my new dog and get some things done."

"We can look for records on the painting," Juno suggested. "Where do you think the documentation might be? Under 'P' for painting?"

"Or 'F' for Fairy, or 'O' for Orchid," I sighed. "It might be under 'N' for North or 'C' for California – or 'J' for Japan if Delphina is wrong about the origin site." I shook my head. "Who knows what my father was thinking that day?"

"Juno and I should take our things upstairs," Cadence said. "And then we will start hunting for clues."

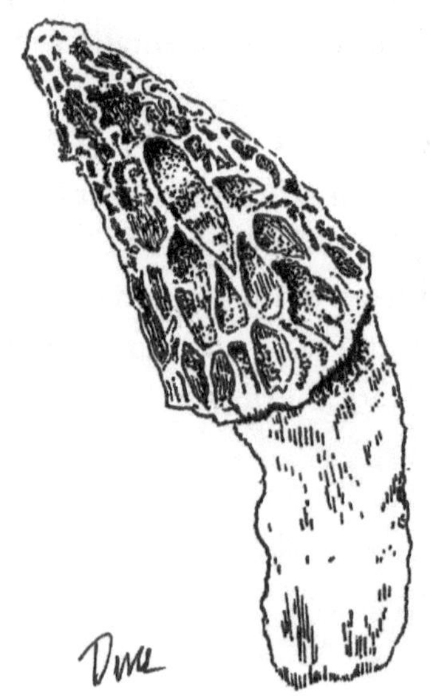

Morchella
importuna

Chapter Twenty-eight

All warfare is based on deception.

Sun Tzu

Sunday, May 3 – 5:30 p.m.

MY NEXT TASK was to shift the sheets in the washer to the dryer. Glynnis opted for a long soak in the old-fashioned tub, and the young women began hauling bedroom clutter to the garage.

Truffles carried the sock and followed me, stopping occasionally to worry and shred his new toy.

I was returning to the kitchen when I heard the Douglas squirrel begin an alarm call. A quick look out the front window revealed a visitor walking up the drive. It was Ivy, and she was carrying a small animal carrier.

"She'd better not have a cat," I muttered.

Truffles came scampering into the kitchen, nails clicking, then sliding on the linoleum. I picked him up as he began to bark, silencing him with a hand on his muzzle.

Carrying the dog, I went outside to meet Ivy.

"I have the world's most adorable kitty," she said.

"Good for you." I hoisted a squirming Truffles so his nails didn't dig into my stomach and said, "And I have the world's most aggravating dog. We're bookends."

I could see a gray-striped tabby through the carrier door. It was a slender animal, hunched and warily studying me through the wire-grid door.

"I was thinking," Ivy began.

"Don't." I cut her off. "Hear me. I'm not a good home for a cat. Not an indoor cat, and not an outdoor cat. I know my limits. If you really care about that cat, you'll find it a home that works."

To my surprise, Ivy accepted the brush off. "Sorry. I know things are really busy for you."

"It's been incredibly nuts," I said. But because she was being reasonable, I found the patience to be sociable. "Do you feed vegan cat food?"

"I do. It's not hard. There are several cat food lines that are excellent." Ivy studied me with caution, then added, "It's not black magic. It's just a soy protein with added amino acids."

"Okay." I shifted topics. "Did you know Flint?"

"Not really. I met him when he arrived at Briar's, and I've watched his talks online. He was a gifted speaker. We're all just devastated by his death."

"Juno says he 'weirded' her out."

Ivy looked away, then brought her eyes back to me. "I only met him the once when he arrived at Briar and Thorne's place. His hug was enthusiastic."

"A tits and ass grab?"

"No." Ivy shook her head. "It wasn't crass. It was more intimate. I was surprised."

Glynnis's comment about wet panties jumped into my brain.

"Did you go to the protest?" I asked.

"I did." Ivy sighed. "We had a great turnout. So many people hate the cruelty of animal industries. I wish Flint had been there, because I think he would have loved it."

I could agree with that.

Two vans came down the road. The vehicles slowed to a stop near Dr. Jaeger's drive. People emerged, some carrying drums, others turning to unload firewood.

"The memorial?" I asked.

"Looks like it." Ivy peeked into the cat carrier. The tabby inside hissed and backed away from the door. "I should get this guy back to my place. He won't like the sounds or smells of a large crowd."

"How many are expected to come?"

Ivy looked at me with a sympathetic smile. "I would expect two or three hundred."

"Two or three *hundred* people? Ah, shit!" I'd been zig-zagging all afternoon on how seriously to take the coming evening. Now it seemed 'serious' was the right level of concern.

"Sorry. Flint's death is a major trauma in the anti-cruelty community."

"I gotta go, Ivy. We need to batten down the hatches."

"Battle clichés are really not necessary," she huffed. "People are grieving, but they're not barbarians." She tucked the kitty carrier under one arm and left.

I didn't bother with a goodbye. I was already half way back to the house, muttering, "People are people. They need to poop and pass out eventually."

Setting Truffles down in the kitchen, I tried to visualize where a large crowd might go as they needed to rest, urinate, or sleep.

Juno came down the staircase carrying a stack of puzzles.

"Got an idea," I said. "Let's get a couple of folding tables out of the garage and set them up at the front of the lawn. We'll put the puzzles out with a 'Free' sign, and let's move the lawn chairs off the porch to the street. We'll make it semi-welcoming."

Juno called for Cadence, and the two followed my directions. We set up a table, a semi-circle of chairs, a water cooler, paper cups, a barrel for trash and a bin for recyclables.

One of the early arrivals on the road walked over, and I greeted him. "Hi. We have a few things to help support you," I said.

"That's really nice. Any chance of a restroom?" He was a lean and very hairy man in his mid-twenties.

"No, and that is going to be a problem." I introduced myself and said, "My parents died recently." I was using 'recently' a bit broadly, but figured no one would be checking for death certificates. "The house is a mess. I have been working non-stop. We have students staying over. We are sympathetic and so sorry to hear of Flint's death. At the same time, we are really feeling overwhelmed right now."

"Bummer."

I wasn't getting a great vibe of caring from the guy. He didn't give his name. His friends already had a fire started, and drums were booming. I could smell the sweet smoke of blunts drifting our way. People would be hungry before long. Three more vehicles arrived, parking near Bob's drive.

"How can we do this?" I asked the Hairy One. "There needs to be a port-a-potty."

He shrugged. "I'll take a whizz in the bushes." With that he left.

I could hear Truffles barking and howling inside the house. He was giving it his all.

"Great." I swore a few F-bombs, throttling them off as Sky and a tall blonde came striding down the road. Gretchen and Bob appeared at the head of Gretchen's drive. I waved an 'over here' to signal a meet-up.

Juno and Cadence came down the drive just as Sky introduced me to his mother, Monika.

Monika extended a hand that went with a firm handshake.

"We've spoken on the phone. It is good of you to employ the young people."

"I've appreciated your practicality," I told her.

She gave a curt nod to the young women and to Gretchen and Bob as they joined us.

"Nothing like a clusterfuck to start a Neighborhood Patrol," Bob said, earning him an eyeroll from Gretchen.

"We are concerned about this evening's gathering," Monika said. "We've closed and locked our front gate, and we've covered our farm sign with a tarp. My wife has sprayed a Christmas wreath with black paint. As soon as it dries, we will put it on the gate with a sign."

"I hope you die, you fucking murderers?" Cadence suggested.

Monika's smile was wintery and fleeting. "We were thinking, 'We mourn the death of a great leader.' We had a head hen named Queen Olivia who we quite adored."

Truffles had been barking non-stop. Now the kitchen door opened, and he surged forward until he hit the end of a pink extension leash. Glynnis stepped out, holding the handle and let herself be towed like a water skier down to join us.

I spoke to Monika. "You're most at risk because of being a farm. My place and Dr. Jaeger's may also be at risk because we're closest to the memorial spot."

"Go ahead and say murder location," Bob said. "Call it what it was."

Truffles came plowing forward, straining against his leash. Monika bent over, and cooed. She had my little dog calmed and curled up at her feet in moments.

I was impressed. Maybe Monika gave dog-wrangling lessons. Yanking my focus back to the moment, I asked, "How do we keep the crowd temperature down?" I yanked a thumb to our set up. "You can see we put out water and trash cans. What else?"

"I'd put away the puzzles," Gretchen said. "It's a memorial, not a senior party."

"We can move them back," Juno offered.

"What about bathrooms?" Cadence asked. "Do you want strangers in the house?"

"Absolutely not." I couldn't imagine that going well.

"Ditto that!" Glynnis shivered. "The plumber took the downstairs toilet out. People would have to come upstairs."

I had forgotten we no longer had a downstairs toilet.

Life had been busy.

More vehicles were arriving. A woman in purple rain pants and a Guatemalan poncho directed four cars to park nose-in at the edge of Dr. Jaeger's lawn.

"Turn off the lights," Gretchen counseled. "Lock the doors. We'll have poop piles in the bushes in the morning and maybe people sleeping on your lawn."

"Sounds like the voice of experience," Monika said.

"Most of my middle age was spent at poorly-planned outdoor events." Gretchen spoke with a half-smile. "I'm glad to smell the grass. We want a mellow crowd."

"When do we call the cops?" Monika asked.

"Hopefully, never," Bob said. "Cops are an accelerant. Especially if they get out of the car with a head-busting mindset."

"I agree," I said. "How do we tell Dr. Jaeger that?"

"Let me get my mom to call him." Cadence started her fingers flying on her phone.

I was surprised. "Your mom knows Dr. Jaeger?"

"She knows everyone in the county who might have a dollar to donate to conservative causes." After a moment, Cadence looked up. "Done. I told her the protestors were peaceful, but had a plan to riot when squad cars arrived – which is probably true. I asked her to rein in Jaeger."

"Jesus, you're scary," Glynnis said.

We heard a ding.

Cadence smirked. "Thumbs up emoji from my mom. She'll handle Dr. Jaeger."

"Any word from my parents?" Juno was looking at Monika.

Monika frowned. "I won't sugar coat this. We had a long message from your mother. She basically said our hens would not have died if we didn't have hens."

With an arched eyebrow, she added, "There is an impeccable bit of logic to that, I suppose."

Juno's eyes brimmed with tears. "I'm so, so sorry. They didn't used to be this way."

"I remember." Monika shifted Truffles off her feet and gave Juno a hug, adding, "If I have moral outrage over their moral outrage, where does that put me? We all have work to do."

Bob stared at Monika. "Man, that should be a bumper sticker. If we all have moral outrage about someone else's moral outrage…"

"Bob, focus." Gretchen interrupted. "We need to get through this evening."

"Right." Bob looked at me. "I think you called it right. Your lawn and Jaeger's may be turd-pile city in the morning. If we can keep things mellow down here, Monika's place is safer. Gretchen's place and mine are probably okay. The drive is too long for much more than lovers and stupid parking problems."

He spoke to Gretchen. "We've got the back trail and the short cut trail. If we're blocked in for the night, who cares?"

Bob flicked his head to the west. "I called Delphina. Same thing. Arkady is staying over. She should be okay."

The drum circle was expanding to accommodate new arrivals.

"That's about to get loud," Gretchen said. "Just to memorialize an S.O.B."

"Did you know Flint?" I asked.

"Flint?" Gretchen laughed. "That's a name straight out of a

Western romance or a he-man six-shooter tale. 'Flint' is a name I'd remember if I ever ran into it."

The drumming took off, breaking up our gathering.

"We're going to have pasta," I yelled to Sky. "You are welcome to eat with us."

He looked a question to his mother. Monika shrugged, then shouted, "Text before you start walking home."

Truffles was glad to head for the house. He strained against the leash, pulling Glynnis along. Sky and Juno walked up the drive hand-in-hand as Cadence collected the stack of jigsaw puzzles and followed us.

I could hardly hear myself think until we were back inside.

Sky and Juno moved to the dining room, perhaps to work. I put the pasta pot in the kitchen sink to fill.

Glynnis unclipped Truffles, then stepped over to speak to me, her voice low. "Kami. Your buddy Gretchen didn't answer your question."

"I noticed."

Chapter Twenty-nine

BENJAMIN FRANKLIN

Sunday, May 3 – evening

GLYNNIS SURPRISED ME. She flapped her hands and said, "You have a ton of stuff to worry about. You go. I'll do the dinner."

I didn't waste time leaving the kitchen. I barged into the dining room, intent on capturing a few thoughts for my story line and ended up surprising a lip-locked half-naked pair of young lovers.

Sky and Juno leapt apart.

"Sorry," I mumbled. I ignored them and reached for my folder and pen. Keeping my head down, I scribbled *misdirection from main buddy character. Who is guilty? Of what?*

I ran my eye over all my notes on the file folder, feeling foolish. This was an awful way to organize a story idea. Among other things, I had no back up. If the file folder was misplaced, or worse, thrown out, I would lose all the threads I had developed so far.

The drums pounded in the distance. Cadence walked in and snorted as Juno finished buttoning her shirt.

Cadence looked at me. "I stacked the jigsaw puzzles in the garage. What would you like me to do next?"

I leaned back in the chair and made sure to focus on her, even as I was fairly certain everyone was now fully dressed. "More file folder searching, please. Glynnis will have dinner for us in a bit."

My own laptop was nearby. I opened it and started a file, typing rapidly as I transferred the story ideas from my scribbled file folder, with the intention of backing up to Dropbox next. I was aware that Juno joined Cadence at the table, and Sky fetched another stack of files from my father's office, but I was primarily focused on deciphering my handwriting and capturing my story line thoughts.

"Kami."

"Kami."

"Kami!"

"What?" I looked up to see the three teens looming over me.

"We found something." Cadence's face was lit with a wide grin. "You'll love this." Juno and Sky were also smiling.

Cadence handed me a file folder labeled 'Colonoscopy Results.' "It was in the Ms for Medical. Buried, but not too far."

I opened the file folder. The top page had a letterhead from a local gastroenterologist's office. Next was a report that went into detail about a polyp removal.

The third page was a treasure list.

It was written in my father's hand and was titled 'Deep Dark Secrets.'

There were twenty items listed, each with a value of at least two thousand dollars. One of the katanas was listed at ten thousand dollars.

At the bottom of the page, my father had written,

Kami and Kent,

I am so glad you found this list. I didn't know where to file it. I finally decided to put it "where the sun don't shine." Have fun turning these goodies into cash or keep if you want the job of dusting things.

Love you so much. Dad.

P.S. The sake bottles aren't listed with a price, but I think they may have the largest value.

I blinked back tears. "My God, Cadence. You just saved my life. We can work on finding these things and let an auction house deal with the rest."

Glynnis came in, "Dinner's ready!"

I stood up, extending my arms. "Group hug first!"

The teens crowded in. Glynnis looked confused until Sky explained, "Cadence found the treasure list!"

Glynnis took a look at the list, saw the numbers and whooped.

We needed a second group hug. And a third.

Dinner was a celebration. We cleared off enough of the dining room table to sit in chairs instead of crowding in at the kitchen dinette.

Juno carried in the enormous pasta casserole. Glynnis paired it with a green salad, a cheese and fruit plate, and baguettes baked from a frozen dough I didn't know we had.

I unearthed a bottle of red wine from the back of the pantry and found a bottle of sparkling cider.

It was the best meal I'd had in weeks. Success is the best of sauces.

The drum circle booming in the street barely registered as I helped myself to thirds on pasta.

We passed the treasure list around. Cadence was beaming.

"The Fairy Slipper picture really is a Marianne North painting. That is so cool."

Juno read, "Roman collectible coins. Coins in the cigar box on the top shelf of the bookcase." She smiled. "Can we look for this after dinner?"

"Absolutely." I thought a moment as I chewed. "We can make a pile of the good stuff. I should call Kent and let him know what you found."

"Send him a photo of the list," Glynnis said. "That way you're covered if you lose that piece of paper."

"Good idea." I looked at the list again. "This is going to save us so much time."

"Did we work our way out of a job?" Cadence asked. "I'm not ready to move back home."

I thought for a moment. "There's still the locating to do. It may take us several days to assemble the items and make sure we have the documentation. We'll need photographs and sales descriptions. I can keep you on the payroll for after school hours for at least the rest of this next week."

Eloise Eliopoulous' biopsy popped into my mind. I hoped she'd have good news to share as the week unfolded.

Our high energy made short work of dinner and dishes. We were back at the dining room table, beginning on the treasure list when there was a rap on the kitchen door.

Truffles went scrambling towards the kitchen, barking as he went. I followed and was relieved to see Gretchen's face through the door's upper window. The evening sky behind her was fading into streaks of red, purple and gold.

I had been able to ignore the drums during dinner. Opening the door let the rumble in. I had a hand on Truffles and kept him from dashing out.

"We're making progress in here," I said. "How is it out there?"

"Getting crowded." She hesitated. "We should talk."

"Come on in." I manhandled Truffles so Gretchen could get by. Still in a half stoop, I told the dog, "We're going to have to work on this people-at-the-door stuff."

He ignored me and went to sniff Gretchen as soon as I let go of his collar.

"We're in the dining room," I said. "We found the treasure list!"

"Buried treasure?"

"Sorta. It's a list of the top twenty things of value that my parents collected. Cadence found it in a file folder marked 'Colonoscopy,' – a bit of dark humor from my dad."

Gretchen smiled at that. She greeted the teens and Glynnis and took an offered chair.

"What happens next?" she asked.

"We see if we really can turn up the items and their provenances," I said. "If we can get the listed items found and documented, then I'll be in a space to have an auction house in. There will still be work after that, but I'm hoping we can get the house on the market soon."

"Summer is peak selling time," Gretchen acknowledged. "So, no more going through all the file cabinets?"

Cadence said, "Kami tells us we're hired for the week. If we keep after it, we might get through most of the folders."

"What's up outside?" I asked.

"The drumming hasn't been too crazy," Gretchen said. "There are lots of people out there and more are arriving."

She looked at Sky. "I floated around the crowd a bit. I didn't hear anyting about your farm. There will be a special speaker about nine thirty. That's when Flint was killed."

"Really?" I blinked. "Didn't I trip over him later?" I honestly could not remember. Too many things had happened.

"Ivy left the Writers Group just after nine," Gretchen said.

"She would have seen him. You stayed for a few minutes. Remember? He had to be killed after Ivy left us."

My memory was that Flint's body was in the shadows of Dr. Jaeger's rhododendrons. Ivy could have missed the lump on the ground. Heck, I hadn't seen him. I'd fallen over him.

Now I shrugged my shoulders. "Okay. We get a speaker at nine thirty. Does everyone go home after that?"

"I doubt it," Gretchen shook her head. "That's why I thought I'd pop over." She turned to Sky. "I am going to put my oar in your life. I know your mothers are highly capable people, but they have got to be worried about their farm and your safety this evening. I think they will be much, much happier if you go home. Soon."

Sky compressed his lips. I thought he was going to argue. Instead, he inhaled, looked at Juno, then nodded. "I should go. If someone starts hassling the llamas, they will want my help."

"There's more," Gretchen said. "Kami, I think you should go out and talk to Briar and Thorne."

"Me?"

"Yes. The speaker tonight is a rising star in the anti-animal cruelty movement. She calls herself 'Joan of Snark,' and she can be vicious."

"Shit," Glynnis swore. "An agitator."

"A rabble rouser who can turn a crowd into a mob," Gretchen agreed.

"What do you think I can do?" I was not feeling any joy in any of this.

"Talk to Briar and Thorne. They can get a few minutes to speak to the crowd. They can tone down the mood. They were Flint's hosts, for God's sake."

"And I'm telling them, what?"

"That it remains to be seen who killed Flint," Gretchen said. She nodded to Juno. "And we don't need innocent lives in danger because of an angry mob."

CHAPTER THIRTY

The mouth is the source of disaster.

JAPANESE PROVERB

Sunday, May 3 – evening

THERE'S NO QUESTION that I am agreeable to awful missions when I don't see an alternative. Juno was staying with me. If Juno spoke to her parents, they would likely brush her off, but if I spoke about Juno's safety, they were more likely to listen.

I checked my watch. It was already after eight. The evening light was fading fast.

"Sky, let's go now, together. We'll circle the crowd and get you to your gate. That will let me see where Briar and Thorne are."

Juno wiped her face, gave Sky a brief hug, then stood back, face stoic as a statue. Cadence moved to stand next to Juno, extending an arm in a hug across Juno's back.

"How can I help?" Glynnis asked.

"Keep Truffles quiet, if you can," I said. "Call Kent and give him an update." I paused, marveling at how Glynnis had become an ally.

She looked down at Truffles, "I've got tablets of an anti-anxiety drug for him. They really knock him out. Would it be smart to dose him?"

Gretchen said, "Absolutely. If we have drumming going on all night, you don't want him barking and whining too.

I picked up my cell phone, a headlamp and my jacket on the way out the door. Truffles whined when he realized I was leaving without him.

Glynnis chirped to him and promised, "Tuna fish and heavy drugs."

Gretchen led the way down the drive. Even though Ivy had said there might be two hundred or more mourners, I still was surprised by the size of the crowd. There were cars nose-to-tail all along the perimeter of the road.

There were people standing, sitting, milling about, and dancing on the pavement, lit by Dr. Jaeger's portable lights. Smoke rose from a grill on Dr. Jaeger's drive in front of a long line of waiting people.

A hand-lettered sign read, "Veg kabob. $8."

There were also people sitting at the table we'd set out, and the trash receptacle overflowed.

The drum circle quieted for a moment as a young man recited a poem into a microphone. There were speakers on stands to his left and right. We could hear his angry verses clearly.

"Food and sound system, but no Porta-potties," I grumbled.

Sky stayed with me as we moved to the left, circling the densest congregation of people. We were like salmon swimming upstream, trying to navigate to his front gate as new arrivals swarmed down the road, moving the opposite direction.

Most ominous to me was a pickup with a tarp in the bed holding a pile of broken bricks and fist-sized rocks. I fervently hoped it was for a garden project somewhere.

We made it to the llama farm's front gate. The news truck was still there. I didn't see a cameraman or reporter, but the black wreath and mourning sign were out. I took it as a good omen that there was no graffiti. Sky parted after a quick hug and did a fadeaway to his drive. I trusted he would go straight to his parents.

Now I needed to find Briar and Thorne.

I joined the incoming river of people, stepping left when I could. I lucked out. I came to Gretchen's driveway and saw Thorne, his high, balding head reflecting the light from the bonfire.

Briar was with him.

I checked my watch. Almost nine p.m. It wasn't long until the memorial speeches would begin.

Moving forward with intent, I marched up to Briar and planted myself in front of her face.

"You need to rein this in," I said. "Before people get hurt."

Her eyes bright with excitement, Briar bubbled out her words. "You are seeing the will of the people. We are mobilizing to protect the animals of the world."

"Goody." I looked to Thorne. "Honestly, I'd be tickled pink if there is never another animal in pain. I am serious about that. You've got a speaker coming up in a few minutes who is inflammatory. If you don't set the stage, this whole neighborhood could be destroyed. Not just trashed. Destroyed. And that could put your wonderful daughter in harm's way."

Thorne blinked. "I think you're over-reacting," he said. "People have a right to express their feelings. Our friend was murdered. We have a right to grieve."

"No objections there," I said. "There's a difference between a group mourning and a violent mob." I yanked my thumb in the direction of Dr. Jaeger's place. "There's a grill going. It's an open fire source. There's probably charcoal, firewood or butane. There's definitely alcohol around, which is also a fire accelerant."

"No one is setting fires," Thorne said.

"Not yet. Your daughter would be at peril, should conditions change."

"You are overwrought," Thorne insisted.

"Nope, but people can be wound up to a rage and then lash out. Don't be a blithering idiot."

Briar, her face furious at my words, put her hands out and shoved me, shouting, "GO AWAY!"

I put my right forearm across her chest and stepped in to flip her with a hip-roll that took her crashing to the ground, a move practiced a thousand times with my twin who almost always had twenty pounds on me. In this case, I had forty pounds and three inches on Briar. There are times when momentum plus size and height matter.

She went down with a thump.

I dropped to put a knee on her chest as the people around us pulled back. I yelled, "Call the police. This woman assaulted me!"

That generated a lot of buzz. I didn't hear any calls being made. I kept my knee on Briar as Thorne started forward. "Touch me, and I'll break her sternum!" I yelled.

A slender woman in black slid through the crowd, calling, "No violence! No violence!"

"Tell that to your disciples," I snarled. Thorne had his hands up in a sign of surrender.

"Joan," Thorne said, "This is our neighbor, Kami Schmidt."

"Easy," the woman soothed. "No need for violence." She knelt down next to me and put a hand on Briar, who was white-faced with shock and fury.

"Please let Briar up," the woman asked.

"If you're the playground monitor for this sideshow then I'm pleased to meet you," I growled. "If you are Joan of Snark, please tell Briar to keep her hands to herself. She shoved me, and I took her down. She's staying down until she behaves."

"Briar's not going to shove you again, right?" Joan looked down and Briar nodded, her eyes bright with tears.

I eased my knee off and stood up.

Briar scrambled to her feet, face pale and wild. Thorne embraced her from behind, whispering into her ear.

The evening was full dark now. A tall, burly man carrying a television camera on his shoulder was cutting through the crowd followed by Dontel, the reporter we'd seen on television.

I turned to Joan and said, "This turns to shit, and it's on you."

Chapter Thirty-one

*Glory ought to be the consequence,
not the motive of our actions.*

Pliny the Younger

Sunday, May 3 – 9:15 p.m.

I POINTED TO the television crew. "Let them through! Let them make a record of this!"

Joan took a step back and called, "Everybody record on your phones!"

We were quickly bathed in the bizarre lights of cell phones.

Dontel put his hand on the big cameraman, said something in his ear. A moment later and we were flooded with extra candlepower from the video rig.

"I live here," I said to the camera and the crowd.

That earned me a chorus of Boos.

I pointed to my parents' farmhouse. "In the morning there will be piss and poop throughout this neighborhood because nobody on your team thought to set up Porta-potties." I wanted to complain about the lawns and road edges being torn up, but I felt Joan and friends would discount those issues.

Cell phones moved all around us as people recorded me.

"You have every right to grieve," I shouted, "but you also have a responsibility to keep people safe. I am terrified that your speech will rouse people to action and we'll have windows broken, vehicles destroyed or fires set."

My chest was heaving. Bonus points to me for using an 'I' statement.

"We don't give a flying fuck about your property," a man yelled.

His language worked for me. As profane as we are as a nation, profane protesters don't resonate well with a television audience. It was a good reminder that I needed to watch my own potty mouth.

"Animals are being tortured as we speak!" Joan's voice rose.

"We have not called the police!" I yelled this. I stepped back and addressed the crowd. "We don't know who killed Flint! We support your grieving. If you take a poop in the bushes, we'll deal with it in the morning. But don't crowd us to calling the sheriff. You are already making local and national news." I waved at the cameraman.

"Don't kid yourself," I shouted. "The security cameras on the corner have already recorded your vehicles and license plates."

That caused some shuffling and eyeblinks.

I had no idea if the Eliopoulous house had security cameras, or if they were trained on the road – but it was the kind of house and family that might.

"Tonight is for peaceful grieving!" I yelled.

"Fuck that!" came from the back of the crowd. "Kill the killers!"

There was a shocked hush. I inhaled to say… I wasn't sure what.

Thorne pushed forward into the circle of light. "I live here too," he said. "Briar and I live on the northeast corner." He pointed in the direction of his place. "If you feel a need to destroy, come destroy my house. We were the ones hosting Flint. We were with him on his last mission. We were the ones who failed him."

That kneecapped the rage. You could feel the crowd deflate.

Dontel, the reporter, thrust a microphone at me. "Care to comment on this gathering tonight?"

"I appreciate the love and concern everyone has for animals," I said.

"Are you vegan?"

"Not today." I looked into his camera lens and added, "I am an exhausted woman who has recently buried her parents. The people grieving tonight do have my sympathy. I hate to see grief followed by injury to others."

Joan pivoted with the mood change. She called out, "We will reject violence tonight. We can and will take action against those who attacked Flint. We can and will take action to stop animal cruelty. Let me see this concerned citizen home, and we will unite in a time of grieving."

She held a hand out to me and said, "Let us walk and talk together."

What a manipulative reversal! It was astonishing to hear and even more astonishing to see that it worked.

I wanted to be mulish. I didn't want her to have the last, camera-friendly word. But my brain was functioning enough to manage a risk analysis. Thorne had delivered an out. The crowd that was trending-to-mob was now back to being a crowd.

I took the win. I pasted on my most grateful looking face and took the offered hand. I gave her fingers a squeeze and dropped the handshake. "Good television," I said as we passed through the group.

We could hear Dontel interviewing Thorne. No doubt the reporter would want a follow-up with Joan. I'd have this woman's attention for just a few minutes.

"Are you the one who found Flint?" Joan asked.

"Yes. I fell over his body when walking home from a neighbor's."

"Do you have any idea who the murderer might be?"

"I'd go with someone who really didn't like him."

Joan halted. "We're not the enemy, you know."

"Tell that to Briar's kid who is living with me this week because her parents are off the deep end with their animal rights passion." I kept my voice down, but kept going. "Tell that to the multi-level marketing expert staying with us who labeled Flint as a player within five seconds of laying eyes on him."

I kept walking. Joan took a long stride to catch up with me. "You think Flint was insincere in his work?" she asked.

It was my turn to slow to a halt. What did Joan know? How well had she known Flint?

"You tell me," I said. "Flint seems to have had other names."

It was now full-on dark, but there was enough light from the houses, cell phones and fires for me to see Joan's eyes shine with interest.

"Really?" A quick smile flitted across her face. "I did not know that."

"I'll make you a deal," I said. "I'll get his previous names for you if you'll make sure to give a super-duper calming speech here in a few minutes."

"How did you learn his other names?" Joan asked.

"Connections," I said. "To an excellent researcher."

"I'd have to change up my talk," she mused. "People have expectations."

I stopped and planted my feet. "Tell them a plan is coming. Talk about accuracy. Or completeness. Or big visions of things on the horizon."

"You're good at this."

"I write fiction." I began walking again.

"I can't promise I can control the actions of others."

"I don't see rocks being thrown or vehicles being burned if you lead a midnight-to-dawn meditation," I fired back.

We were near the foot of my drive.

Joan insisted, "I am very sincere about stopping animal industries. All of them."

"So, property destruction is fine by you." I made my tone level and uncaring. "Don't waste your time telling me that you have to destroy to rebuild. That's been said and done before."

I stopped and fumbled for my headlamp. "You have to decide when a partial win is a good day. You've got a reporter over there who will be covering your speech in a straight-forward way. You have Thorne and Briar as loyal foot soldiers. You've got people here ready to hear your message."

Sliding the headlamp band over my head, I continued, "And you've got me ready to share some information. All that can change if you orchestrate a rampage."

I pointed to the north. "The big house on the corner belongs to a mover and shaker in the local Republican party. How pissed do you want her to be?"

"We're not afraid of her."

"Too bad. Because she's the one who called around asking for no calls to law enforcement. If she changes her mind, we won't have a squad car out. We'll have the SWAT team and the national guard." I was exaggerating. Maybe. "And she's a local. You're not. You and your followers will be painted as raging thugs. Animal industry publicists will love that."

I paused, then added "Our county prosecutor is a law-and-order Republican who grew up on a cattle ranch." This was a bit of insta-fiction from my innards that surprised me with its authentic ring. "He has senatorial aspirations."

"I'll see what I can do." With that Joan left me, sliding through the crowd in the direction of the reporter.

I trudged up the drive, using the light of the lamp to make sure I wasn't going to find a poop pile with my feet or, God forbid, another body. The downward look had me half way up the drive before I realized there were two people sitting in lawn chairs smack in the middle of the road.

Bringing my head up, the light went from a pair of elegant loafers and a large-sized pair of trail shoes up to the faces of Dr. Jaeger and Arkady. They each held up a hand to shield their eyes from my light. Arkady's left hand held a baseball bat on his lap.

"Sorry." I clicked off the light. "I didn't expect to see people here."

"Delphina sent us over," Arkady said. "She felt your place is most at risk from troublemakers. We're here as a line of defense."

"Oh." I looked at Dr. Jaeger. "You don't think people would go after your place? It's fancier."

"I think my place will be alright. Eloise Eliopoulous called me earlier," Dr. Jaeger said. "She strongly advocated no calls to law enforcement. I could see her point, so I set up the lights and invited the kabob grillers to set up. I told them I was vegan."

"Are you?"

"As a matter of fact, I am."

"Aren't you a Republican?"

"The two are not mutually exclusive."

The doctor had another surprise for me. He asked, "Weren't you at CalTech?"

I sighed. "I was in graduate school there for almost two years. I bombed out of a Ph.D. program. Why do you ask?"

"Arkady and I are discussing college paths. Staying on the West Coast seems desirable. There's Stanford, of course. My alma mater. But would you recommend CalTech for an undergraduate degree?"

It dawned on me that my two defenders in lawn chairs were thinking of Delphina's baby-to-be.

"Ahhh." I took the question seriously and replied, "CalTech is notoriously challenging. It can be a good fit for someone science-minded."

"There's also excellent schools here in Washington," I said. "I earned an undergrad math degree at Whitman."

"There's nothing wrong with a solid, pragmatic foundation," Arkady agreed. "Washington State is an excellent value."

"And they have strong athletics," Dr. Jaeger conceded. "But driving to see games would be dreary. I suppose one could stop at Moses Lake for birding."

"No East Coast colleges?" I asked.

"Too far," Dr. Jaeger's tone was completely dismissive.

"Too expensive," Arkady said. "Although for the musician, you can't beat Juilliard."

I laughed. "You have a point. I will leave you to your discussion." I paused. "And thank you for being here."

I felt surprisingly jubilant as I went up the steps to the house. Briar had surprised me with her attack. Thorne had surprised me with his willingness to take responsibility. Joan was a bit too predictable, but Dr. Jaeger and Arkady chatting about colleges for a future child was mind-blowingly wonderful.

My fingers itched to develop a backstory for each of the characters in my nascent novel. I tried the kitchen door, remembered the emphasis on locking up and changed the knob turning to a rapping.

I expected to hear Truffles barking and to have him run into the kitchen, but there was no doggie greeting. Glynnis emerged from the dining room and came to let me in.

"Where's Truffles?"

"Totally stoned," Glynnis said. "I gave him a double dose of the anti-anxiety meds."

"Is that safe?"

She frowned at me. "It says 'give one or two' on the bottle. For Pete's sake, I can follow directions."

"Sorry. Been a crazy evening."

Glynnis found a smile for me. "I found a bottle of bourbon,

and I'm tempted to follow Truffles into dreamland. How crazy is it out there?"

"Let me grab a glass of wine, and I'll update you. Cadence and Juno still here?"

"Yep. They have earbuds in. They're actually getting some work done."

CHAPTER THIRTY-TWO

The best cure for insomnia is to get a lot of sleep.

W.C. FIELDS

Sunday, May 3 – night

I CARRIED THE wine glass into the dining room, which I now was thinking of as 'brain central' for my life. Tacked-up receipts, certificates and lists covered the interior wall. File folders and piles of paper topped most of the dining room table.

The recycling bins under the table were overflowing.

Cadence and Juno were each working through stacks of folders, laptops open, as they evaluated, researched, made notes, and discarded papers.

They had moved the television in from the living room. Now it was set up on the sideboard, the local news feed on but muted.

Truffles was curled up at the far end, showing no interest in my arrival. I was surprised at how I missed his dancing, toenail-clicking greeting.

The young women looked up, each with an easy smile.

My heart expanded with a burst of affection. I enjoyed having the young people in my world.

Of course, not being alone with the job of evaluating four filing cabinets worth of paper would make any heart happy.

"I am amazed at how much you've done!"

"Making progress." Juno's happy smile disappeared when she asked, "What's it like out there?"

"Your father was really great about addressing the crowd and lowering the temperature of anger," I said. That was truthful. I omitted telling of my brawl with Briar.

I reassured Juno, "Sky got to his gate without any problems. I was able to speak with a woman named Joan who is going to be giving the eulogy about now. I think she heard my concerns."

Concerns about being overly optimistic I kept to myself as Glynnis walked in, bourbon glass in hand.

"Your mother's call to Dr. Jaeger helped," I told Cadence. "He's out there on our drive with our other neighbor, Arkady. They're sitting in lawn chairs. That may not sound like much, but I think they are a deterrence to intrusions or rock-throwing."

I sipped my wine. "If we're lucky, we're moving more to expressions of grief instead of actions of fury."

"Look," Glynnis pointed at the television. She grabbed the remote and unmuted the sound just as Dontel, the reporter, spoke about the gathering. The camera cut to Joan, who was standing on a wide, high rock near the entrance to Gretchen's drive. Joan held a bullhorn.

Her voice boomed out. "We are gathered this evening to mourn the loss of our leader, Flint Heroux. He was murdered on this spot last night."

"Lie number one," Cadence said. "The police tape is thirty feet to your right."

"Close enough," Glynnis said. "Shh."

"We will have justice," Joan bellowed, earning a cheer from the crowd. "We will persevere. But we will do this on OUR terms."

By the time she was finished, she had the crowd cheering and stomping their feet.

"Impressive," Glynnis admitted as the television clip ended and gave way to a traffic report. "She's almost as good as a top-level MLM conference king."

Cadence looked at Glynnis. "You've been to an MLM conference? I've heard they're intense."

"Definitely," Glynnis agreed. "It's a life experience, for sure. Everybody should go to one. Or be born again at a church rally. It's a ton of fun, and you feel like you can climb mountains." She snorted. "Even if it is a buncha B.S. and beeswax."

With a grin, Glynnis added, "When that Joan gal watches the news clip, and you can bet your bottom dollar she will, she'll see she needs some powder on her forehead. It's too shiny."

"Anything else?" Cadence asked.

"She didn't give a specific call to action. Rookie mistake. You want people to sign up for a newsletter or join an on-line club," Glynnis said. "That's where you make your real money. People remember the signing up, and the excitement they felt. You can get a lot of donations or purchases from an email list of the charmed."

"Get your Flint Heroux T-shirt, on sale this week only." Juno shuddered. "My mom would so buy that."

My phone warbled with a call from Gretchen.

"Hey," I said. "We just watched Joan's speech. I think we might be okay."

"I hope so," Gretchen said. "Bob is going to go linger around the edges in a minute. How are you holding up?"

"Fine. Dr. Jaeger and Arkady are set up in lawn chairs on my drive to deter foot traffic. They are making college plans for Delphina's baby."

"No kidding. That's hilarious."

"I'm amazed," I agreed. "I imagine we'll all call it a night soon. Juno and Cadence have classes in the morning."

"Are you going to be able to sleep?" Gretchen asked. "That drumming may pick up again."

"Our bedrooms all face the back. Glynnis is prepping with bourbon. I've got a glass of wine going. We'll manage."

"How's Truffles doing with all this drumming? Did the medication help him?" Gretchen asked.

"Glynnis gave him a double dose. He's out to dreamland," I said. "How about you? Do you feel safe?"

"I do. My driveway is long, and Bob will be staying over."

Gretchen said goodbye with a promise to call if there was trouble. I finished my wine as we listened to the drum circle begin again.

Juno and Cadence headed for the stairs at half past eleven, with Glynnis following them a few minutes later.

Truffles snoozed on. I checked all the doors, stopping to peer through the sidelight windows of the front door. The lawn chairs were empty. Arkady and Dr. Jaeger had called it a night.

I felt good about that, thinking they would still be on guard if the mourners had seemed at all threatening.

The lights from a car executing a turn illuminated a few shadowy dancers gyrating to the drum beat, but much of the crowd had departed.

I found I still wasn't ready to go upstairs.

Watching television seemed silly. The sound might carry upstairs, and there was nothing I wanted to watch.

Part of me longed to be in the woods, seeing the trail by the light of the stars and hearing the sounds of the night creatures. Gretchen had mimicked the barred owl for me, promising I could hear it one evening if I took time to listen.

Unfortunately, this was no night to wander the woods.

I decided to sleep on the sofa. I fetched my headlamp and

cell phone from my jacket pocket and kicked off my shoes, before laying down, and spreading a lap-robe afghan over my body. I soon found my raging thoughts kept sleep at bay.

Fetching my mother's old computer tablet, I watched dog training videos on YouTube, learning abundant exercise helped many dogs. So did thinking things through from the dog's point of view.

Fourteen videos later, I was still awake.

I started thinking about just how much product Ashlee had to sell.

Not my problem.

Eloise Eliopoulous had her biopsy in a few hours. Juno's college admission plan might not work. Would she have to wait a full year for college?

Truffles was so deep in sleep in the dining room. What if Glynnis had given him too much medication?

Could I think of something positive?

I was positive that Briar was wound as tight as a cocked cata-pult. Oh, I could take positivity further. I was positive that Joan of Snark was on her way up and would let nothing stop her rise.

The boxes stacked all around me weren't helping my mood as they turned the familiar room into a sci-fi landscape of looming shadows.

For sleep to come, I needed to do something to address my feelings of unease. Despite my companions and a normally very barky dog, I felt astonishingly vulnerable. Flashbacks of Flint's brain matter oozing out of that deep gouge weren't helping.

I tossed off the afghan and sat up. Weapons we had. Moving as quietly as I could, I slid on the headlamp to light my way to the dining room/research command center where I retrieved the razor-sharp katana from its cradle on the sideboard.

Carrying the sword tip down, I walked back to the living room with immense care. This was no time to stumble and do myself injury. I laid the sword across the low coffee table, and shed the headlamp, placing it next to the blade. The mantle clock read 2:32 a.m.

All was quiet.

I tried to snuggle under the too-short afghan. It was time to get serious about anxiety bashing.

Which took me to commas. Internet sites opinionated that there were four rules for commas. Or eight rules. Or fifteen.

I stared at the ceiling and began my own count. There were listing comma rules. There were rules for commas that joined segments. There were bracketing commas.

Sleep came, and with it came bizarre dreams of drummers, dancers and lecturers who wove in and out of shadows while chickens ran for their lives, wings flapping.

A metallic 'click' woke me.

I knew the sound. Someone had inserted a key into the lock of the front door.

Could it be Kent? That seemed so unlikely.

Who else had a key to our house?

My heart thudding at a galloping pace, I lay as still as I could, listening to the swish of the front door opening, followed by the sound of a sleeve brushing against a jacket.

I reached out and put my hand on the katana handle. If it was Kent, it would serve him right if I started yelling and waving the blade about.

Unfortunately, the sword was wicked sharp. I could do terrible injury with it, including to my own shins.

Mind racing, I thought of Sky. Maybe he'd purloined a key and was coming to stay the night with Juno.

Now a smaller swish and click came, signaling the door was closed.

I froze as two shadows passed the living room entry, each person stepping quietly.

Folding back the afghan, I swung my legs off the sofa and stood, then reached for the katana.

Light might be enough to scare the intruders off. With my free hand, I slipped the head lamp back on, feeling the elastic band scrunch up my hair.

I hesitated over calling 911. Back up would take half an hour. I thumbed off the ringer and slid the phone into my jeans back pocket.

My hands were sweaty. I put down the sword, wiped my hands, then picked up the weapon, all while trying not to breathe too deeply. Heart still pounding, I stepped over my shoes and slid my feet carefully forward, navigating around the boxes.

As I reached the hallway, I could hear whispering voices from the direction of my father's den. One voice I recognized.

I also heard a creak from the staircase.

Who else was up? Juno? Cadence?

Please, dear God, let them have the sense to stay silent.

Chapter Thirty-three

*An object in possession seldom retains the
same charm that it had in pursuit.*

Pliny the Younger

Monday, May 4 – 3 a.m.

I STOPPED IN the hallway outside my father's den and listened as a file cabinet drawer slid open.

"It's total chaos," came from inside the den.

I reached around the door frame to the light switch and flipped the light on as two bodies reared back with stifled shrieks.

"You are so right, Bob," I said. "My father's filing system is an Augean stable." I moved the katana tip in a small circle. "Mind telling me the purpose of your visit?" I kept my tone mild, hoping the eavesdropper on the stairs would be able to tell that I was in no danger.

Gretchen started to giggle. She leaned against a filing cabinet and snorted back a guffaw.

"Baby, I think you better get a grip," Bob said.

"This is too bizarre," Gretchen hiccupped. "We end up hacked to death by the most brilliant woman I've ever known, and I didn't even leave a bad book review."

The phrase "most brilliant woman" was certainly distracting. I tried to keep a fierce look on my face, then failed.

"Come on, guys," I said. "What's up?"

"Could you put the sword down?" Bob asked. "I about skidded my shorts, and you're making me really nervous."

"I am making you nervous?" I blinked. "It's three in the morning. You're creeping around my house, and I am making *you* nervous?"

Bob nodded. "I'm kind of a mess," he said.

"We're looking for an article," Gretchen said. "On juggling."

"Juggling." That seemed just weird enough to be true. I stepped over to my father's desk and laid the katana down before turning to cross my arms over my chest. "And why the sudden interest in juggling?"

"Bob and I were jugglers thirty years ago," Gretchen said. "We traveled the West Coast Renaissance Fair circuit." She smiled. "Bob was my third husband."

"Wha?" I stared at her. "Bob?"

"Yes. Donnie, the motorcycle guy and my kids' bio-dad, was Number One. Marlin, the Army guy was Number Two. You've heard me talk about Marlin as Donkey Butt. And Bob was my Number Three."

Gretchen looked at Bob with love on her face. "I was thirty-six years old with three kids. Marlin had killed himself, and I was a traumatized mess."

Bob smiled back. "After the Reagan years, who wasn't?"

"The kids and I were living off the grid near Eugene," Gretchen said. "I was making ceramics and growing pot. Bob lived in a cabin up the hill from us. He was collecting mushrooms for restaurants. We hit it off, and I started to get my head together."

She sighed. "My kids loved him. They still do. After Donkey Butt's screaming and belting, Bob comes along and has the patience of a saint."

Gretchen put her hand on Bob's arm. "We came up with a Punch and Judy puppet show and started juggling. We'd load the kids up in my Volkswagen camper van and take off on Thursday night for wherever there was a Renaissance fair."

Bob's smile was sweet as he put a hand on top of hers.

"Then Stone shows up at a fair," Gretchen said with a sigh. "And he was enchanting. We ran into him all over Oregon. Eventually, he charmed the pants off me." She arched an eyebrow. "Literally."

"Ouch," I moaned.

"He was twenty-six," Gretchen said. "Handsome, and he knew it." Her eyes went up and to the right, a poker tell for someone ready to be cagey with the truth.

"And?" I prompted. "No bullshit, Gretchen. I'm not having it."

There was a moment of silence. I wasn't sure Gretchen would say more. There were no creaks or gasps from the staircase, so the eavesdropper was staying still.

Gretchen took a deep, shaking breath. "Heather, my oldest, was fifteen. She came to us one night and said I couldn't have Stone because he was her lover, and they were going to be married."

I gasped.

Tears spilled over as Gretchen added, "My whole world blew apart. The worst of it was Stone walked in. When he realized Heather had spilled the beans, he smirked and told her he'd been kidding. Her mother was a better lay. Bob had his hands full to keep Heather from the knife drawer. Stone laughed like a maniac, and I just stood there and howled. He ran off, and we were just destroyed."

"We should've killed him right then," Bob said. "It's taken me thirty-five years, but I finally got the bastard."

"You killed him?" I blinked. "Weren't you baking crab puffs?"

"I set the oven on low," Bob said. "The S.O.B. had called Gretchen for a meet up, so we timed everything."

Gretchen wiped her eyes. "Stone, or now Flint, called me about five. He'd done his homework. He knew where Heather lives these days."

I'd met Gretchen's daughter just once. I knew she lived in Richland, had two little boys, liked knitting, and had a husband who taught middle-school math.

"Flint wanted money," Gretchen said. "A donation, he called it. If I'd donate to his vegan operation, he'd not call Heather to talk about old times."

"Does your son-in-law know about all this history?" I frowned. "I mean, you're incredibly frank."

Gretchen snorted. "You're correct. I am. Heather and Jason are good. I wasn't going to give Flint any money. I just wanted to tell him to his face that the age of consent in Oregon has been eighteen for decades. If he contacted Heather, he'd find himself up on charges."

"There weren't charges when she was fifteen?" My stomach squirmed. There should have been, but what an ugly, ugly story it was to go to court and have your friends know your lover had literally screwed your mother.

"Shelve the question," I said. "I can see where you might not have filed charges."

"Things were different then," Gretchen said. "The cops would have labeled us as sluts. Heather was hysterical. I was too. For weeks. We were in no shape to testify."

"Why are you looking in the filing cabinets for a juggling article?" I asked.

"I gave your Dad a field guide on mushrooms," Bob said. "It had an old newspaper cutting in the back that I must have put in as a bookmark. It was about Renn Fair juggling, and it had a photo of Gretchen and Stone, hamming it up."

Bob nodded at the filing cabinets. "This was years ago. Your Dad called way back then and asked if I wanted the article. I told him to toss it. He said he wanted to keep it."

"Cadence found that article and photo," I said. "It's on-line."

Bob's shoulders slumped. "Hell. I should have known." He looked at Gretchen. "I have to turn myself in. We're not going to be able to keep this quiet."

"Let's not call the cops just yet," I bared my teeth. "There might be vegans passed out on the lawn."

"There are," Bob nodded. "Cops before morning could be messy."

"How did you get above Flint?" I asked. Bob was so short.

There it was. The physics my mind had been seeking.

Whoever split Flint's head open like a melon had to have been attacking from above. It required a downward arc to create the wound I saw.

Gretchen and Bob stared at me.

"What kind of weapon did you use?" I asked. "On Flint."

"Weapon?" Gretchen shook her head. "We didn't have a weapon. Bob just clocked him with his fist. Then we went back to the house and served the crab puffs."

"Flint was sitting on his butt in the gravel," Bob said. "I musta given him a split blood vessel."

He looked down at his hands. "Never thought slugging his face would kill him, but he sure as hell deserved it."

"Flint's head was bashed open," I said. "From a downward arc with some heavy, narrow object that now has brain matter on it."

Gretchen stumbled to the desk, fumbled for the wastebasket, and threw up.

She wiped her mouth and croaked, "Sorry."

"No worries," I told her. "At least you weren't wasting Bob's crab puffs."

CHAPTER THIRTY-FOUR

Never cut what can be untied.

PORTUGUESE PROVERB

Monday, May 4 – 3 a.m.

WE AGREED THAT three in the morning was no time to think clearly.

I ended up joking, "Why don't we remand Bob into Gretchen's custody?" which earned a weak laugh.

"We'll call the sheriff's office in the morning," Gretchen assured me.

Bob nodded an agreement. "I'm not looking forward to that," he said. "I'm glad I'm not a killer, but I was kinda groovin' with the Bad Boy vibe."

"You can be naughty with me later," Gretchen promised. "Let's let Kami get some sleep."

I locked the front door behind them after receiving back the key that Gretchen had been given by my parents some years previously.

"We watered the plants when they went on one of their trips to Japan," Gretchen said. "I put the key in my junk drawer and never got around to returning it."

By the time I'd ushered out my friends and checked on Truffles, the eavesdropper was gone from the staircase. I had a passing thought about the katana parked on my father's desk, but I was too tired to do anything about it.

I trudged upstairs and fell into bed, just as a haunting "Who-cooks-for-you?" hoot floated in from the woods.

"Barred owl," I muttered, turning my face into the pillow. "I should go see it." That was my last coherent thought as sleep crashed down and took my brain on a much-needed vacation.

My phone rang at 6:30 in the morning. The scroll bar read 'Jay's Roofing.' I managed to focus enough to swipe the call and croak a "Hello."

"Jay's Roofing. We'll be there in half an hour."

"My God, you're early." I blinked and yawned.

"We start at seven. We'll do the tear off today and quit about three. Then we'll roof tomorrow."

I found my manners. "Thank you. I know we're a substitution."

"Glad to have the work." There was a pause, then Jay said, "Sorry about your folks. They were nice people."

A lump filled my throat so my next "Thank you" came out as a croak.

After saying good bye, the pillow called for my return. So did the quilts.

I resisted. By the time Jay and his roofers arrived I had limped through a shower and started a pot of coffee.

The roofers only took about ten minutes to set up. Roof deconstruction began, sounding like a rain of hammers.

Glynnis was the first to show up in the kitchen. "For the love of God," she said. "Has this turned into a madhouse?"

I poured her a mug of coffee and waved her to the dinette. "The roofer had a cancellation. It is either today or in September."

"September sounds great."

Cadence and Juno showed up a few minutes later, each looking weary. Cadence said, "We could sneak into my house and crash. Mom will never think to look for us there."

My mental electrons fired up enough to recall that Eloise should be at her biopsy. I was saved from thinking of a diversion by Juno.

Juno said, "I'm waking up. I need to get a transcript ordered."

With a shrug, Cadence agreed. "Okay. I'll do yearbook stuff."

No one mentioned our late-night visitors.

Fine by me.

I dangled the keys to the Mazda, and the young women were out the door, discussing a stop at McDonald's as they left. Briskly.

The whacking sounds changed to a screeching of shovels and prybars as the roofers peeled off the old asphalt tiling.

"I'll buy you breakfast out," Glynnis yelled.

"You're on." As I set my coffee cup down in the kitchen sink, Truffles came trotting down the hall, whining.

"He hates construction," Glynnis said. "Makes him anxious."

"Me too." I guided Truffles out the back door and kept him company as he took a whizz. I could see workmen all over the roof.

It was a big roof in poor condition. It would not be a fast prep process.

And I needed to call in to the insurance about getting the flooring replaced in the downstairs bathroom.

Oh, and I needed to figure out who murdered Flint, and if that was a problem for anyone I cared about.

It was a blessed relief to climb into Glynnis's Prius and let her whisk us away to breakfast. She chose the Blue Heron Bakery on Harrison, which had outdoor seating. I sat at a table, holding Truffles, as Glynnis went inside to place our orders.

I didn't care what I ate. What I needed was more coffee.

Glynnis returned with coffee and a promise of hash plates to come. She'd even ordered eggs and toast for Truffles.

"I heard you talking to your friends last night," she said.

"You! I wondered who was on the staircase." I slurped my coffee. "Were you frightened?"

"For a couple minutes. Who wouldn't be?"

After a long moment of quiet, she added, "But that Bob fellow wasn't the killer."

"No. I don't think so." I exhaled. "Any ideas who came along and expressed their opinion a bit more strongly?"

Glynnis chewed on her lower lip, thinking. "Someone really pissed off. Like, duh."

I laughed. The coffee was working its magic. The May sunshine sparkled on the windshields of the Subarus and Priuses parked along the bakery's sidewalk.

A waitperson in dreadlocks, t-shirt and jeans delivered our meal. Glynnis put the extra egg dish on the ground, and Truffles ate along with us.

My cell phone pinged with an incoming message from Gretchen. I read it to Glynnis. "Been interviewed by deputy. Waiting for Round Two."

"Does she have a lawyer?" Glynnis asked.

I poked the cell phone keyboard with my broad, clumsy fingers to ask.

"Yes," came pinging back.

"Good." Glynnis settled back in her chair. "What's next?"

"Why are you asking me?" I could feel my shoulders come rolling forward into a solid, protective hunch.

"Sweetie, you're not just smart." Glynnis rolled her eyes, apparently impatient with my denseness. "You're a natural leader. You're also fair and logical."

I blinked. I thought of Kent as having these attributes, but I thought of myself as barely coping.

"You empower people," Glynnis said, lifting her coffee cup in a salute. "I've been around enough military and church people to know the real from the fake. You've got the real."

My heart expanded. "I was voted T.A. of the year," I told her. "In graduate school. Before my life imploded."

"What were you teaching?"

"A college physics lab." I paused. "At CalTech."

"That's a brainy school?"

"Yes. Sits on top of the brainiac list, in fact."

"Makes sense you're the one to decide what's next. And I just bought you breakfast. And coffee. That means it's your turn to do stuff."

"We're keeping score?"

Glynnis didn't get a chance to answer. Truffles had finished his breakfast and now he started to lunge in the direction of an elderly Labrador who was entering the outdoor nook with his owner.

I yanked Truffles to my knees before he could launch his machine gun barking. "No," I told him as I lifted the little dog into my lap.

Truffles shuffled his feet, whined and gave up. He gave my chin a lick and settled.

"I'm impressed," Glynnis said.

My phone chirped again, this time the incoming call read "Yo Mommas' Llamas."

I put the phone on speaker so Glynnis could hear.

"This is Xiolen, Sky's mother."

"Hey! How was your night?"

"Fine. Thank you for all that you did to calm the situation. We were glad no police were called. All was quiet for us."

"It was Cadence and her mother who nixed calls to the sheriff," I said.

"But you were the person who connected our situation to their network. Which is why I am calling now."

Xiolen continued, "We have a connection to share. Sky said your brother's family has essential oils to sell?"

"Yes!" I glanced at Glynnis, who leaned forward, avarice lighting her eyes.

"We have a friend," Xiolen said, "Who raises milk goats and makes goat milk soap. She's part of a soap co-op. The group might be interested in bulk purchasing, if the price was workable."

Glynnis's lips parted. I sliced a finger through the air, cutting her off.

"I'm in town," I said. "Could I please give you my sister-in-law's phone number? Normally I'd connect with her to call you, but today is really crazy." Truthfully, I didn't want Glynnis to hear a contact name or number.

"We hear the roofers," Xiolen said. "I am glad to call your sister-in-law."

Relieved, I recited Ashlee's number, added profuse thanks and hung up.

I looked at Glynnis and said, "Thank you for breakfast. You've been a peach. And if you put your oar in on this goat soap deal, I'll rip your little shark's heart out and feed it to Truffles with red eye gravy."

Glynnis laughed. "Fair enough. Where to next? Are we going back to the house?"

"No. Not yet." I thought for a moment.

"Let's go to the woods," I said.

CHAPTER THIRTY-FIVE

The devil is in the details.

ATTRIBUTED TO MANY

Monday, May 4 – 10 a.m.

WE ENDED UP on the Munro trail near The Evergreen State College campus. Truffles walked on the leash like an almost gentleman as I mumbled a prayer of thanks to dog trainers who posted YouTube videos.

I praised the little dog when he ignored a chattering squirrel. Still, I kept to the right on the trail and let Glynnis take the inside. I wasn't ready to trust Truffles should we meet up with little kids or a bold dog.

We had a nice walk, meeting and passing several other people on the popular trail. The path was heavily shaded by trees, creating conditions for moss communities that I did not recognize. I longed for Gretchen's company and insights.

I tried not to think about how her day must be unfolding.

Bob didn't bash in Flint's skull.

Who had?

Glynnis walked along, unusually quiet.

"You okay?" I asked.

She shook her head. "I hope Ashlee is paying attention to price points. An organic soap co-op will be all about the bottom line. I'll bet there's not an impulse buyer in the lot. Hard to make a profit there."

"Ashlee needs to unload product and pay off her credit card bill," I grumbled. "Profit be damned."

Glynnis held up a hand. "See? I'm not texting her. I'm not telling her what to do." She muttered, "And it's about to kill me." With a grin, she added, "Parenting is the pits."

"Stick to babysitting," I suggested as our pace slowed for an incline.

We topped out on a shaded hill to find a half dozen young people crouching in the bushes. Three young men were looking at a tree trunk through loupe glasses and one young woman lay prone, on her stomach, arms outstretched and holding a cell phone. She clicked several frames and scrambled to her feet as another person moved to take her place.

"Mushroom yoga," grinned a shaggy young man. "We found a great cluster of Molly Winks."

"I don't know that one." I stopped and joined the gawkers, keeping Truffles close.

"We can get you in the queue," the young man said. "You'll have to wait a few minutes, but the Mollies are really cool."

Glynnis shrugged an agreement to wait. The May sunshine sparkled. We were in no hurry to return to the land of roof replacement, so we might as well sight-see in the woods.

As we waited for a turn, two of the college students engaged in a heated debate.

"You have to put in just the genus, *Scutellinia*. You can't add the species name without doing a microscopic confirmation." This came from a student in cargo pants and a neon-yellow "Fun-guy" T-shirt.

"That's stupid," argued a near twin in cargo pants and a green "I'm lichen it" shirt. "We have *Scutellinia scutellata* here. *Scutellinia setosa* is on the East Coast. They don't overlap."

"Evan's right." This came from a small, blonde male in a tie-dyed sweatshirt. "We post it by genus, then confirm with microscopy. We don't know if East Coast or European species are here until we do due diligence. He shrugged. "Come on, Jan. The details matter."

These confident words had my brain jump to visualizing Flint's broken head. Details matter.

Bob's fist had knocked Flint to the ground. Flint had stayed down. Knocked out, or playing possum?

Flint on the ground meant anyone of any height could have made a swing down to split open the skull.

Had Flint been prone, like the student now taking photos?

Doubtful, I decided. The gory groove I had seen went from the forehead back, with a deeper gouge towards the front.

He must have been sitting on the ground, facing his attacker. Did he not see the weapon? Did he see it and ignore it? Laugh at it?

It was easy to picture Flint sitting on the ground, hands on his knees, lecturing and confident of his abilities to persuade.

The students had their photos. It was my turn now to see the Molly Winks. I handed the dog leash to Glynnis and laid down in the needle duff next to the paved path, expecting to see the stem and cap of a mushroom.

To my immense delight, the Molly Winks were a cluster of orange-red discs, each with dark filaments circling the rim, looking all the world like a fashion model's long eyelashes.

The Molly Winks were beautiful.

"Cup fungus," I was told by the expert in tie-dye. "Ascomycetes."

At my look of non-comprehension, he explained, "Yeasts, cup fungi, morels all are ascomycetes. The gilled mushrooms, shelf fungi, and puffballs are basidiomycetes. Different reproductive paths."

I took his word for it and returned my attention to the Molly Winks. After taking a dozen photos, I withdrew and asked, "Is this a biology class?"

Mr. Tie-Dye said, "Unstructured mushroom club. We meet up and canvas a part of the campus a couple times a week."

My heart and soul winced. I'd forgotten how wonderful it was to gather with others just for the sheer fun of nerding out.

Glynnis had no interest in laying in the dirt, but she did look at the photos on my phone.

"Are they edible?" she asked.

Mr. Tie-Dye shook his head. "Not recommended." He smiled as Glynnis turned away, as if acknowledging that edibility trumped beauty for many.

A student with blue hair and a nose ring leaned forward and asked, "Are you Kami Schmidt?"

"Um. Yes!" My supposedly superior language skills were sleeping in this morning, apparently.

"You look just like your author photo!" Blue Hair said. "Loved your book! Awesome concept!"

"Thanks," I stuttered.

The students moved on, with Blue Hair sketching a goodbye wave.

"You stink at business," Glynnis said. "You should have gotten that kid's name and contact info."

"That was a student!" I protested.

"That was an adult who buys books," Glynnis shot back. "And who has some friends."

"Augh!" I kicked a fir cone off the path. "I hate that you're right."

My cell phone pinged, signaling a text. Next to me, Glynnis's phone also chimed.

"Gretchen says she and Bob are headed home," I read.

I looked up to see that Glynnis wasn't listening. She had her own phone out and was thumbing a message.

"Ashlee has a meeting this afternoon with the soap co-op people," Glynnis said. "She wants me to watch the girls."

"Excellent! I hope she sells a ton."

"You could watch the girls, and I could go with Ashlee," Glynnis suggested.

"No way!" I pointed at Truffles. "I'm on dog duty."

"Worth a try." Glynnis grinned at me. "I should take you home. I'm to take some samples with me for Ashlee to use in demonstration."

We walked back to the car in silence, enjoying the spring sunshine. I ran through a mental list of things to get done. There was the home insurance phone call for starters. No doubt that would be followed by research on who could do the repairs.

If the roofers did finish around three, then there was a chance Cadence and Juno could get some work in. Did I want to have them just clear out the file cabinets directly into recycling? Were we finished with treasure hunting? Why or why not?

Glynnis interrupted my thoughts when we reached her Prius. "Gretchen and Bob were headed home?"

"That's what she said in her text."

"Then that means the sheriff doesn't think they killed off Mr. Charismatic." Glynnis looked at me, and added, "But you were already thinking that."

"Right." I exhaled. "I think he was sitting on the ground, facing the person who clocked him with something that has a sharp edge."

"Someone he wasn't worried about." Glynnis looked at me, and blurted, "It's not one of the kids, right?"

"One of our three?" My heart squeezed with anxiety. Surely

not. I felt such love for the three young people who had arrived on my doorstep and walked into my heart.

Why would Glynnis have such awful thoughts?

And why would I even consider the suggestion?

Because Glynnis and I knew that in addition to being sweet and smart and hardworking, each was a teen in troubled times. And with the teen years came impulsiveness.

The sheriff's deputies would look at the teens if they knew what I knew about the pressures they were under.

Juno hated what strident activism was doing to her parents.

Sky mourned the death of his flock and was in love with Juno.

Cadence had inner griefs from years of conflict with her mother. I could put her as least likely to strike out at Flint, but then, again, Cadence had a deep-seated disgust toward adult's acts of hypocrisy.

"I feel like a rat even going there, but I have to. Which one might lash out?" Glynnis asked.

I shook my head. "I have no idea."

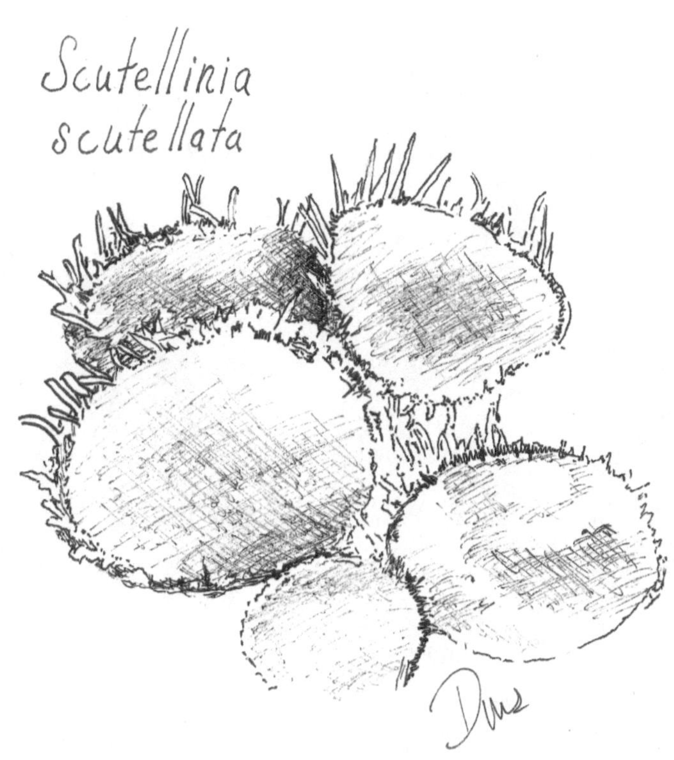

Scutellinia
scutellata

CHAPTER THIRTY-SIX

Love truth, but pardon error.

VOLTAIRE

Monday, May 4 – noon

THE ROOFERS HAD more than half the old shingles off when Glynnis delivered us back to the house. The guys were taking a break, sprawled out on the lawn with drinks and sandwiches.

I waved to the workers and hustled Truffles into the house. By the time we had identified and loaded three boxes of oils into Glynnis's Prius, the workers were back on the roof.

The overhead racket was less in my father's den. I'd forgotten the katana was still out. I carefully restored the sword to its elegant wooden cradle before setting up my laptop on my father's desk.

I could not have worked at his desk the week before. Today, my many memories took a back seat to the needs of the moment.

Nothing like a little murder and mayhem to crowd out sentiment.

While on hold with the insurance company, I reviewed the

happenings of Saturday night. I wanted to eliminate the possibility that one of my dear young people had struck a fatal blow.

My memory was I had paid the three teens and they had all left, happy.

Sky wouldn't find the dead chickens until the following morning. He had no reason to attack Flint. Not on Saturday night.

Unless Flint had made a move on Juno.

That seemed unlikely. Cadence and Juno had left my place arm-in-arm, heads together. They'd been talking. The topic had been college destinations. They had not been happy campers, I recalled, but no one seemed murderous. And why would they be angry at Flint?

"Disgusting," I grumped to myself. "Something bad happens, and you immediately think teenagers are responsible. Kami Schmidt, you are a worm."

Recalling Cadence's non-pregnancy, I let myself squirm. The distant scrape and shovel of the roofers had me think of being buried in muck. Served me right.

I was thinking awful things of three young people I admired.

Truffles lay under the desk, tucked into the back shadows of the knee hole. He'd been curled on top my feet until I insisted he move. He had, retreating inward like a child desperate for a safe hiding place from an angry world.

"Wherever we end up, it won't be at a construction zone," I promised him. "We should look for a place where you can keep squirrels in line."

My phone finally chirped with a connection to an insurance liaison. He walked me through the steps to have the downstairs bathroom repaired.

I called the approved vendor for flooring and amused the saleswoman by adamantly dodging the opportunity to come in to view samples. She agreed to look at a photo of what we had and to send out computer links to photos of products that might fit.

Feeling victorious at this small progress, I hung up. "If anyone has to go look at linoleum samples, it can be Ashlee," I told Truffles. "Store visits are not in my wheelhouse."

I wasn't sure if Truffles would leave his cave space as I went to photograph the bathroom floor. He did linger in the kneehole for a moment, then came rocketing out to shadow me down the hall.

Photos were accomplished by me kneeling in the hall with arms resting on the floor while a trembling dog took refuge under my navel. The noise from the roofers continued, unabated.

My phone began to ping with messages. Glynnis first, complaining about Mai leaving bite marks. That one I ignored, but I rocked to my heels when a text arrived from Eloise Eliopoulous.

Imperative we speak with Cadence, she sent. *Is she with you?*

This suggested the biopsy news might be very bad, and Cadence wasn't responding to her mother's messages.

As I was mulling a response, the phone pinged again. This time it was Cadence.

Skipping last class. Juno & Sky too. Got work?

Sure, I answered. I checked the time. Two-thirty. The roofers would be knocking off about three. Only half an hour more of scraping and screeching to go before my brain could start functioning again.

I added, *See you at 3,* before switching to tell Eloise, *Teens to be here at 3.*

A heart emoji bloomed on the screen. A heart from Eloise Eliopoulous? Few things have unnerved me more than this small red emblem from my formidable neighbor. I pulled Truffles to my chest for a snuggle and said a prayer for Eloise.

The noise of the roof scraping was starting to diminish as I exchanged photos for links with the flooring saleswoman. We finished with an email agreeing to a product called "Farmhouse Hexagons," which looked like chicken wire on a white background. It was a supposedly stupid-proof choice for a farmhouse.

"Classic," the saleswoman said.

Worked for me. We also agreed to a Thursday morning measure and tear out, to be followed by an install a week later after the subflooring had a chance to dry completely.

The saleswoman complemented Hector, the plumber. He'd done us a favor with the toilet removal. "We don't need a plumber in to get started," she said.

My brain mused, *When I need a good guy in one of my future novels, I will name him Hector.*

I hung up realizing that I was thinking of not just one more story, but of "future novels."

"Interesting," I said to Truffles. "Light is beginning to dawn around here."

Recalling Hector's suggestion for a real estate agent, I found his cousin's name on the internet. I called and left a message with our address, saying we hoped to put the house on the market soon.

My brain was full of flooring, toilets, and real estate to-do thoughts when I heard a knock on the kitchen door.

Truffles raced to the kitchen ahead of me and barked, but he fell silent when I joined him. His dark eyes seemed to say, "I told you someone is here. Now it's your job to do something about it."

Things were looking up, Truffles-wise.

Jay, the head roofer, stood on the stoop. I could see his crew departing to their trucks with calls to each other and easy waves. My Mazda was waiting to turn in at the bottom of the drive, Cadence at the wheel. A handsome and huge Lincoln Navigator lurked behind the Mazda. Eloise and her husband, I guessed.

"I'm double checking with you on the color," Jay said. "We've got the Pondicherry to install tomorrow."

My brain was not on roofing. "My sister-in-law says it'll work," I said.

"She has a paint choice in mind?" Jay didn't wait for an answer.

He said, "Makes sense. Your gutters need replacing too. Get the roof in, and you'll know what you want to do there."

The worry on his face disappeared, which worked for me.

Jay hustled down the steps and waved to the waiting cars. A moment later he had his truck rocketing down the drive with a speed that matched Sky's driving enthusiasm.

Cadence brought the Mazda up the drive, parking it next to the stoop. She and Juno climbed out with Sky unfolding from the back seat with some effort.

The Lincoln Navigator rolled up next, triggering a frown on Cadence's face.

"We're here to work," Cadence called to me. "I'll tell my folks I'm booked."

"My stuff can wait," I called. "No worries."

Eloise opened the passenger side door and stepped out, looking oddly waifish in an oversized purple sweatshirt with a Northwestern Wildcats logo.

A lean man exited the driver's side, wearing a matching sweatshirt and purple ball cap.

I grinned at Cadence, whose look was priceless. "Looks like there's some Wildcat fans in the neighborhood," I said. "Maybe Northwestern is a decent school."

Cadence burst into tears and ran to her mother, who enveloped her with a hug. Her father joined them, laughter on his face.

Juno and Sky came to the steps with careful looks of curiosity. "Everything is cool?" Juno asked.

"We'll see," I said with a smile. This was no moment to let my worries show. Eloise would share her health news on her terms.

Cadence now tugged her parents my way. "Kami, this is my Dad."

My arms were full of Truffles, so I went for a "Hiya."

"We'd like to borrow your worker bee," Eloise said. "We want to take her for a slice at Brewery City Pizza."

"You hate that place." Cadence stared at her mother. "Faux trendy fast food?"

Eloise's shrug was an elegant dismissal. "When one capitulates to the notion that a daughter has grown up and has her own preferences, one might as well do a complete job of it."

"Go," I said. "We'll save you a musty file for dessert."

To my immense surprise, Cadence charged up the steps to engulf me and Truffles in a hug.

Then she hugged Juno and Sky before hustling down the drive to the Lincoln Navigator.

As she yanked open a car door, she yelled, "Love you!"

Sky, Juno and I all waved her a farewell with goofy grins on our faces.

As the big car sped away, Juno heaved a sigh.

"How'd the day go for you two?" I asked.

Juno's long eyebrows slanted up as she waggled her hand in a so-so gesture.

Sky draped an arm over her shoulders and said, "Mine would be better with sandwiches."

I snorted and jerked my head towards the kitchen. "Food first," I offered. "Then we'll start tackling problems."

Chapter Thirty-seven

Monday, May 4 – 3:30 p.m.

"I HAVE A transcript ordered," Juno said around a mouthful of tuna fish. "And most of the application is done. It's not too late to be considered for fall term."

"And?" I asked because clearly there was more.

Juno put down her sandwich and slumped against the dinette bench back. "I can pay the application fee, but I don't have the bucks for a dorm deposit. If my parents won't pay, I'm stuck."

She blinked back tears. "My mom is being difficult. She sent a text telling me I had to come home. If I don't, she'll donate my college fund," Juno held up fingers to make quote marks, "For a good cause."

Sky, sitting next to Juno, put an arm around her shoulders and pulled her into his chest.

Juno leaned in and gave way to a rain of tears, her long eyebrows V'ed into deep grooves of misery.

"That's an intense threat," I said. "When people sound very angry, it can be that they are frightened."

"Of what?" Juno wiped her face. "That I become a botanist?"

"Kami, could you go talk to her?" Sky asked.

"Me?" I could feel my own eyebrows moving up.

"She's not that keen on me," Sky pointed out. "And the time to do something is now, before the money goes someplace where Juno can't get it back."

"Briar's not starting a fan club for me either." I rolled my shoulders to relieve a sudden tightness. "We got into it last night."

Was it just last night? So much had happened. I picked up a corn chip and wondered how Ashlee was doing with the goat soap crowd.

Sky had a point. No doubt Joan of Snark was putting out appeals for Flint memorial contributions. Joan wasn't the sort to let time pass.

I temporized. "Can I send her a text or an email? See if she *wants* to talk to me?"

Juno shook her head. "She's turned off her phone. She told me I could show up, or she'll donate. She's in the garden waiting for me to come help with weeding."

"How about talking to your dad?" I'd been impressed with Thorne when he'd spoken to the crowd.

"He'll do what she says. Always has." Juno picked up her sandwich. "It's okay, Kami. I'll be alright."

"No. You won't." I made a decision, "You guys can start boxing paper for recycling. Do a fast pass through the files. You know the kind of thing we're looking for. If it's a receipt for a big-ticket item or a historical record for something that looks expensive, we'll keep it. Everything else can go."

I stood up and carried my plate to the sink. "I'll walk Truffles up the road and see if it's possible to have a conversation with Briar. No promises, but I'll do my best."

Truffles was keen for the excursion. He scrambled down the stoop stairs, but he didn't dash off. He waited for me to clip on the leash.

The roofers had stacked roofing tiles for the next day's installation on the far side of the garage. I recalled Jay's question about the color and thought to take a look. I chirped to Truffles and took him to the plastic-coated stack.

I peeled back a corner of pink plastic and gasped. The roofing shingles were blue.

Bright blue.

"No, no, no." I took a photo and sent it to Ashlee's phone. Surely, she was home from her sales excursion.

Truffles and I walked down the drive and were on our way up the lane when Ashlee called.

"Those aren't the right roofing tiles!" Ashlee's voice came booming through my cellphone. I thumbed the volume down. "They're blue!"

"I know they're blue," I said. "That's why I sent you the photo. Did you want bright blue?"

"No! That would look horrible."

I heard Ashlee speaking to her daughter. "Mai, Mommy needs the tablet. Now. It's an emergency. If you fuss, I swear I'll hang you by your toenails until Tuesday."

Perhaps I wasn't the only one watching training videos on YouTube.

Ashlee's voice came back, high and rushed. "I'm on the shingles product page. I see the problem. We have Pondicherry. I thought Jay was bringing a color called Fond of Berries. The Fond of Berries is a wine-red that would have gone with the olive house color."

"Pondicherry is blue?" I asked.

"Yes." After a moment, she added, "Pondicherry is an ocean resort town in India. As a color, it is a bright ocean blue."

"And we can't make the blue work?" I knew the answer. Even someone as fashion unconscious as I am could grasp the concept of 'clash.' At this point I was half way up the road to the Whirled Peas sign, Truffles high stepping in front of me and enjoying the May sunshine.

"We need the Fond of Berries," Ashlee insisted. There was a pause, and her voice came back on, shaking. "It's backordered. Available early July."

"What is the weather forecast?" I asked. Again, a superfluous question. There was no way we'd have clear skies for six weeks. Olympia is famous for 'June Gloom.' We'd have rain.

Ashlee confirmed this. "Nice weather tomorrow. Switching to heavy rain on Wednesday." Her voice was almost a wail. "We're screwed."

Truffles stopped to wee on a bush. His leg-lifting inspired me. Piss on the world. That's what we'd do.

"We're fine," I said into the cell phone. "In fact, this is fabulous."

"You sober?"

"Yep. The roofers put on the blue roofing tiles tomorrow. You figure out what color the house needs to be painted. Jay says we need new gutters. Please pick out something that will fit the new color scheme."

"It will cost so much money!"

"But it won't be my parent's home anymore." I inhaled. "Dad's berry trim will be gone. The downstairs bathroom is going to look different. Heck, we get the auction house people and the cleaners in and the whole place will be transformed. Kent and I will be moving on, hopefully with a check in hand."

"Alright." Ashlee's voice came level and clear. "I'm thinking the house in light yellow. Blue and yellow is a very popular color combination right now. I'll play with some on-line software tonight. The front door could be a red, but it'd be a different shade than berry."

She paused. "Think your teen workers could paint?"

"No!" I was not going there. "It's a large, two-story house, and we don't need a kid falling off a ladder. We do this with a licensed, bonded professional. The end result will look sharp. Let's make it happen. You get us started, and the pros will execute your vision."

"Kami, you are so amazing. You have such a talent for turning shit into sunshine."

"Thanks." I stopped on the lane as Truffles irrigated a mailbox. "Is Mai listening?"

"Oh, shit. I mean, shoot. Shoot!"

I laughed. "How were the soap people?"

"Sharp. Awesome. We shook hands on a deal for the essential oils. I'm to get their written offer tonight." Ashlee's voice now was confident and lilting. "Four thousand, five hundred."

"Score!" I tugged at the leash and Truffles came along. We turned down the driveway to Juno's home. I could see Briar. She wore a floppy garden hat and stood at a long potting bench near a hedge that hid their extensive vegetable garden. I waved and kept talking to Ashlee. "Can you squeeze five hundred out of the other gear?"

"I will try. Although who it is that wants tote bags and T-shirts with last year's conference logo is beyond me. I think I'll try to place the diffusers next. Maybe a booth at the Wooden Boat Fair."

"Go get 'em, Tiger."

"Gotta go. Thanks, Kami."

My mind and heart were light as I clicked off the cellphone and stored it in my rear jeans pocket.

"Hi, Briar," I called. Truffles and I came to a stop next to the potting bench.

Briar's eyebrows were as expressive as her daughter's. The

eyebrows came down now, in a straight line like artillery units aligning for war.

I suddenly remembered our last encounter had been ever so ugly.

"It's clean," Briar said. "It is really clean."

Her hands motioned to a plastic dish pan full of suds sitting on the potting bench. She reached into the dishpan and pulled out a short-handled garden knife. It was ferocious-looking with a stout grip topped by ten inches of hardened steel. One edge was serrated, the other beveled to razor sharpness.

"See?" she said.

I recognized the piece. "That's a hori-hori," I said. "A Japanese knife for digging."

Briar nodded. "It's a wonderful garden tool. You can do so much with it." Her chin came in, and she repeated, "This one is clean."

"My mother had one." I kept my tone of voice light. I remembered the tool. It had a real heft to it, and was her favorite for slicing through compacted dirt.

It could easily be a weapon.

Briar giggled. "Come see." She held the hori-hori up and moved her fingers back.

My mother's initials were painted on the handle.

"Ivy saw it at your place and brought it to me. A nice tool should be appreciated." Briar turned and plunged the hori-hori into the suds. "It's clean. I'll make sure it's clean for you."

I hate when life imitates art. Briar was Lady McBeth in a garden hat.

Pretending all was fine was the only card I could think to play.

"You're giving it back?" Again, I kept my tone light. "I'd appreciate that. A lot."

"It will be clean. They'll think you did it." Briar's eyes jittered. "You're not a nice person. Your mother was nice. You're not nice."

"I'm trying to improve." I was closer to Briar than was wise. She clearly wasn't stable. Unfortunately, Truffles was straining forward on the leash, eager to collect a head pat.

"You need to send Juno home!" Briar's head nod was emphatic. "She'll be safe with us. She needs to be home."

"Where's Thorne?" I upped my volume just a bit, hoping he'd be close enough to hear there was a visitor.

Briar giggled. "On the computer. He's trying to get Juno's college money back, but I was too fast! It's gone. Juno will be home soon."

Her face flushed as she pulled the hori-hori out of the suds. "They will think you did it."

"Hit Flint?" I asked. "Because that's what happened, right? With the hori-hori?"

For a moment there was a lucidity in Briar's eyes. "I can't go to prison. Juno needs me. I can't go to prison. It would be too embarrassing."

"You want embarrassed? Try writing a book that's labeled a derivative flop," I kept my tone light as I tried to reel Truffles in closer. He wasn't having it. I kept up an encouraging patter. "We can get past being embarrassed."

"You can." Briar's mouth firmed. "Not me." She dropped the hori-hori back into the suds.

Her eyes suddenly went wide. "How do you know? How do you know what happened? No one saw!"

CHAPTER THIRTY-EIGHT

The worst deception is self-deception.

PLATO

Monday, May 4 – 4 p.m.

"FLINT HAD AN ugly past," I said. Truffles had finally twigged on to my agitation and was at my feet. I picked him up, thinking to run, which was a scary thought. I'm no sprinter.

I tried to get through to Briar, "Flint seduced a married woman years ago. Then he seduced her teenaged daughter. He thought it was funny, but it just about destroyed the girl and her mother. It makes sense that he might repeat the pattern."

"What did she do?" Briar licked her lips. "The mother?"

"She got help for her daughter and herself. They survived. They are okay now." That may have been stretching the truth a bit. I suspect no one ever truly 'gets past' major trauma. We could, however, rebound enough to live a satisfying life. Gretchen and her daughter had.

Right now, all I wanted was to live through the next few minutes. I didn't like how Briar's eyes kept skittering back to the tub of suds holding the hori-hori.

"Extreme emotional distress is a legal condition," I said. "The detectives will keep going until they solve this case. Thirty years ago, a woman in anguish would not be heard. Today there is a chance she would be. Especially a hard-working woman who is trying to save the world."

Briar seemed to be listening.

"Juno is fine," I told her. "She just had a sandwich at my house." I omitted the 'tuna fish' part, and added, "She's stressed out about college, but Flint didn't get to her. Juno is okay."

Briar took a great shuddering breath. "Thank you," she said.

"Do you want to tell me what happened?" I was making this up as we went. I had no idea if hearing more was a good idea. Phrasing it as an open question let Briar decide.

Her voice was dull now, but she sounded sane. "We opened the chicken house doors. It was so exciting. After all the talk, talk, talk, we were actually taking action. Flint said he had to go meet with Gretchen. He told us she was an old friend who would donate money."

Briar's eyes came up to mine. "I bet Gretchen is too smart to be a friend of that rat."

"She knew him years ago," I said. "But she agrees on the rat part."

"Flint told me to send out an email to our followers reporting on our success in liberating animals." Briar's words plodded out now. "But Thorne had a Zoom call. I knew Flint's password for his laptop."

Her eyes lit with a passing moment of humor. "His birthdate. Very egocentric and rather stupid."

"You had watched him type it in before?"

Briar nodded. "I was naked as a jaybird and sitting in his lap.

He reached around me to log in. Zero-five-zero-five. May 5." Her eyes filled with tears. "His birthday is this week."

"And this time?"

"I logged in on his laptop, and the screen opened to a Mommy-daughter forum. It took me a minute to understand what it was."

"Predators."

"Yes." Her breath went in with a ragged inhale. "Flint had posted under the name SharpStoneOne. He'd posted, 'Nailed mom. Leggy Lovely next.' "

Briar's shoulders started to shake. "It's my fault. I invited him in."

"Flint is responsible," I corrected. "Does Thorne know?"

"That we had sex?" Briar shrugged. "Of course. We have an open relationship. We talked about having a threesome, but we couldn't get our schedules to align."

"Oh." I had no comment. For a reasonably intelligent person who is normally highly verbal, I was at a loss.

"You don't approve."

"It's your life," I said. "I'm more self-absorbed than judgmental. It seems everyone in the neighborhood is up to something, and I'm growing old sorting papers."

"Juno can't work for you anymore. She needs to come home. She has to stay safe."

With that, I could see the tired, lucid Briar was gone and the jittery Briar was back. She plunged her hands into the soapy water and began washing the blade again.

I needed to separate Briar from the hori-hori before someone, namely me, got hurt. An invitation to walk to my house might work, except Juno was there with Sky. If they had all their clothes on, I'd be surprised. And Glynnis, Queen of the Frank Comment, might be arriving.

Should I shout for Thorne? He had calmed the crowd the night before and could reassure his wife now. But I rejected the idea of a shout. We needed a peaceful intervention. And fast. Briar was crooning, "This is clean. Really clean."

I also rejected my earlier notion of bolting for freedom. Not only am I not a runner, I had Truffles. We wouldn't make it fifty yards if Briar decided to come after us.

"Could you show me your garden?" The words popped out of my mouth. What the hell? Why would I go further into Briar's property? There could be no pulling back now. I added a bright smile on what I hoped was an I-am-interested face.

Briar's eyes narrowed. "You're not a vegan."

Somewhere I had read it was never smart to lie to the paranoid.

I shifted Truffles. For a little dog, he seemed very heavy. No doubt I'd been too easy with the cheese bits.

Truffles licked my chin. He was trusting me to lead.

Lead I would.

"You're right, I'm not a vegan, but Meatless Mondays are a possibility for me." I found I could put some edge of seriousness behind this. "I may not ever give up cheese completely, but I know I need to eat better. And I'm actually all for fewer government subsidies for animal industries. That would help with the federal deficit and be better for the planet."

There. A truthful offering.

I held my breath as Briar considered.

She nodded. "You might like a lentil stew. With onions, ginger, and spices. Adding chopped kale provides iron."

"I'm not keen on kale," I admitted. "It has a strong flavor. Are there other choices?" Just about any garden topic would be a great alternative to hori-horis.

"With kale it helps to remove the stem and massage the leaves before chopping." Briar pulled the hori-hori out of the suds and laid the heavy tool on the potting bench.

I looked down the drive. This would be a wonderful time for

Delphina and Arkady to stroll by. Or Gretchen and Bob. Surely the mail had arrived.

No strollers.

"Aren't there several kinds of kale?" I croaked. I made a fuss of Truffles and shuffled my feet a few inches further from Briar.

"Of course," Briar said. "I can show you four that we grow. "

"Awesome. Super. That's great." Stop babbling, I scolded myself.

Briar turned and stepped towards a path that led through a gap in the hedge. I surged forward and was almost at the potting bench when we heard Thorne calling.

"You out here, darling?" Thorne's voice came floating over the hedge.

I stopped at the bench, using my body to shield the hori-hori from Briar's view. The tool was wicked sharp. I'd have to be careful with it.

Thorne came to the gap in the hedge. "There you are."

"Kami is here," Briar said. "We're going to look at kale."

"Excellent." Thorne searched his wife's face, seemed assured, then looked over Briar's head at me.

"I cleaned the hori-hori," Briar said. "Kami did it. It's her tool. It's not mine." With a furious inhale, she added, "Juno needs to come home. Kami did it."

"Right," said Thorne. "You are so very clever."

Chapter Thirty-nine

Nothing is pleasant that is not spiced with variety.

Francis Bacon

Monday, May 4 – 4:20 p.m.

MY RIGHT HAND snaked out to grab the hori-hori as I held Truffles to my chest with my left.

And then my cellphone rang.

Thorne looked over Briar's head and made eye contact, his face unsmiling. He nodded at me with a quick chin bob as he encircled Briar in a hug. He murmured into her hair as I yanked the phone out of my tight rear pocket.

"Hello?"

"Hi. This is Marta Moreno, of Moreno and Sons Real Estate Sales, returning your call. I am actually very close to Grand Fir Lane. I was wondering if I could stop by and see your property."

"You bet!" I spoke rapidly. "I am visiting my neighbors. Could you please turn down the drive next to the _Visualize Whirled Peas_ sign? I really, really could use a lift home."

"Alright." Marta Moreno sounded a bit taken aback, but like any realtor worth having, she wasn't going to let a little seller's quirk interfere with a property listing.

If Ms. Moreno got me out of this jam, she could sell the house. Heck, she could sell my next house too if I survived long enough to have one.

I clicked off, jammed the phone back into my pocket, grabbed the hori-hori and tucked it under Truffles, saying, "Gotta Go! That's the real estate agent. She's coming down the drive any second now and as soon as we get the house sold, I'll be moving!"

"I thought we were going to see the kale," Briar complained.

"Raincheck, please. So sorry. Ride's here!" A dark sedan was coming up the drive. Ms. Moreno hadn't been kidding. She must have been as close as the mailbox when she called.

I didn't want to turn my back on Briar and Thorne, so I started walking backwards down the drive. The hori-hori dug into my ribs but, so far, I felt no wounds forming.

Thorne had his arm across Briar's shoulders and was continuing to speak to her gently.

As soon as the sedan came to a stop near me, I dashed to the passenger side and yanked open the door. I made an awkward entrance as I lifted my left leg into the car in a move that brought my thigh into the point of the hori-hori. I shifted Truffles, then the garden tool, plopped my butt in the seat, pulled my right foot in and slammed the door shut.

"I'm Kami, and it'd be really smart to leave now."

Ms. Moreno clicked the door locks, put the car into reverse and had us backing out the drive at a rapid clip, all without asking questions.

When we reached the pavement, she did ask, "Which way?"

"My house." I waved down the street.

Ms. Moreno drove us to the house, pulling up next to the

kitchen before putting her car in park behind Glynnis's Prius. "What next?"

I exhaled. I'd been holding my breath. "I need to call this in to the sheriff's office. I'd appreciate it if you would wait with me."

"Alright. Anyone else here?"

The woman was wonderfully unflappable. Her dark hair was swept up in a neat bun and a name tag sat utterly horizontal on her blue blazer. Ms. Moreno was all business. She could sell a house for me anytime.

My answer came after another deep breath. "My friend, Glynnis is here and two teens who are helping me sort estate paperwork."

I spied the lawn chairs folded up and leaning on the garage. "Let me wait out here for the sheriff, and while I'm waiting, we can get you a tour of the house with Glynnis."

"Are you sure now is a good time?" Ms. Moreno cocked her head, assessing.

"Yes. I'm going to face down the driveway. If anyone troublesome comes by, I'll sprint for the kitchen."

It took just a moment to call in the kitchen for Glynnis and explain my needs.

Glynnis rose to the occasion, taking Ms. Moreno inside. A few minutes later and I was sitting in the lawn chair, cradling Truffles. I had the hori-hori on the ground beneath the seat. After a bit I realized how stiff my arms were. "Down you go," I told my dog, setting him on the ground.

Truffles was a different dog today. He settled at my feet, head up, paws lying straight out and alert like a miniature Sphinx.

I heard the back door open, and Glynnis's voice floated out. "You can see the expansive backyard and mature landscaping. There is a community trail at the rear of the property that wanders through the woods. Absolutely beautiful."

Had Glynnis been for a walk on our trail? I couldn't remember. But she sure was selling it now.

"Sold by an expert," I mumbled. It'd be great if the sheriff's deputy would show up and take the hori-hori. Then Truffles and I could hit the trail and get a much-needed jolt of greenery and sanity.

Juno appeared at the kitchen door, her face pale and strained. She came to me, with Sky trailing a few feet behind.

"Kami, my Dad called," Juno said. "He's taking my mother in for a mental health evaluation. He asked if I could stay with you. He said it might be for several days."

"Of course, you can stay here." I moved my feet slightly to hide the hori-hori.

"He said you knew what had happened and should tell me. Tell me what?" Juno collapsed into a cross-legged sit at my side.

She had to be seeing the hori-hori.

Sky sat down on the stairs. He probably could see the hori-hori too.

I wanted to curse Thorne, leaving this ugly task to me, but I could also understand that he had his hands full with Briar.

Now I could see down the drive, across the road and to the tall Douglas firs towering behind Gretchen's cabin. Our community trail really was one woodland, containing within this loop a fraction of the insanity that came from humanity. A right Forest of Mayhem.

And yet, here were Juno and Sky. Soon Cadence would be back from her celebratory pizza with her parents. The young people had such intelligence, goodwill and decency. I felt like a rat for doubting their goodness. And I found myself hopeful for the future.

I looked at Juno. "Your mother may have been overcome with anxiety. It may be that she struck Flint. I don't know this for sure, but it is a possibility."

"Because of me?" Juno's face went even a shade paler.

"No." I shook my head. "Because of Flint's cruel actions. You have done nothing wrong. Don't make it about you. Flint is the one who created the situation."

I reached out to put a hand on Juno's arm. "It will take some days to know more. The next few weeks are going to be very busy here. There'll be work if you want it, or you can just chill."

"I'd like to work."

"Good."

"Me, too." Sky stood and stretched. "I need to go home and feed the llamas, but I'll be back." He leaned over and planted a kiss on the top of Juno's head. "We'll get through this."

With that he waved a goodbye to me and went striding down the drive, his long legs moving fast.

Marta and Glynnis emerged from the house, talking.

It was very bizarre to sit with my dog at my feet and my tush planted in a lawn chair over a murder weapon, but what can one do?

I listened as Marta listed the strengths of the property. She ended with, "I'd love to represent you, but if I did, I would have a list of expectations."

"That's understandable." I waved at the bare roof. "The workers are back tomorrow to put on a bright blue roof."

"Blue?" Marta's eyes went wide as her head swiveled to take in the olive-green exterior of the farmhouse.

"We're going to have the place painted, and the windows washed," I said. "My sister-in-law is choosing a color. Possibly yellow."

Marta smiled. "That would be handsome. We have a list of painting companies to recommend, if that is helpful."

"Absolutely." I could feel burdens lifting. "The downstairs bathroom will have new flooring in a week. I know we need to get a new toilet in, and I've got a plumber who can do that. We've identified some of the more valuable collectibles. We'll have an auction house in to cart off the rest. We'd like to have the house on the market by the end of May."

I couldn't believe how happy it was to be saying these things.

"Will you be looking for housing yourself?" Marta asked.

Clever woman. She was up for two sales opportunities. Glynnis grinned in appreciation of the question.

What was I going to do after this property sold?

I looked down at Truffles and thought of Arkady's fenced backyard. I should chat with him. Perhaps he'd be moving in with Delphina and would want a renter for his place.

Which would mean I needed a job. Preferably one that would give me time to write.

I liked having teens in my life, just as I had enjoyed being a lab T.A. for college students. Seeing Juno's easy smile as she reached out to fondle Truffles' ears, I felt a pang, knowing she'd be gone by summer's end, along with Sky and Cadence.

My autumn would be bereft without the young people.

But I could still have my writing, the woods and my dog - if I was just smart enough to build them into my life.

Looking up, I said, "I suspect I'll be a renter next. I'll be applying to be a substitute teacher for high school science classes."

Epilogue

*Educating the mind without educating
the heart is no education at all.*

Aristotle

JUNO STAYED WITH me all summer. The house sold the first week of June, and we relocated to Arkady's house. September could have been grim with the departure of the teens and Briar's court proceedings. The woods, however, were splendid with fall colors and an abundance of fungi. Truffles and I spent many happy hours on the trail in the slanting autumn sunshine.

By October's rains, I was trained as a substitute teacher, and Briar pled guilty to a charge of manslaughter, not murder. This triggered an in-depth discussion at the Writers Group as manslaughter meant the attack on Flint was unintended.

Carrying a sharp-edged garden tool to complain about the planned seduction of one's child certainly seemed a wee bit premeditated to most of us.

Bob was of the opinion that Briar had evaluated the women's prison in Purdy, Washington and decided it was more pleasant

"

than the Western Washington Mental Health Hospital, resulting in an agreement to a plea deal.

When the teens returned home for winter break, Juno stayed with Sky and his mothers. They and Cadence stopped by often. It was astonishing and delightful to see their growth in confidence and experience.

Eloise Eliopoulous left this earth on the last day of December. Twenty-four hours later, a new Eloise arrived, born to Delphina and weighing in at seven pounds, six ounces. Xiulen crafted an utterly gorgeous baby blanket of exquisite llama wool, and Cadence bawled abundantly, so pleased the new Eloise had a life that began with a swaddling in fine fibers.

January was also the month Kent and I sold the last of the fine collectibles. An anonymous buyer paid forty thousand dollars for the quartet of Nabeshimaware saki bottles. Kent and Ashlee sold their ice cream business, and now Kent is taking time off to work on their bungalow. He'd like to teach middle school math, but he says the salaries offered currently don't pencil out.

Truffles is my constant companion unless I am substitute teaching. Then he hangs out with Gretchen or Bob and is abundantly spoiled.

My second book is finished and will launch at the end of May. It will be another crazy spring, I'm sure.

The forest calls to me every day. The woodland residents have their own stories, and I am ready to leave the mayhem of humanity behind to know more of my quieter neighbors. Even the poisonous ones seem imminently reasonable now.

Amanita
pantherinoides

Ready to try another "Mushroom Thriller?" Turn the page!

From The EvoAngel

---

*"Once the mushroom has sprouted from
the earth, there is no turning back."*

LUO PROVERB FROM KENYA

CHAPTER ONE

**Tuesday morning, September 15
Kamilche Peninsula, Shelton, Washington**

SHE COULD POISON the doctor.

Edna's hands trembled slightly as she lifted the latch on the door to her cabin. There was no lock. There had never been a need for one. Edna entered and hung her purse and jacket on the peg row by the front door. She desperately needed a cup of chamomile tea.

Oh, she knew which mushrooms to use. She could kill the doctor dead, dead, dead and, if she was careful, no one would connect the death to her.

Edna crossed her narrow living room, navigating carefully around the edge of the rug. At her age, she didn't need a fall.

She knew where to collect the Death Angel mushroom. There was a disturbed site behind the school bus barn that produced *Amanitas.* Even if the species she needed happened to be growing in a mixture of other fungi, as mushrooms often do, the Death Angel would stand out to her. She would know, instantly, when she had found any specimen of the Death Angels group. Eighty years of mushroom hunting was good for something. She knew her fungi.

Edna made it to her kitchen and rested her hands on the deep enamel sink. She remembered the day her husband had installed it. There was a chip near the drain hole. The geraniums on the windowsill needed watering. Edna blinked back tears. She had bigger challenges now. Her hands continued to tremble as she filled the teakettle.

She knew a Death Angel signaled its presence with a bright white stem erupting from an egg-shaped sac. Then there was the white ring on the stalk, the white spores, the unattached white gills, and the elegant profile that all said *Amanita phalloides* just as clearly as a nametag.

She would have preferred the prettier *Amanita ocreata,* with its brighter cap, but that was a spring Death Angel. She was going to have to make do with the fall alternative.

As the flames of the propane burner licked the bottom of the teakettle, Edna's nerves steadied. She should think this through.

Amatoxins were not affected by heat. Cooked or raw, they poisoned. Surely a casserole would be a better vector than a salad. Who gave a gift salad?

Edna's mind skittered through the details. It would take several hours for the mushrooms in the dish to begin their poisoning of Dr. Band. The vomiting and diarrhea might not be connected with her offering. A day of intestinal agony might be attributed to a passing virus. She could hope. That weasel of a woman deserved all the agony the planet could deliver.

There would be a rebound day. Her victim would feel much better. It would be on the third or fourth day when the kidneys and liver began to fail.

Edna lifted the squealing kettle off the fire and poured the boiling water over a teabag. She made her mind take a step back from thoughts of murder.

She trusted Dr. Patel. He was a sweet man. None of this was his fault. She had made the appointment with him, trusting that her odd condition would be discretely discussed. And, no, she hadn't been naïve. It was time to tell someone about her changing body.

She had not known there was a visiting doctor at the clinic, an intense, scary woman with a tiny body and ferocious eyes. Dr. Band was a witch of the worst possible sort.

Edna grimaced, a sour taste in her mouth despite sipping the mild tea.

"These days it is 'witch' with a B," she muttered.

Dr. Band was trouble.

As she sipped her tea, Edna considered her options. She could get a dog. A large dog with large teeth. And a *No Trespassing* sign. Her daughter would think her aging poorly, with the fears of old age sprouting like mushrooms after fall rains.

Edna's mind veered back to murder. Weasels sometimes had to be killed to protect a flock. No matter what, she should protect her daughter and granddaughter.

What she had, they might have next.

Feathers. An old woman should be sprouting chin hairs, not feathers. And a feather had emerged on her sternum a month ago and now that odd emergence was adding little friends. Dr. Patel had been kind and soothing. Dr. Band had been… fascinated.

Edna had seen the rectangle of a smartphone in the pocket of

Dr. Band's white coat. When Dr. Band's hand went snaking into that pocket, Edna had leapt off the examination table and she had fled the clinic. There would be no photographs of her chest. Not if she could help it.

Edna picked up a frame from a kitchen shelf and studied the picture of herself as a bride. Marrying a cousin had not seemed so bad as they had no plans of children. She had been a fifty-year-old bride, for heaven's sake.

"*Well, 'oops', as they say.*" Edna replaced her bridal picture on the shelf and took down a framed photo of Lena. Edna hugged the picture frame to her sagging chest. Her daughter Lena was so much more than they could have ever hoped for. More marvelous, more flawed and in so much danger from the modern world. Thank goodness Lena's husband was such a good man. And their daughter, Piper, had the family cunning to go with the family oddities.

Edna kissed the glass of the picture frame, steering her lips to the glowing halo of bright hair surrounding her daughter's perfect oval face. Edna's stomach swooped down with a wave of worry, then stabilized as the chamomile did its magic.

Edna's jangled thoughts began to settle. There was a better way.

She would protect Lena. She would protect her granddaughter. She would forge a back-up plan in case she needed a speedy exit for Dr. Band. Forget the mushrooms that had sustained and enchanted her all these many years. She needed to get out of the cabin and into the woods. She would collect some water hemlock.

Wabi-Sabi – an imperfect, rustic beauty

I work hard on my stories, but I'm constantly aware of short-comings. Too much lecturing, repeated phrases, and confusing plot lines are just a few of my tripping points. The best I can hope for is a flawed beauty as my imperfect efforts meet up with the astonishing ecology of the Pacific Northwest.

The Tuesday Morning Rebel Writers saved my sanity during the many months of the Covid-19 pandemic. Thank you to Connie Jasperson, Lee French, Melissa Carpenter and Johanna Flynn.

I am inspired and educated by Connie's Life in the Realm of Fantasy blog postings. She delivers a scrumptious smorgasbord of storytelling, book reviews and discussions about fine art, all well-seasoned with her insights on grammar and punctuation. I don't know what I'll learn when I open her column, but I always learn something. Connie is also an accomplished map maker. She created the map of Kami's neighborhood, a blessing as I rushed to finish this book.

Melissa Carpenter was willing to read through this story even as her own plate of life has been very full. Your generosity is so appreciated!

Johanna Flynn read the story next and found some inconsistencies that made my jaw drop, and yet her comments were positive and curative. I wish we could have Johanna in charge of all things medical and social. Her leadership inspires.

Stephanie Claire is a treasure who has been astonishingly generous in sharing her time and talents as an editor and beta reader. Thank you, thank you for such a gracious and special gift. Not everyone can provide both an eagle's eye for error and a consistently kind delivery of corrections needed.

I'm also deeply grateful to our neighbors. Sally and Gregg Bennett are perennial supporters of all things good, including mushrooming.

Olympia writers Judy Kiehart and Sheila Rodriquez have been insightful assessors. Thank you, so very much, for your wise comments.

I'm grateful to Duncan Sheffels because working with him is a joy. I always know the results will be awesome. Thank you, Duncan!

Last in mention, but first in my heart, are my husband and sons. I'd be lost without you.

How to Help an Author

Once upon a time, there were publishing houses sending authors on book-selling tours, complete with administrative assistants to manage details like scheduling events and booking tickets.

Alas, the modern indie author is living in a very different universe. For us, we count on book reviews and word-of-mouth marketing.

Book reviews matter. A reader taking time to mention what worked and what didn't work helps other buyers zero in on purchases that will please. Book reviews also help authors grow by highlighting strengths and shining a light on terrain that needs to be better managed.

Please help your favorite authors stay in business. Speak about what you're reading and share your insights. We want to make you happy!

Learn more about my world at my website:
www.ellenkingrice.com